LAKE
SURRENDER

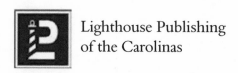

Amy —
Blessings
from Lake Surrender
Carol Grace Stratton

Carol Grace Stratton

Lighthouse Publishing
of the Carolinas

LAKE SURRENDER BY CAROL GRACE STRATTON
Published by Lighthouse Publishing of the Carolinas
2333 Barton Oaks Dr., Raleigh, NC, 27614

ISBN: 978-1941103227
Copyright © 2014 by Carol Grace Stratton
Cover design by writelydesigned.com
Interior design by Reality Premedia Services Pvt. Ltd.: www.realitypremedia.com

Available in print from your local bookstore, online, or from the publisher at:
www.lighthousepublishingofthecarolinas.com

Brought to you by the creative team at LighthousePublishingoftheCarolinas.com:
Elizabeth Easter, Rowena Kuo, Michele Creech, and Eddie Jones.

Library of Congress Cataloging-in-Publication Data
Stratton, Carol.
Lake Surrender / Carol Grace Stratton 1st ed.

Printed in the United States of America

PRAISE FOR LAKE SURRENDER

This delightful story chronicles one woman's journey through divorce, a job loss and a cross-country move (with two children in tow, one of them autistic) to a place of new beginnings aptly named Lake Surrender. Carol Stratton's debut novel is sure to find its way into the hearts of many a reader.

Ann Tatlock, awarding-winner author of *Sweet Mercy*

Carol is a gifted writer. This book strikes just the right balance between the trials and the triumphs of raising a child with autism. I highly recommend it to families living the daily battle with autism.

Pat Hays, www.autismvoices.com

DEDICATION

To John and Tammy VanderVoort

Last summer I saw our dear friends, the VanderVoorts, at our son's wedding. While we chatted at the reception I told Tammy how much I enjoyed the song her daughter sang at her high school graduation open house. She had dedicated the number to her parents. The song's lyrics talked about how she had learned how to love from her parents.

The words echoed what many of us think of the VanderVoorts. They have three older children who have done well in school. Their youngest one, Travis, is severely autistic and fairly non-verbal. These parents have spent years, time, and money getting help for Travis. They have had to hire tutors and assistants to come spend one-on-one time with him. He is relating better to people, but his parents still have to hang pictures high on the walls of the family room and fill in the holes where Travis acted out the frustration of a bad day at school.

What has amazed me about this family is the kindness

and patience his siblings have developed. I know they have watched their parents and learned well from them. Travis is their brother and very much a part of their family.

I know it hasn't been easy. Going out to dinner or just having a social gathering challenges the VanderVoorts because of the unpredictable behavior of their son. I've never before seen such unconditional love coming from a family.

If you asked John or Tammy how it has been to raise a severely autistic child, they won't deny the challenges. But in Tammy's word's, "I can't imagine life without Travis. He's taught us so much. My other children are better because of Travis being a part of our family."

Acknowledgments

Launching one's first novel is an exciting endeavor, and I am very appreciative for the people God has sent to help me get this story off the ground. So many friends from my past have held up my hands, cheering me on.

Many thanks to my beta readers: Chris Bos, Frankie Tipton, Deanna Mundy, Tammy VanderVoort, Laura Carroll, Debbie Cox, Tami Kincer, Lanie Van Wijk, Milei Cook Yardley, Patricia Hays, Linda Schwert, Mary Heaton, Kelly Rosloniec, Mollie Bond, Jo-anne Gardener, Chris Kramer, Sue Ciullo, Suzanne Ruff, Barbara Hall, Marge De Young, Kathy Cranston, Jeannie Romack, and Jackie Roadlander.

Thanks to Gloria Graham, who early on saw some value in my story, and for my great critique partners, Suzanne Ruff and Lisa Glase. I love meeting with you on Wednesdays, and you always give me the truth with kindness.

And to Julia Crandall, a special education teacher who loves and understands autistic children. She showed me how to connect with the students when I was an aide in her A-I (autistic) class.

Thanks to Jennifer Fromke for her honest evaluation, and to Linda Schwert. I've only met you in person once, but you've been a great cheerleader all the way from Chicago.

Thanks to my great launch team, including Linda Schwert, Billie Sue Strawder Corley, Glorianne Schultz, Debbie Callaghan, Sue Wilson, and Kelly Rosioniec. I am rich in "Barnabases"* in my life. You're doing the heavy lifting for me.

For information on burn injuries, my dear cousin, Kathy Wickware, gave me valuable medical information.

Of course, I own a huge debt of gratitude to my publisher, Eddie. I appreciate you taking a second chance on another of my books. I've loved working with Lighthouse Publishing of the Carolinas.

Elizabeth Easter, what a blessing you've been, taking my manuscript with its possibilities and many awkward passages, and in brutal but loving honesty spelled out what worked and what didn't. Writers are often blind to their own story's weaknesses, and you helped me strengthen the story to give it muscle. Thank you, Elizabeth, for your challenging critiques to make my book more believable.

Allison Gardner, thank you for writing insightful questions for book clubs to use.

I'm grateful for a husband who willingly gives me feedback on my story. He's my muse, my best friend and critic, and someone who gets me "unstuck". I still picture us sitting on our porch in Wheaton five years ago as I bounced ideas off him. He's always been in my corner. Thank you, John.

Thanks to my kids, who love to give me their opinions on what works and what doesn't in my story: Joel, for helping me get my Michigan facts straight; Seth for being our family editor; and Erica and Caitlin for their feedback and unwavering faith in me.

"But thanks be to God, who always leads us in triumph in Christ, and manifests through us the sweet aroma of the knowledge of Him in every place." 2 Corinthinians 2:14 (New American Standard Bible)

* Barnabas was a fellow believer who traveled with and encouraged the Apostle Paul.

CHAPTER ONE

"If you're going through hell, keep going."

Ally thought about Winston Churchill's quote as she pulled into her driveway and slammed on the brakes of her emerald green compact sedan. Seeing the *FOR SALE* sign freshly pounded into the front yard set off her inner tornado, and ruined a perfect Northern California Friday in March.

She jerked the key out of the ignition. *Didn't waste much time, Bryan. Would like to have told Kylie first.*

"Let's go, Benjie," she said, glancing in the rearview mirror at her six-year-old.

Ally flicked back hair that sat hot on her neck, a color her ex-husband Bryan called a cross between a burnt cranberry and a persimmon. She opened the passenger door and leaned over the car seat, trying to connect to Benjie's menthol blue eyes. But as a thousand times before, he jerked his head away. Ally sighed and lifted him out of the car. Almost before she planted his red Velcro-strapped sneakers on the ground, her son bolted down the sidewalk.

"Stop," Ally hollered, watching a blur of boney limbs and platinum blonde hair fly down the block. He flew past the neighbor's nanny pushing a stroller of twins, and barely missed the mayor of Mountain View, who looked like his Great Dane was taking him for a walk. Benjie's head turned for a moment before he jumped off the curb and into the street. Ally's heart sped up as a Honda Civic swerved and barely missed him. The driver leaned on the horn before squealing off.

Dashing to the street, Ally felt the heel of her best Jimmy Choos crunch beneath her. She lurched forward on the other good shoe and gripped one of Benjie's arms.

Her whole body shook. "What are you doing? You know you're never supposed to go into the street. That's naughty." She cupped his face, and looked into the eyes that never seemed to look back. "Benjamin, don't ever do that again. I would hate to lose you."

His right hand grabbed his left forearm, pinching it until it turned a reddish purple.

"Oh, honey, it's okay, I'm not mad at you." She wrapped her arms around him for a reluctant hug before scooping him up in her arms. She hobbled on one shoe back to their house.

As she hit the code for the garage door opener, she heard a car pull up behind her. Ally turned her head to see a seventy-something portly man sitting in a silver BMW. He leaned his head out the window. It was Frank, her boss at Shout Books. "Need to talk to you."

Ally nodded, and raised a finger to signal him to wait. She turned back to her son and planted a kiss on his cheek. "Please go to your room, now." She put him down on the pavement, and watched as he scooted through the garage to the kitchen.

Turning around, she reminded herself to paste on her best professional smile. "Hi, Frank, didn't expect to see you here today."

Frank climbed out of the car and headed toward her. "Wanted to catch you before you came in to work Monday. Got a minute?"

"Let's sit on the front porch." She thought it strange for him to pay her a visit at home. They settled into two big rattan chairs with yellow overstuffed cushions overlooking the lawn, and she waved to her gardener, who was finishing up trimming a bush. Turning back to Frank, she asked, "Can I bring you a drink? Wine, beer?"

He took off a pair of gold wire sunglasses, folded them, and slipped them into his jacket's breast pocket. "No thanks."

"Shoot."

Frank bowed his head as if to gather his thoughts. "You know you're a great editor, and you're the go-to girl when we need to be represented at conferences. You also have a natural ability to sniff out a children's bestseller."

Ally shifted forward in her chair, and focused all her attention on the CEO of Shout Children's Books. As good a friend as Frank was, her instinct told her this wasn't a social call.

"Thanks for that appreciated and rare compliment, but you didn't drive down the peninsula to praise me. What gives?"

He stood and started to pace the length of the porch. After two loops, he stopped and motioned to the *For Sale* sign. "Looks like you've got the house on the market."

Ally put her hands palms side up to show she had no choice. "Yeah. Since the divorce, I can't maintain the payments by myself."

"That's probably providential." Frank paused to wrangle a cough drop from his pocket, and popped it in his mouth. "I'm afraid I have bad news for you. I wanted to catch you before you read about it on Twitter and *Publisher's Weekly*."

Ally's stomach did a one-eighty. Her fingers sank down into the arms of the chair as she absently traced the relief pattern of the rattan. What was he trying to tell her? "Bad news? Providential?" This wasn't Frank asking her to head up the company's picnic committee.

"You know the financial woes of the children's publishing companies. People just aren't buying their kids books anymore. Video games, yes, print books, no." He took out a handkerchief and wiped the sweat off of his forehead. "We've tried to maintain an independent voice and keep our company going. But I just got word that the board has accepted an offer to merge with Randly House Publishing." He fiddled with his watch strap, repositioning it back and forth on his wrist like a nervous twitch.

"Bottom line?"

"Bottom line—we're downsizing. I was told we have too many acquisition editors and need to eliminate the one that had the least seniority."

Taking a big gulp, Ally inhaled the warm spring air, trying to comprehend his words. All she could hear was, "Eliminate, eliminate, eliminate." The word reverberated in her head like a tiny troll banging a brass gong. She opened her mouth to respond, but her throat felt covered with sand. She couldn't squeak out a word. Was she locked in a horrible dream? She'd climbed the company ladder, starting as an administrative assistant and then becoming an editor, earning excellent yearly reviews. She thought she'd work for Shout for life.

She eked out a hoarse "When?"

Frank leaned toward her and gave her hand a paternal pat. "In about two months. I'm negotiating a severance package for several of you. I'm so sorry, really I am. Just didn't see it coming."

Ally watched Frank's car disappear down the street. Gathering the little bit of strength she had left, she opened the front door and propelled her body toward the family room only to crash lengthwise onto the couch. Her Jack Russell Terrier, Jumping Bean, raced to the sofa and licked her on the arm. "At least you love me, J Bean."

Kylie, her daughter, walked into the family room from the kitchen, a couple of oatmeal cookies in her hand. "Mom, are we really selling the house?"

Ally put up both hands in front of her, a "don't even ask" gesture. She could hear the twelve-year-old angst in Kylie's voice, but was in no mood to start in with her daughter. She needed to control her own tsunami first.

"Sweetie, give me a moment." Ally pried herself off the couch, hobbled to the refrigerator and grabbed a can of Coke, then collapsed once more onto the family room couch. Bringing her feet up to her lap, she leaned over, massaging the balls of her feet. She was too tired for two-and-a-half-inch stilettos. The cool can felt good to Ally, pressed to her forehead, but it didn't calm her throbbing headache. How was she going to explain to Kylie about the house, and now her job?

"I already ate at Jamie's and, anyway, you guys promised we could stay here in this house. No fair, Mom."

Ally stood and walked over to the kitchen bar to thumb through the day's mail. Pulling out a bill, she turned around only to see her daughter had followed her. Kylie's look—two dark eyebrows dipped into a frown—told her Kylie wasn't going to give up until she had an answer.

"I did *not* promise anything of the sort. I said we'd stay here until it sells. We've been talking about selling for weeks, and it has to be sold as part of our divorce."

Her daughter's lip started to quiver like a diving board after a jump. "But all my friends, Mom. We *can't* move. We just can't."

How am I going to plow through this one?

She dropped the pile of mail on the counter, put out her arms, and drew her daughter in for a hug. "I know it's hard, but I'm asking you to be mature. Things don't always work out."

Kylie took a step back, crossing her arms defensively. "I'm sick of being mature. I want to be a kid." She lowered her head, long hair falling on either side of her face like two shiny sheets of chocolate satin.

Ally touched her daughter's chin and tipped it up. "Please, Kylie, I know this isn't what you wanted, but—"

Kylie jerked her head away. "If you and Dad could just get along—" Choking anger hung in the air like an invisible cloud.

Ally crossed her arms in front of herself. "That's enough."

"I have a right to say what I think." Kylie turned and stomped off to her bedroom.

"While you're up there, check on your brother."

Ally groaned and sat down on the long leather couch in the family room. Out of habit, she booted up her laptop, clicked open a file, but then shook her head. *Better check on Kylie.* She climbed the stairs to Kylie's bedroom and stood in the doorway. Her daughter sprawled out on the purple spread, crying.

"I'm sorry, sweetie. I didn't think we'd have to put the house up for sale so soon. Maybe we'll find another nearby." Ally curled up next to her daughter and hugged her, pulling up the old pink afghan that Aunt Nettie had crocheted when Kylie was a baby.

"Don't make this any harder. Please, honey."

Kylie shook her head. "You don't understand." She swiped at a tear running down her cheek.

Ally pulled a tissue from a box on her daughter's bedside, noticing the new box was half empty. "I do understand. I just can't fix it. Honey, we live in the most expensive part of the country. It comes down to money." *Yeah, money from my now non-existent job.* She massaged her daughter's back, waiting for the crying to subside before she slipped out.

She passed the office located in an alcove off the upstairs hallway, trying not to think about the vacant bookshelves or the empty spot in the middle of the large walnut desk where Bryan used to keep his computer, phone charger, and a row of family photos. Now it sat oddly clean and uncluttered, a piece of furniture that had lost its importance in their lives. *It looks empty and useless, like me. The desk and I, we've both lost our identity.*

In her bedroom, Ally threw her suit jacket on the bed. She had taken to sleeping in the middle now. It kept her from waking and seeing one side of the bed still made up. Now at least the whole bed would be messed up when she woke. She stared at the wall painted Heavenly Blue, and the carved four-poster bed with its gauzy peach-colored panels. The sanctuary now felt more like Ally's personal morgue. *And I hate the color Heavenly Blue.*

She pulled on brown leggings and a lacy stretch top, reminders of her ballet days. In the bathroom, she turned on the faucet to rinse off the day's stress. Georgia, her sister, used to say she could pass for a woman in her late twenties instead of thirty-five. But, since the divorce, her skin showed her stress. She probably needed to go back to the spa for a face peel to get rid of the latest crop of crow's-feet.

It didn't help to brush her hair and see dark red strands left in the sink. *I can't be losing my hair, can I?* Ally pulled back her hair to see her forehead. Yes, it did look higher.

While wrestling it back into a ponytail, she heard banging on the closet wall next to the bathroom sink. Ally turned toward the closet. Bryan's empty belt rack on the back wall vibrated, preview to an earthquake. The thud came from the other side—Benjie's room.

Just a few more minutes to myself, please, little man.

She flung herself onto the silky bedspread and rolled over onto her back.

Bam, bam, bam. The noise grew more demanding.

She jerked open her son's bedroom door to discover Benjie pounding his head against the wall—his head the drumstick, the wall the drumhead.

"Oh, baby, don't do that to yourself." Ally grabbed her son and cradled his head in one arm. With the other, she pulled her phone from her pocket and dialed Benjie's therapist. The dog pushed open the bedroom door, barking frantically.

"Quiet, J Bean. I don't need your opinion."

She tapped her foot, waiting for Maria to pick up.

The call went right to voicemail, and Ally spit out a terse message.

Why won't she pick up? Benjie squirmed out of her arms and returned to his head banging. Ally yanked a Transformers blanket off the bed. With one hand she wrapped the blanket around the top of his head as a cushion, and with her other hand she pulled a surgical sponge from the bedside table. Using firm strokes she put pressure on his limbs. His teacher promised the technique worked miracles in calming autistic children. It only took five minutes, and she felt him stop straining in her arms as his little body went limp.

"Me bad, me bad."

Ally tucked a wisp of hair behind his ear. "No, sweetie, you're not bad. You just can't run into the street. We want you to be safe." *Note to self: Buy son a helmet.*

Benjie took the lock of hair she had just tucked back and twirled it around his finger, around and around and around. Ally suppressed a scream. If she had to watch him flip his finger around that swatch of hair one more second, she'd be a candidate for the local mental health facility.

Ally disconnected his finger from the strand. "Why don't you play with your button collection instead?"

Grabbing a shoebox from a shelf above his desk, she dumped out the contents onto an oval braided rug. In just a few minutes, her only son had lined up all the buttons from small to large, dark to light.

"Whatever it takes."

Before closing the door, Ally glanced down at Benjie, lost in his world of buttons. He never looked up.

That night after dishes, she joined Benjie in the family room. Pulling out more paperwork from her briefcase, Ally settled onto the couch and looked over the pile. She estimated a couple hours of work ahead. Her analysis of two key manuscripts needed to be submitted by Monday. Might as well finish on a good note.

Kylie padded down the stairs, rubbing her still swollen eyes, and slid into the leather club chair across from her mother. "Mom?" she said as she fingered the curves of a vase next to her.

"Hi, sweetie." Ally patted a spot next to her, inviting Kylie to sit beside her, before looking back at her computer.

"I have to know—can we at least stay in this neighborhood?"

"I don't know." Ally finished the last sentence of an email then looked up.

"Are we moving?"

"Somewhere."

"When will you know where?"

"Not sure."

The corners of her daughter's mouth flipped up. "Mom, you always say that a lot can happen in twenty-four hours. You never know."

Ally gave her a thumbs-up and flashed her a smile. *Bless that girl for her eternal optimism.*

"Twenty-four," added Benjie as he used toothpicks to outline the gray and brown hexagons in the patterned rug.

"Yep, so hop to bed so we'll have a new twenty-four hours sooner." Ally kissed her daughter goodnight, then turned and watched her go down the hall, taking her long skinny legs with her. Dad used to say to Ally, "You have long legs to take yourself to places faster. But where will you be when you arrive?"

Where *had* they taken her? Would Kylie be in a hurry, and as impatient, too?

*   *   *

"What's this about a new twenty-four hours?" a low voice interrupted her thoughts. Bryan had slipped into the family room and into the conversation. He leaned over to ruffle Benjie's hair and give him a kiss on the top of his head. "Just came by to give you the real estate brochures."

Ally glared at the tall lean figure she used to be married to; the sight of him caused her jaw to lock. "Where have you been? I had to tell Kylie by myself."

Bryan shook his head. "Sorry, I had no idea they'd stick the sign in the yard so soon. I want to sit down and talk to her."

"As usual, your timing's impeccably bad."

The moment the cutting words escaped her lips, pain slashed across his face, and Ally wished she could take them back.

"As usual, your role in life is to remind me I'm not the perfect father."

Ally bit her lip, trying not to say anything more, but the

poison slipped out again. "If you had been around more—"

"Here we go again."

"—maybe we would have had a semblance of a normal family."

Bryan lowered his head and pinched the bridge of his nose, a sign of trying to control his anger.

She gulped. "I'm sorry, that just slipped out."

"Not the first time. Or the last, Miss Wordsmith."

CHAPTER
TWO

Ally woke up early that next Saturday morning to the dull plinkety-plink sound of rain on the roof. The downpour matched her soggy mood. She rolled to the side of the bed and stood. In the darkened room, she slid her way into her cozy fleece slippers. Ally yanked up one blind a few inches above the window. Only a sliver of gray light peeked through. She sat on the edge of her bed, listening to the hammering drops, trying to block out last night's fight. She could admit Bryan hadn't meant for her to break the news alone, to tell their daughter about selling the house, but her temper couldn't keep her from lashing out. Yes, she occasionally shot her mouth off, but Bryan could be so unreasonable. It hadn't always been that way. Things hadn't been perfect, but how did they ever end up at this level of ugly?

Ally's head throbbed as she tried to reconstruct the final argument that ripped their marriage apart. Bryan's comments—"That son of yours" and "*You* wanted another baby" and "A hot meal would be a treat. Shall I show you how to turn on the oven?"—still haunted her.

Just let it go, she thought as the memory tightened the knot in her stomach. She trudged to the bathroom to find an antacid tablet, only to find the bottle empty. Back in her room, she picked up the phone on her bedside table and scrolled down to her sister's number. "Hi, Georgia. Hey, I know it's early, but I needed to talk."

"No problem. Spill."

Ally stretched out her body on her bed. "Just thinking about the last argument Bryan and I had. It still haunts me."

"Give your brain a rest, Sis. You've been through a lot."

Ally rocked back and forth on the side of the bed. "I know, but the things he said I can't forget. It's almost like the Devil came to call and stayed, if you believe in that stuff."

"You can't keep thinking about it. Focus on the kids."

"Yeah, the kids. You're right. Thanks, Georgia."

She hung up the phone but another memory appeared— their last anniversary. What had usually been a weekend in the wine country turned into a hectic meal, both of them on the phone the entire time. She wanted to stomp the memory, but it popped up like an unwanted gremlin.

Snap out of it, Ally. She walked back to the bathroom and turned on the tap to wash her face. Cool water soothed her swollen face, bloated from tears. Again, her untamed thoughts ran ragged.

Why the comment about Benjie? His teacher said Benjie needed both of his parents to be involved in his life, but the more he acted up, the more Bryan threw himself into growing his new software company. *I'm the one who always talks to his teacher.*

She opened a drawer and pulled out her favorite corduroy jeans and a plum cardigan sweater. Thank God it was Saturday. She stepped into a pair of ballet flats, then walked down the hall and peeked into Benjie's room. Good, he was still asleep. In Kylie's room, she glanced around at her daughter's favorite girl band posters and travel posters of Michigan. Ally tiptoed past the bookshelf full of DVDs, CDs, and miscellaneous stuffed animals, many not played with for several years. Two Barbie dolls stood guard at the end of one of the shelves. Ally sighed, knowing playing dolls would soon disappear. Kylie was close to becoming a teenager. The ache started as a wave from Ally's toes, moving in a fury until it reached the top of her head. *Slow down, honey. Just stay this age for a while.*

"I'm going to Jolly's. Watch your brother if he wakes up," Ally whispered into the ear of her half-asleep daughter. She smoothed the long bangs off of Kylie's forehead and found a pimple hiding.

"Can you buy a bag of doughnuts there?" Kylie murmured. "Daddy buys doughnuts on Saturday."

*   *   *

It took an hour meeting with the bank and her money manager for Ally to recognize she was headed down a slimy slope to a dark lagoon called bankruptcy. Where should she go now?

Back at the house, she pulled out her wallet to pay Benjie's overpriced therapist, who was leaving. When the front door closed, she put her arm around her daughter and pulled her son out of the corner. They sat huddled together, motionless around the kitchen table. All she could hear was the rattling of the ice-maker in the kitchen.

After a few minutes, Ally headed to the refrigerator, grabbed a pop, and slammed the door shut.

What could have gone wrong? She had a special-needs child. No, change that. She *and* Bryan had a special-needs child. Benjie's autism diagnosis had turned their marriage upside-down.

Ally leaned against the stainless steel refrigerator as she tried to avert the beginnings of a splitting headache. The coolness soothed her forehead.

She thought they could survive anything together, but having a child that would never play golf or take over Bryan's company was a dream-killer.

Ally stroked her daughter's hair then opened the freezer for the ice cream carton. She turned around and saw Benjie twirling in circles on the kitchen floor.

"Where's my big boy Benjie?" Ally held out her arms and, for the first time in weeks, Benjie ran to her. Her arms closed around his tiny body as she felt his rib cage expand and retract.

Thankful for small miracles. She scooped two bowls of Moose Tracks ice cream for the kids.

"When can I see Dad?" asked Kylie. "I *miss* him." She dragged out the word *miss* to be sure Ally got the point.

"I know, but he'll be by on Wednesday. You'll stay at his house on Wednesday nights and on weekends. Probably see him more now."

Kylie licked the ice cream off her spoon. "Why can't he live here? Doesn't he like us anymore?"

Ally walked to the refrigerator and grabbed another pop. "We've been over this before, Kylie. Your daddy doesn't want to be married anymore. But that doesn't change how much he loves you. He's just—he's very confused right now."

"Do you think he'll get unconfused and come home?"

Ally studied the ingredients of the soda can, avoiding her daughter's eyes.

"Mama, answer me." "Mama" meant upset.

"We can only pray," Ally replied, taking a swig of her soda and wishing she had a few ounces of rum to add to it. "Yeah, pray. Ha! That's a concept."

"Pray, ha! Pray, ha!" echoed Benjie. He climbed into his chair, and held onto the edge of the seat rocking the chair side to side. Droplets of ice cream dribbled down both sides of his mouth.

In spite of this being one of the worst days of her life, Ally let out a chuckle. "Benjie, you sure know how to enjoy life. Give you a bowl of ice cream, and you're in heaven."

If only her life could be that simple.

*   *   *

"Are you positive we'll have an offer if we lower it?" Ally quizzed her realtor the next day. She'd figured out many people cruise through open houses as a weekend lark, never meaning to buy, and her checking account was a reminder her personal *Titanic* was about to sink. Earlier in the year, she assured Kylie that they wouldn't move, but the divorce meant liquidating the house. As much as she wanted Kylie to be able to stay in her own neighborhood, hanging onto the house would be impossible.

"I've read about the real estate bubble collapsing, but it's about all I have, Tim, and we need to extract every penny out of this property." She opened the hutch in her dining room, pulled out two delicate china cups and saucers, two slim gold lines decorating the perimeter, and placed them on the mahogany coffee table. As she closed the door, an idea flashed through her mind. *The hutch could be another way to round up extra cash.* She'd call Atherton Antiques in the morning. She tried to blot out the memory of Bryan purchasing it for her birthday during their first year of marriage.

Tim tapped her shoulder. "Are you hearing me?"

Ally shook her head. "Sorry, got distracted. How much did you say?"

"You probably should list it for $1.3 million."

Ally's jaw tightened. "I'm not in the mood for jokes, Tim."

"I know you paid $1.4 million five years ago, but as you know, the housing market is in a slump in the Bay Area. Nothing is moving unless it is priced under appraisal."

"I know." Ally slumped onto the leather couch holding her coffee cup. She'd like to have the money they paid for that couch in her savings account right now.

Tim handed her the papers to sign for a price change. "We'll both think positive thoughts. By the way, do you have a place in mind when you sell?"

"Haven't thought that far. Maybe a rental in my kids' school district. I love their school, and hate to move them now."

"I'll keep my ears open for a good prospect. We'll sell it quickly, even in this market."

The front door burst open and Kylie marched in, holding Benjie's hand.

"You forgot school got out early today. You were supposed to pick us up at two o'clock." She rolled her eyes so Ally wouldn't miss her message. "Ember brought us home." Then she squatted down to eye-level with her brother. "You buckled your seatbelt all by yourself, didn't you?" She clapped her hands together, and Benjie mimicked her.

Ally felt her throat tighten. How could she have forgotten? She poked her head out the front door and waved to their neighbor who was parked in the driveway. "Sorry." Ember honked and pulled into the road.

Kylie whipped her head around to her mother and narrowed her eyes. "Why is Mr. Lee here? We didn't sell our house already, did we?"

Tim glanced at Kylie's face. "Hey, need to go, 101 is bumper-to-bumper this time of day. We'll talk later."

The roar from Tim's sports car pulling out of her driveway almost muffled the wailing from Kylie as she fled to her bedroom in tears.

Almost but not quite.

Chapter
Three

Shout Books prided itself on being the cutting-edge publishing company: books for the modern child. "Exciting reading for today's children, stories for the plugged-in generation," was their motto. Now, in the Shout conference room, a strident monologue bounced off the walls, rattling the windows.

"Lately, I've been seeing a lot of namby-pamby crap floating through here. Let's take a look at the titles coming across my desk: *The Gypsy Moth's Ball, Alex and His Pet Llama Take a Vacation.* Oh, and how about *Derek the Daredevil Becomes a Professional Snowshoe Guide?* These stories are lame at best, dated, and not of any interest to the average reader. We need manuscripts that are sellable. There's a writer's conference back East next month. Who's volunteering?"

Ally looked around the table. Not one hand went up. She reined in the urge to walk out of the meeting. Why should she care? She only had her job for another month. Still, she needed a good reference.

Frank turned to her, a smile that begged cooperation. "I guess you're it, Ms. Cervantes. There's a Northern Children's Writers' Workshop coming up in Traverse City, Michigan, in three weeks. One of the main speakers couldn't make it, so I gave them your name. I expect you to snag a sitter for your children and cover that conference like a mother hen covers her eggs. I want a few good hatched ones."

"Come on, Frank, send Travis." She needed the time to start job hunting.

"Will be on his honeymoon."

She turned to Kim. "What about Kim?"

"Mother's in hospice, can't leave," Kim replied.

"Give me a break, Frank. You know I have a hard time finding a sitter, and Bryan is traveling the whole month of May."

Frank laughed. "I *am* giving you a break—a free vacation in beautiful Northern Michigan, whatever that looks like."

Ally leaned forward in her chair. "For your information, it's a beautiful state, especially this time of year."

"Then, by process of elimination, you're it."

Ally groaned inwardly, but the more she thought about it, she figured a few days away might be fun. Working full-time, commuting fifty-five minutes on Highway 280 and coming home to grumpy kids was no picnic. She could try to scrape up a little loyalty to Frank. It wasn't his fault. He didn't want the merger.

She sighed. "I'll see if my mom can help."

A snappy little tune announced her ringing cell phone to the whole meeting.

"Must be your travel agent," said Kim.

The whole room chuckled as Ally silenced her phone. She'd talk to Aunt Nettie later.

Later that evening, Ally settled on the couch and dialed her aunt's number. "Aunt Nettie? It's Ally."

"Why, what a treat to talk to you, dear. How are you holding up?"

"You don't want to know." Ally swiped at a tear sloping down her cheek.

"I *do* want to hear. I've been talking to your mother, and she's kept me updated. I'm so sorry about what happened to you and Bryan."

"It came out of the blue. *I* didn't see it coming. We just kept fighting, and I hated that for the kids. Thought we could fix things, but at the end, it fell apart. So now I'm a single mom raising an autistic son and a daughter who cries herself to sleep nightly."

"I wish I could be there to give you a big hug. It takes a lot of persistence on the part of both parents to raise a special-needs child."

"Obviously, Silicon Valley Man of the Year had his mind elsewhere; otherwise he'd have been there for us. He can be a mover and shaker in the world of software companies, but he bailed on me." Ally glanced down at her nails. She'd chewed off most of her red polish. "I'm sorry. I'm making him out to be the bad guy. I take responsibility for some of it."

"I see this so much with our families. I could tell you so many stories, but I don't want to depress you even more. How can I help you now? You know you and Kylie and Benjie are in my prayers."

Lot of good that does, but even out of touch, her aunt had always been there for her. Ally could depend on her for a listening ear and a few Bible verses. A widow, Aunt Nettie lived in Northern Michigan, and had taught special education classes until she retired.

"I have a huge favor to ask you. Shout wants me to go to a writers' conference in Traverse City and I was wondering if you—"

"Might be able to fly out to babysit?" Nettie finished the sentence. "Why, of course. I'll make you one better. Why don't you stay at my cottage while you're at the conference? I moved from my old house. I'm now in the Lake Surrender cottage, right around the bend from where your parents used to rent. Remember how you used to hang out with that kid, Willy, who lived a few doors down? You and your sister spent hours swimming out to his family's raft in the middle of the lake."

"I'd love to stay in the cottage. I asked Mom to come, but she and dad have a trip planned to Cancun. It's their fortieth anniversary."

"I miss my little munchkins. Just plan on me."

Ally let out a sigh. "I can't thank you enough. It will be my last trip for Shout. I got downsized a few weeks ago."

"Oh Ally, I'm so sorry."

"A merger. It's part of being in the publishing world right now. I'm already sending out résumés. Anyway, I hope I won't be gone more than four days."

"You just take your time. I'll fly out, bring my paints, and work on a portrait of the kids."

Aunt Nettie loved to paint, and when she wasn't painting children's furniture for a local store, she was painting children's portraits. She claimed she wanted to be buried with her paintbrushes resting on top of her chest so she could render a portrait of St. Peter when he let her in the pearly gates.

"Leave a few favorite photos out, and I'll see what I can start. I'll leave the key under the geranium pot by the front door, and you just make yourself at home. Freezer will be full."

"You're a lifesaver."

*   *   *

"Mommy's not going to be gone long," Ally whispered into Benjie's ear as she sat him down on the chair next to her bed. They had just greeted Aunt Nettie's taxi and settled her in her room for the evening. Now Ally needed to pack. She pulled the suitcase from under the bed and dumped it on top.

Thump. Thump. Thump. Thump.

Here it comes, another tantrum. How many times had she

watched his left foot stomp, signifying the volcano was about to blow? She just didn't have time for that tonight. She folded a couple of blouses and laid them on top of her open suitcase.

"I promise to call you every night before I go to bed."

But that didn't slow the stomping cowboy boot pounding harder and faster.

Ally sighed. "Aunt Nettie will be here the whole time, and she—"

Benjie crawled onto the bed. Ally grabbed for his thin torso but couldn't catch him in time. He flipped the entire contents of her suitcase onto the floor. Wool trousers, jeans, her olive cardigan, her best brown heels, and underwear piled into a heap. Then he opened the makeup kit, and mineral powder and blush scattered all over the carpet. Ally lunged for his arm, but he jumped off the bed and squatted down by her ankle. Sharp pain shot through her leg.

"Ouch!"

Tiny drops of blood dripped from the teeth marks. That did it. She raised her hand to slap his leg, but Benjie fled down the hall.

"You're not running this household yet," she shrieked, trying to catch him.

Kylie popped out of her room, waving a book. "Mom, you promised you'd help—"

"Hold on." Ally caught Benjie by the edge of his ragged green Chuck E. Cheese T-shirt. *Thought you could scoot downstairs. No way, buddy.* "Bring paper towels, Windex, and the Dust Buster," she ordered Kylie.

Kylie took one look at her mother's expression, dashed to the laundry room, and appeared back with all three requested items.

"I'm winning *this* round," Ally shouted as she flipped on the switch to start the machine.

Benjie let out a high-pitched squeal, putting his hands over his ears. She pried his hands off of his ears and wrapped his fingers around the vacuum's handle. Ally planted her hands firmly on top of his; together they swept up the powder strewn all over the carpet and bedspread—until Benjie wiggled out from underneath her grip. Ally placed the small vacuum down on the carpet. Benjie grabbed the screaming machine, flew into her bathroom, and pitched the tool into the toilet for a 3-pointer that would make any NBA player proud. The Dust Buster gurgled a few seconds and then, with a hiss, gave up the ghost.

Ally looked at the mess. The sight of the red vacuum drowning in her toilet was priceless. She chuckled. How could her life become any more absurd? Her chuckle turned to a full belly laugh until she slumped to the floor, holding her stomach.

Kylie ran into the room. "What's going on?"

Benjie stood in the doorway with a confused look. Ally pointed to the toilet and then wrestled her son onto the floor in a clumsy embrace. "It took one of your tantrums to make your mama laugh. Bless you."

*   *   *

She collapsed into the Ford Taurus she'd rented at the Traverse City airport. A light mist covered the road as Ally turned west onto Highway 72. Her trip would take about a half hour, just enough time for her to unwind. All that dashing to the San Francisco airport and barely making the connection from O'Hare in Chicago to Traverse City had left her with a headache that started from her neck and reached all the way to the top of her head.

Sometimes life is just too tough.

Ally zipped around a curve, barely missing a squirrel. "Stupid animal."

People talked about how their cup runneth over, in a good way. Her cup was overflowing like a plugged toilet, badly in need of a plumber.

She took a shortcut, a winding road veering off the highway, and gunned the engine as she followed the road through the empty pastures with patches of green grass and thick wooded countryside. Spring pushed tentatively through the soil, not convinced of its welcome in the cool temperatures. Still, white three-petal trilliums and bright yellow marsh marigolds peeked through wet leaves matted on the forest floor. Pale green points burst through the tips of the branches, giving life to what had been dead only a few weeks ago. Ally's favorite trees, northern birches with their graceful trunks and peeling silvery-white bark, reminded her she was actually in Northern Michigan. Her dad referred to the trees as "ladies in nightgowns" when he drove the backroads of Lake Surrender. Oh, how she loved those trees from her childhood memories.

Being in Michigan brought back the promise of summer days long gone when her parents would rent a cabin on Lake Surrender. She could still remember the smell of early morning coffee brewing and pancakes frying on the griddle. The aroma of summer breakfast mixed with the scent of pines and the remnants of last night's campfire.

Maybe I'm trying to recapture a place that only exists in my mind. But a strange pull, like the desire to see an old love, enveloped Ally as she pushed down on the accelerator. A tingling of dormant joy rippled through her body.

Pulling into the wooded lane, her car crunched over a gravel road. Just another half mile and the memories poured in. Built from the remnants of old log cabins in the area, Aunt Nettie's place stood on the east side of Lake Surrender, with a picture window looking out over eighty feet of lakefront. A stone path led up to the front porch decorated with pots of violets and pansies. The front door, the color of a ripe banana, sported a floral spring wreath. *Vintage Nettie. No one ever accused her of liking dull colors.*

Once inside the cottage, Ally plunked her suitcases down on a pine floor so shiny Aunt Nettie must have polished it daily. She gazed around the cottage at Nettie's projects: cheerful tables and a desk likely hauled out of a nearby junk store or flea market. Each summer, Nettie toted home treasures to keep or to paint for a local art store. The couch, for instance—though the cushions were soft chartreuse green, the frame was painted white with a pink trim. Two pink and green floral print chairs flanked the sofa.

White eyelet lace curtains framed the front windows, showcasing the glossy deep blue lake, the surface rippled only by an occasional fish coming up for its dinner. All was well with the world. Late afternoon sun filtered through the family room as she opened up the blinds, letting in just enough light to create a pensive mood. She watched the rosy hues of sunset that lingered wistfully on the outlying silhouette of the lake as two swans built their nest on the shore of the vacant lot next door.

Ally cranked open a side window. A dove called to its mate with a throaty lilt. Ally let the sound flow over her, surrounding her as she shook off the accumulated stress of living in the San Francisco metro area. Every muscle in her body started to loosen.

Ally removed her ponytail holder and shook out her hair. *I forgot how slow things move up here.*

She pulled out a bag of coffee from a kitchen cabinet and made a pot of French Roast. Bryan's favorite. She commanded the lump in her throat to go away. Opening the refrigerator, she searched for a carton of cream, but wrapped her hands around a small pan covered with aluminum foil. She pulled back the foil: chicken enchiladas. Awesome! Aunt Nettie knew her weakness. She preheated the oven and poured a cup of coffee before sitting down at the kitchen table. *Lots of good memories and meals at this table.* She fingered a photo of her aunt on the shelf next to the table. Smiling, Nettie showed off her prize-winning pie at the State Fair. Ally's mouth tipped up into a grin. On the plump side, Aunt Nettie could cook circles around Mom, especially with Blueberry Crumb Bread and Italian Cream Cake—her aunt's specialties.

Ally picked up her cell phone from the kitchen counter. As she hit *Home* in her contacts list, another call beeped in. What did Frank want now? He'd just have to wait; the kids came first. He seemed to have an annoying way of knowing exactly when she'd landed, and always wanted an update on her schedule.

"Hi, Aunt Nettie, how's it going? I just got to your place, and I'm unwinding. Found the enchiladas in the refrigerator. You're amazing."

"Just a little supper after your long flight. Kids are doing great. Kylie is helping Benjie play Twister. After that, they want to help me make peanut butter cookies." She paused for a minute. "Kylie is growing up so fast!"

Ally grabbed the pan of enchiladas and slid them into the oven. "I know—scares me. I'm not ready for the teen years. Hey, can you put her on quick?"

Kylie's voice sounded bright. "Mom, we're having a great time. Aunt Nettie is so cool. And guess what? She got Benjie to hold a pencil, and she's working on having him make the letter B. Benjie's trying hard, and he hasn't stomped his feet all afternoon."

Thank heavens for little things. "I'm so glad things are working out."

"Oh, we got to go now. Aunt Nettie is taking us to rent a DVD. Benjie is in the car or he'd talk to you."

"That's fine. Give him a kiss for me." Ally ended the call. *I forgot to tell Aunt Nettie to stay away from the Dust Buster.*

Ally washed and dried her plate, and put it up in the knotty-pine cabinet. She looked out the front window, feeling the magnetic pull of the lake beckoning her out to the front porch. She breathed the cool air, an enchanting potpourri of blooming lilacs, wood decks mildewed from the winter, fish smells, and fresh-cut grass. The breeze picked up, and she pulled her cardigan snugly around her. The San Francisco airport and freeway traffic jams didn't exist right now. Tomorrow would be full of appointments and two classes she'd been tapped to teach on writing for the young adult market.

She smiled in anticipation of teaching her classes. She probably should review the keynote speech she'd be making on the last night. No, not now. This moment was a gift, begging her to empty her mind of all the stresses of the last few months. It was like an invisible hand reaching to loosen a guitar string pulled too taut. That was her life—six strings ready to burst. Ally rocked back and forth on the white peeling porch swing, lowering her eyelids as she remembered how she and her sister would sit on it during many a July evening. She missed Georgia.

Georgia lived in Baltimore and rarely flew out to the West Coast, but the sisters kept in touch with occasional emails. She'd married a high school principal, and ran herself ragged with carpooling three little boys to sports teams and Cub Scouts. On a whim, Ally fished her phone from her pants pocket and scrolled down to find her sister's number.

"Hey, Georgie-girl, guess where I am?"

"Knowing you and your exotic, high-powered career, you're probably sitting in a quaint French bistro in Manhattan after nailing a multi-million-dollar book contract," Georgia answered.

"Hardly." Ally still didn't want to tell her about the layoff. "I'm at Aunt Nettie's. Got a horse and pony show, and I'm the keynote speaker. It's a kick to be back here."

"You lucky dog. While I'm doing school runs to three different schools, you're lapping up pure lake air. I'll bet she still has that ancient front porch swing."

"Yep, I'm doing swing therapy as we speak. Brings back a lot of summer memories. Remember when we collected pine cones and sold them at the old General Store to tourists?"

"Yeah, and how we played all day, digging for gold in the sand? That dumb kid who lived by the post office told us pirates dumped their loot there."

Ally grinned. "My favorite was sneaking off after dinner in Aunt Nettie's old leaky rowboat to spy on those cute guys at the Boy Scout camp. It got dark, and we couldn't remember how to find home, so Dad had to come rescue us with the speedboat. That was one of those grounded-for-life moments. But, hey, I'm doing all the talking. Is Jarrid still goalie for his team?"

After a few minutes, she closed the phone, but not before reassuring Georgia she'd visit Baltimore soon.

She watched the outdoor plastic thermometer's red ball drop to 39 degrees. Ally shivered and slipped inside the front door. She took one last look at the lake before bolting the deadlock and heading for bed. She slipped into a pair of pajamas and a soft cotton robe. In the guest room, she pulled back the creamy yellow quilt covered with a daffodil pattern. As she settled into the sheets, she slid into the deepest sleep she'd had in months.

CHAPTER
FOUR

Something kept ringing. Eyes closed, Ally fumbled for her phone.

"What desert island are you on?" boomed Frank. "I called you yesterday, and you never got back. And now the conference director has put two calls into me asking why you haven't shown up. What's going on, Cervantes?"

She raced to the kitchen and looked at the clock, a black cat with a pendulum. It read ten o'clock. Yikes. A knot tightened in her stomach. She forgot to change her alarm to a.m. and, because of the three-hour time difference, she had overslept.

"Frank, I'm leaving in three minutes. Had car trouble and I'm at the service station. I'll give the director a call."

Why did I just fib?

Ally threw on her gray dress trousers and a cream-colored silk blouse, and pulled a comb through her hair. *Keep it together, Cervantes.* She grabbed her makeup bag and threw it in the car. She could put her makeup on at a stop sign.

She pushed down on the accelerator and shot out onto the county road. Groggy from lack of caffeine, she tried to focus on what she needed to do next. *Oh yes, call the director.* She flipped through a notebook she'd pulled from her purse to find the number. While dialing, she slammed on the brakes to miss a wild turkey.

"Oh, sorry, Mr. Tournquist, I didn't mean you! I'm yelling at a stupid turkey. I'll be there in fifteen minutes." Her hands shook as she grabbed the steering wheel to stabilize herself.

Pulling into Little Traverse Bay Conference Center, she leaned down over the passenger's seat to grab her briefcase on the floor. No briefcase. All she saw was her purse. A cold fear shot through her body. She racked her mind to remember where she had put the briefcase. *Did I leave it at work?* She grabbed her phone.

"Looking for something?" Ally heard coworker Kim's voice snicker on the other end of the phone.

"Hey, Kim, what's going on?"

"I think you might be missing your notes. I just passed your desk and saw your briefcase sitting on top."

"What? I was just checking and couldn't find it. Are you positive it's mine?"

"Aren't you supposed to be teaching three writing classes? I think I'm looking right at your notes."

"Are you kidding?"

"Why would I kid about that?"

Ally hit her forehead with her palm. Her right eyelid

started the old twitch, her body's sign for too much stress. "I think I'll shoot myself."

"Hey, girlfriend, you're in a pickle. Do you want me to fax them to you?"

"Oh, that would be fantastic." She pulled out a business card for the conference director. "Here's the fax number. You are awesome."

Ally slipped in through the front door and scurried past the reception desk, trying to avoid the director's eyes. Luckily he was tied up with another faculty member, his back turned to her, but he caught up with her in the second class, faxed pages in hand. She thanked him, the heat of embarrassment creeping up her face like the mercury in a thermometer. In Ally's eyes, unprofessionalism ranked high on the list of cardinal sins.

In late afternoon, she scoured through the manuscripts she'd critiqued. *Doesn't anyone know how to write tight?* Other manuscripts either dripped with flowery descriptions or read like a Stephen King novel for children. She lugged her jetlagged body home after eating orange chicken at the local Chinese restaurant with conference members.

The next day went better. After being introduced as one of the industry's rising stars, Ally walked to the platform. At the speaker's podium, she surveyed the eager new authors ready to absorb her every word. Pens poised, ready to write her wisdom of the publishing world. She basked in the moment but then thought, *If they only knew, I'm more like one of the falling stars.* But now she was in her sweet spot. She'd shine, and show Shout what they'd be missing.

"Children's literature is changing, just like our society is evolving. Today I will share three observations any children's writer should regard to keep on the cutting edge. Miss these points, and you'll be back to writing non-profit newsletters or letters to the editor." Ally continued for an hour to expand her points. Successful and potential authors furiously jotted notes. At the end, she smiled and looked over the crowd standing and applauding. The glow continued as she counted ten in line by the podium, ready to pelt her with eager questions. *This is what I've worked for. They love me.* Confidence that had taken a huge dip, rose, buoyed by today's accolades.

After answering questions, she nabbed a potential author, Jeremy, a young man who wrote in the style of *Eragon*, the popular fantasy novel that had come out a few years ago.. "Great story line. I'd love to see the first three chapters. This has possibilities."

With a half-hearted grin, he agreed.

Probably thought he'd walk away with a book contract.

Ally picked up her purse and meandered towards a group of her colleagues, enjoying the fellowship, catching up on the industry gossip.

Her phone rang as she hiked back to her car. She checked the number. Frank again. She didn't have a lot to report; she'd call him back later. Instead she dialed home.

"Hi, hi, hi!"

"Benjie, it's Mommy. I've missed you. I hear you are learning to hold a pencil and write a B."

"B, Benjie."

"And I'm proud of you. Are you having fun with Aunt Nettie?"

"Aunt Auntie, Aunt Auntie."

"I'm glad," said Ally. "I'll be home soon. Love you. Is Kylie there?"

"Sorry," interrupted Aunt Nettie. "Kylie had to stay after school to work on a project. I'll tell her you called."

After a few more remarks about Benjie's schedule, Ally ended the call and put her cell phone in her purse. *Time for a quick dinner before heading back to the cottage.*

She pulled the car onto the narrow highway that led to Mission Point. Rolling down the windows, she welcomed the light spring air.

Pangs of hunger reminded her she needed to eat dinner soon. She passed a friendly burger joint called Hamburger Haven, perfect for dinner. The waitress seated her by the window overlooking a small patio filled with pots of red geraniums and umbrella tables advertising an Italian wine. She placed her order with an older woman who might have been there since the restaurant's beginnings in 1935. "One tuna melt and a small Caesar salad, please."

Ally pulled out a couple of manuscripts she'd been reading, but was interrupted by a woman's musical laugh. She peered up from her work to see an attractive couple in their thirties walking toward her. He was about five feet ten with a thick thatch of brown hair, deep-set black eyes, and a trimmed beard. The woman was tiny, with long blonde hair and tiny hands that would make Snow White swoon with envy. Her thin body looked like she rarely ate three meals a day. *She desperately needs a double cheeseburger and a shake.*

They scooted into a booth across from her.

Being an avid people watcher, she sneaked a peek out of the side of her eyes. Cozy in the same booth, the man put his arm around the woman, and she had his complete attention. They talked about an orphanage in Mexico, and high school memories. There was something familiar about the guy, but Ally couldn't place where she'd seen him, a vague resemblance to a person in her distant past. He raised his hand to summon the waitress, and Ally noticed the tip of his left pinky was missing. She only knew one person who had a digit missing, a boy she knew from summers past who'd been in a boating accident. *That can't be that kid, Will, who used to play with me when we visited here in the summer?*

He was three years older than she, and a know-it-all. She was a city girl, he a country boy, and he had loved to tease her. Even still, his memory irritated her. He had convinced her and her sister there were rattlesnakes in the lake, bats in the rec hall, and pirate treasure in the lot next to the post office. She and Georgia spent two weeks digging around the post office until the postmaster called her parents.

What's he doing here?

He glanced up, and she found herself looking into dark brown eyes that crinkled at the edges. Yes, she remembered that large wide grin from the past encounters when she positively *knew* he had been secretly laughing at her. *Guess you never outgrew your annoying smile.*

"Great burgers here," he said to Ally.

She nodded back with a polite smile.

Ally stuffed down her sandwich, and pulled out a ten and four ones from her wallet to pay for dinner. She scrambled to put on her trench coat, and jumped up from the table. As she stood, her foot caught the strap of her purse sitting on the floor by her feet, and Ally fell, within an inch of kissing the floor in the aisle between the two booths.

Trying to rescue any dignity left, she looked up to see the guy squatted down next to her. "Need help?"

He held out his hand. The large palm had thick calluses, like a builder's. Ally hesitated, and then put her hand in his. It felt rough as it covered hers. *Wonder what this grownup version of Will does for a living?* An unexpected but pleasurable shiver went through her body as she released his hand. *If it's you, please don't recognize me.*

Ally brushed dust off her pants, wanting to restore an ounce of self-respect for herself. A quick thanks and she scooted straight for the front door. Georgia wouldn't believe this one.

Once in her car, she headed for downtown Traverse City. The evening loomed long and lonely ahead, and she needed to fill in the hours. She turned onto Front Street. Maybe she'd kill some time by getting a coffee. Cherry County Coffee, packed to the rafters, seemed to be the place to hang out. A local bluegrass fiddler had drawn a crowd of college students who surrounded the wooden makeshift stage. The audience roared as they tried singing along with the dark-haired soloist in time to an Irish jig. A short bald mandolin player kept the time, picking faster and faster. Clapping along, Ally looked around and became conscious she was the only one not paired with a significant other. Dropping her hands to her sides, she pinched her lips together and stared out the window, feeling alone. *Sitting at a table by myself, pretending to have fun, is pathetic. I'm not a couple; I'm just another divorced woman trying to cope.* She could have kicked herself for choosing a coffee shop. Too many memories. Better a quiet bar and a Cosmo.

We both chose to end it. Stop whining, Ally. She stirred an extra shot of cream into the mug and took a big slug. *Here's to my new life. I'll survive even if it kills me.*

CHAPTER
FIVE

The plane touched down in San Francisco. A balmy seventy-five degrees, but Ally hardly noticed. Weather, the god many worshipped in California, seemed unimportant right now. She was coming back to one more week of employment, a house to sell, and unhappy kids. A side of her wanted to just stay in Michigan. With a shaky hand she started up her car in the parking lot and headed south for home. The South Bay hills had turned their characteristic straw yellow. Green in the rainy months, they were dry in late spring. *Dry as my soul.* All she wanted to do was hug her kids, drink a cup of tea with Aunt Nettie, and have a good cry.

At the exit, Ally flipped the right blinker on. A few more turns, and she pulled into her driveway. She didn't have the energy to take her bags out of the trunk. That could wait.

She put the key in the front door and turned the knob.

"Is that you, Ally? I hope so because I'm up to my elbows in pizza dough and can't fend off even the mildest-mannered burglar." Holding up dough-covered hands, Aunt Nettie came into the living room and leaned over to give her a kiss hello. Ally got a whiff of Nettie's familiar scents, a combination of lavender soap and Pond's Cold Cream.

Ally hugged her neck. "Glad to be back. Even though I love Michigan, it was hectic. But I received good feedback on my talk."

"Excellent. I'll fix you a cup of peach ginger tea, and you can tell me all about it." Nettie went back into the kitchen, and before long the tea kettle whistled.

Anticipating the soothing beverage, Ally plunked herself in front of the breakfast bar. She breathed in the steam from the hot mug and reached for the cream and honey. Fresh peanut butter cookies piled high on a red stoneware plate called to her, and her resistance flew out the window. *Might as well eat away my depression.*

"Where do I start?" Ally paused to sink her teeth into the cookie. "The trip back east went fine. I got to the cottage the first night and just unwound. By the way, I love your new place. The next day, I overslept because I forgot about the time difference and had jet lag. I woke up to my cell phone going off. It was my boss, Frank. He wanted to know why I wasn't at the conference. The director had called him and wondered if I had missed my flight."

"Good Heavens!"

"I said a few stronger words than 'Oh dear.' Anyway, I raced to the conference, and when I got there, I reached over to grab my briefcase, and it dawned on me I had left it in the office. So I called Kim at Shout, and she faxed my notes to the conference center, with a promise that she'd keep quiet and not let Frank know."

"Seems, my dear, she didn't," Aunt Nettie replied. "I got a call from Frank wondering if you got your faxed papers. Evidently, your cell phone was off and he doesn't text. They thought I might be able to get a hold of you. Looks like you had better steer clear of Kim when you need a friend to keep a secret."

"That weasel woman. Figures. I've had a hunch she's been talking behind my back and making me look bad—always wanted my job." She took another sip of tea, enjoying its soothing aroma. "Hey, it doesn't matter now. Anyway, I tried to snag this new author everyone is talking about, but he ended up talking to the competition. Then I went out for a hamburger last night, and ran into this weird guy I remember from summers at the lake. What are the odds?" Ally stood and paced the kitchen, her voice growing louder and her speech faster. "I just wanted to fly out of that restaurant fast, but I tripped on my purse strap and fell on my face. The guy picks me up off of the floor. Total humiliation." Ally sighed and took a sip of tea. "It's my last week at Shout. I'll go out with a bang."

"Sweetie, I know you're a great editor. You'll find another position. They're going to miss you more than they think."

Aunt Nettie came around the counter and wrapped two plump arms around her. For a moment neither talked. Then two high-pitched voices broke the silence as the kitchen door banged open. The wrench in Ally's stomach tightened another turn. She had put off telling Kylie she'd lost her job. This week she had to let her know.

* * *

Hmm. Aunt Nettie must have worked her magic. Benjie grabbed Ally's hand and led her to the bathroom sink where he showed her how he had learned to brush his teeth. Amazing, no fights or tantrums for his most un-favorite chore. His hatred of a bristly toothbrush inside of his mouth caused many a nightly uproar in their house. His therapist, Maria, told her how autistic children often had severe reactions to certain sensations, but tonight Benjie hopped up on his stepstool and stood watching himself brush his teeth in the bathroom mirror.

"Me teeth!"

After Ally read him his favorite book, *Diary of a Worm*, and squeezed in a quick snuggle, Benjie closed his eyes. *Such a beautiful angelic face. I missed him. Who wouldn't be captivated by this adorable little imp?*

"Thanks for my Benjie."

Benjie smiled. "Thanks, Benjie."

Ally walked down the hall to Kylie's room. A light still burned. *Probably engrossed in her latest fantasy novel.*

"Bedtime." Ally flipped the switch on and off, waiting for her daughter's protest, but Kylie just yawned and put her book down. Ally walked to the side of the bed, pushing aside the weekly accumulation of tee shirts, jeans, CDs, and socks Kylie had plopped on top of her bedspread.

"You're a great daughter," Ally said, and kissed the top of Kylie's head, sniffing the smell of her daughter's favorite grapefruit-scented shampoo.

"Missed you, Mom, but, no offense, Aunt Nettie rocks. Wish she lived nearer."

Ally plumped up a pillow. "One of the best, and she loves you kids. How did school go?"

She listened to the latest updates on Kylie's friends. After a few minutes, she flipped off the bedside lamp and walked out the door to her own big empty mattress. It grew larger each time she walked into the room.

CHAPTER
SIX

Ally surveyed her empty office, the walls stripped of her photos and awards. Without them, it became a sterile square room devoid of any personality. The grayish green walls had nothing to say anymore. She grabbed a couple of empty boxes, dumping her heavy reference books on the bottom. Gingerly, she fingered a red ceramic mug that said "Shout it out!" The mug and a hefty check had been a prize for signing up the most authors in one year. She closed her eyes for a minute and then reached for more newspaper to pack the mug, the three framed photos of her kids and her college diploma from UCLA. Funny how a career could fit into three small boxes.

She took little comfort in knowing three other editors had been let go too, one who had been at the company twenty years.

Ally surveyed the nearly empty top drawer housing a lone stapler and three paper clips. She fingered the edge of the drawer, sliding her finger across the smooth top one more time. *So many memories of this desk.* Kim popped her head through the doorway. "Hey, best of luck," she said.

A few more co-workers came by to say their goodbyes. Then Ally headed toward the elevator with her boxes piled high, her eyes almost too misty to see the floor buttons to push. This job was like a second family.

She looked up to see that even Frank, ever the gruff papa bear, had a tear in his eye. He had met her at the elevator, and when they shook hands goodbye, he squeezed her hand.

"You're a gifted editor, and if things improve, you know we'll hire you back in a flash." Then he pulled out an envelope from his coat pocket. "I had to do a little bit of finagling. It's your Christmas bonus—a little early."

"Frank!" She held the envelope close to her face, not wanting him to see her blinking back tears. "I appreciate this more than you know."

"You'll make it, Cervantes. You've got guts."

Ally gave Frank a hug around his neck and walked to her car. She ripped open the envelope. Five thousand dollars. Five times more than she ever received at Christmas. She'd have to make it last.

* * *

"Spaghetti," called her favorite aunt as they filed into the dining room to eat.

"Thanks for staying a little longer." Ally wrestled Benjie

into his booster seat. His stubborn legs never slipped into it easily. "I needed the moral support."

She handed Benjie two bowls, one with spaghetti sauce and one with pasta. He sat with a satisfied look on his face as he dipped his spoon into the sauce. He then took a bite of the noodles with his fork. Back and forth, he took a spoonful from one bowl and a forkful from another. After a while, he took his garlic bread and nibbled all around the sides, leaving the middle alone. He reminded Ally of a tiny field mouse savoring a great treat.

"Doesn't Benjie eat funny?" said Kylie.

"We're just happy he's eating. Remember when he was four and would only eat soft things, like pudding and scrambled eggs? He didn't like the 'mouth feel' of so many things. We've had to encourage him to try different textures." Ally exchanged looks with Nettie, who had heard of the many food battles.

"I dread going back and leaving my babies," said Aunt Nettie, passing the salad down the table. She wore her usual pink bandana and smock top. "I'd like to see more of all of you."

"We'll miss you, Aunt Nettie. Why can't you live with us?" Kylie asked.

"Great weather here, but too expensive. Maybe you can come live by me in Michigan," said Nettie.

"What made you say that?" Ally raised her eyebrows.

"Just a thought."

The next day Ally dropped Aunt Nettie off at the airport before driving the kids to Bryan's condo. He was renting in an upscale complex that catered to young professionals. Ally turned around to the back seat as the kids grabbed their inner tubes, ready to head for the pool. Kylie would tell her later all the details about the condo's mini waterpark and the cool game room.

Here we are at Disneyland North. Ally gripped the edge of the steering wheel as she caught Bryan's outline headed toward the car.

"How's my best girl?" Bryan leaned into the passenger window, not bothering to greet Ally.

"I missed you, Daddy." Kylie squeezed Bryan's hand. Benjie rocked back and forth in his seat.

Ally bowed her head over the dashboard, not wanting to see Bryan's face.

"Miss," said Benjie.

Bryan tousled Benjie's hair and unbuckled the seatbelt. "Hope you guys like spaghetti and meatballs."

"We just had spaghetti last night." Ally talked into the steering wheel. "Anyway, Benjie doesn't like meatballs with his spaghetti. You know that, Bryan."

"Guess I forgot. We'll figure out something else." He reached into the back seat to grab the two backpacks with the kids' overnight stuff. "How about picking them up about six o'clock Sunday night?"

"Whatever."

Coming back to an empty house, Ally poured a glass of her favorite Napa Valley Shiraz and nibbled on hummus and crackers. Closing her eyes, she breathed in the quiet. But, after a while, the stillness triggered her mind to start talking. Ally flipped on the television to drown out her thoughts, and then snapped it off, not in the mood for another reality show or the latest detective drama. She booted up her laptop and looked on Monster.com for jobs, only to see few available in the publishing industry. No surprise there. She put a comedy into the DVD player, but her mind wandered. Her Jack Russell terrier brushed by her legs, and she bent to pat J Bean. He settled down at her feet.

"I've got to sell this house. It's bleeding us dry, J Bean."

The brown-spotted dog tipped his head as if taking in every single word.

"This area is too expensive for a single mom."

J Bean tilted his head to the other side and let out a little growl.

"Maybe I could move in with Dad and Mom?"

Her little dog hid his head underneath the bottom of the sofa to hide.

"No, they're busy traveling and doing their volunteer stints. Besides, Benjie and Mom would butt heads, and Dad's always giving me his opinions on how to discipline Benjie."

J Bean poked his head out from underneath the sofa just far enough to lick her leg in agreement. Ally rumpled his ear. *If you only knew, Dad. So easy to give advice.*

She decided to be constructive, so she wiped off the kitchen counters, emptied the dishwasher, and then whirled the disposal once more. The house had to shine. Tomorrow, she had the only showing since listing the house two months ago. A Korean couple wanted to live in this school district. Please make an offer, she thought, buffing the kitchen faucet one last time, one last shine before turning off the light.

Ally walked from room to room, remembering the time and money she and Bryan had spent on the house. *Who cares anymore?* She loved to decorate, and had thrown her whole heart and soul into this home. No matter. The wood floors, custom slipcovers, and handcrafted crown moldings gave her no pleasure. It was all about money now, cold hard cash. She remembered waking up a couple of nights ago with sweat dripping off her forehead and panic racing her heart. She had gone to bed after watching KGO's eleven o'clock news report on the latest drop in housing prices. Right now, she could count three neighbors on her block who had *For Sale* signs in their yards.

Saturday morning, five prospective buyers breezed in and out.

Two more showed later that day. One couple moving from Oklahoma City had sticker shock.

"We could buy a six thousand square foot home in Tulsa for the price of this home," they said.

Why don't you just go back and live there? Immediately she regretted her nasty thought. Maybe they had to move here for a job.

Sunday morning, Ally got up and made her favorite, Kona coffee, and popped a couple of slices of bread into the toaster. With the house ready for another showing, she felt at loose ends. She dialed Ember, another single mom and a friend, to ask if she wanted to take in a movie with Ally that afternoon. Ember had a son in Benjie's class, and the women talked back and forth about how to deal with things that came up with their boys. Ally could always depend on an honest answer from down-to-earth Ember, who had been calling Ally once a week since the divorce.

They met at the Century Cinema.

"Good thing we came early—the place is packed. I just read that, during a recession, more people go to movies," said Ember. She tended to be a little bit of an authority on everything. "Know what else is hot in a down economy? Eyeliner. It used to be the lipstick indicator, but now, if eyeliner sales are strong, economists tell us we are heading for a down period. Thought that little factoid was interesting."

"Very," said Ally, studying the latest movie posters.

"Any news on jobs?" said Ember.

"Don't even ask. I'm terrified of the next few months."

"How long can you last without a job?"

"About two more months. We have to sell the house. I'm even considering a short sale to the bank."

"What's a short sale?"

"It's when the proceeds from a sale of a house fall short of what the owner still owes on the mortgage. The bank allows it when the owner can't make the payments."

"That bad? Can't Bryan help you out?"

"He's got his own financial problems, mainly with cash flow. Seems he has a fair amount of back taxes due."

"I'm sorry."

"Lots of people are saying that lately," said Ally, flashing a half-smile.

Later that night, after settling the kids in bed, she called the realtor. "Tim, I have to lower the price forty thousand. I'm fighting the clock."

"That will put us into a different group of buyers. I'll put in the change tomorrow," he said.

She sat on the living room couch, analyzing her financial situation. Ally had toyed with renting a condo, but she would still fork out a huge monthly payment. Most decent condos went for about $3,000 a month. She pulled out a pen and wrote down her expenses. Her severance pay might cover most of them, but she still had medical bills from Kylie's tonsil operation, not to mention the hefty monthly health insurance premiums. Bryan sent monthly child support, but funds still ran short.

There must be a better place to live, where the cost of living is a lot lower. She hated to ask her parents for help. They had just lost a part of their retirement, and even debated going on their anniversary cruise.

She glanced at a lone postcard plopped in the middle of the coffee table. Aunt Nettie had sent the kids a photo of

Lake Surrender. The photo had been shot in summer and showed a couple in a kayak with a trail of ducks behind them. The caption said: "Come join us at Lake Surrender, where the living is good and time moves slowly." Ally wished she could crawl right inside that postcard and float away on the deep blue water.

She scrolled down to her mother's number on the phone, and hit the send button. The phone rang six times before her mother picked up.

"Hi, honey, just unpacking from the cruise."

"I'm glad you guys got to go."

"Yes, but my fundraising work for Legal Aid is backed up. I will have to be in the office all next week. We've got a big telethon. How are the kids? Sorry I won't be able to come over there 'til next weekend."

"I thought you'd be busy. Anyway, I wanted to run an idea by you. Now don't freak out, but—what do you think about the kids and me moving to Michigan?"

A deadly silence answered her question. Finally her mother spoke.

"Why in the world would you want to do that? You've got your life here. Things will eventually shake out."

Ally covered her face with her hand, taking a deep breath, trying to keep her tone civil. "Mom, do you know I am two months away from a short sale on my house? I don't know if I can afford to live here anymore."

"Honestly, Ally, you always exaggerate. Things can't be

that bad. You'll find a job. Maybe you can economize on groceries and cut down on eating out."

I am not going to lose it. Ally drummed her fingers on the countertop. "Mom, the last time I ate out was a business trip. I am in major financial meltdown."

"Suppose you need to have your father come over and help you with a budget?"

Ally hated her mother's casual tone. *What do they know about saving money?* They had plenty.

"Thanks anyway, Mom." She closed the phone.

Three weeks later, Ally walked into the bank lobby to close on her house. It was a cash deal, and the transactions went fast. A friendly forty-something woman with short blonde hair greeted her.

"I'm Janet, please follow me." The receptionist led Ally into a long room where Tim Lee waited with another realtor and the branch manager around a conference table. After a short discussion, Janet handed her a pile of papers to sign.

"We're sorry it had to come to this. Unfortunately, we see this happen a lot. People buy more house than they can afford, and at the first downturn, they unload it," said the branch manager as she handed Ally a manila envelope with the house papers.

Ally bit her tongue, swallowing what she wanted to say. Instead, she picked up her purse.

"Hope we can continue to service you with all your banking needs," smiled the receptionist as Ally walked past her to the front door.

In the parking garage, when Ally clicked her key ring to open her car door, she felt a tap on her left shoulder. Cold shivers went down her back. She turned around to look straight into the face of a twentyish young man with a torn parka and a scruffy orange and green parrot on his shoulder. Ally swallowed a scream until she saw his cardboard sign.

"Lost your job?" she asked.

He nodded as he looked at the ground.

She pulled a twenty from the ATM envelope and put it into his hand, then watched him limp away.

He turned back to her. "Thanks, lady. What goes around comes around."

*   *   *

Later that day she decided to make a statement, to herself if to no one else. *If I don't do it now, I never will.*

Gathering up her nerve, Ally walked a couple of blocks to downtown and turned right. Two shops from the corner, she saw the front window covered with black paint sporting two green dragons facing each other. Above the figures, Chinese symbols connected the dragons together in an arc. Ally held her breath and grabbed the dulled brass door knob. She stepped over the doorstop as a young man with a short haircut and scraggly beard looked up.

"With you in a minute," he said with a nod before opening the curtain behind the counter. Ally stepped up to the counter where she found a couple of binders with plastic sleeves full of designs. She supposed she should pick out one. Flipping through cartoon images, swords, battleships, snakes, and all sorts of devilish faces, she found a section on birds. Any kind of bird she could imagine: eagles, ravens, robins, blackbirds, and even a wicked-looking vulture. She shuddered. She turned to the last page and saw a petite-looking dove with outspread wings. *That's it.*

The artist wiped off the thick vinyl covering with a rag and sprayed disinfectant. Ally lay face-down as he worked on the design. She felt a warm burning sensation like sunburn, and like a dull nail scratching her skin. It didn't feel so bad after all. An hour later, she walked out with a dove and the words *Free Bird* decorating the back of her neck and hidden by her hair.

She had just defined herself. A new woman and a new life.

But what kind of life?

*   *   *

"Kids, I just went to the bank and gave them their house back. It's now official."

Ally threw her coat on the sofa and flipped off her shoes. "Kylie, can you stop texting your friend for a minute? I want to talk to you."

Kylie looked up. "So where are we going to move? Can we rent one of those cool condos?"

"That's what I wanted to discuss. I've been checking into rentals, and they are pricey. I've got an idea, and want to know what you think."

Ally paused until her daughter put down the phone, her gray blue eyes open wide.

"Okay, what would you think about moving to another state? It wouldn't have to be forever, but maybe we could have an adventure."

Kylie's words came fast and furious. "Move out of California? What about Dad? We can't leave him. That's no fair."

God give me patience. Ally counted to ten. "I know, and I don't want to keep you and Benjie from your father. But please just listen to me. I've been toying with the idea of moving to Lake Surrender. Aunt Nettie has offered to keep us for a while until I get back on my feet financially. We could stay there for one year and save up money. I don't want to take you away from your father. We've talked. He flies to Chicago once a month, and he can extend his trip to include Traverse City."

Kylie's lower lip protruded. "It's a terrible idea."

"Okay."

"I'd have to make new friends."

"Yes."

"I'd really miss my friends here."

"I understand."

Kylie paused looking down at J Bean, who had rolled over for a belly rub. She squatted down to scratch him while Ally listened to a television commercial for toothpaste drone in the background.

Finally she spoke. "I guess I'd have to make new friends here. I just got into a big fight with Lindsey, and Meaghan has to move to San Diego, 'cause her dad got a transfer."

"I'm sorry."

"Can we move back here?"

"As soon as possible. If we lived with Aunt Nettie, I could sock away my paycheck, and we'd come back here with money in the bank. Maybe it would only take a year. You could do that for a year, couldn't you, Kylie?" Ally met her daughter's gaze until Kylie looked down.

"Aunt Nettie's so nice. Benjie likes her a lot."

"Yes."

"But I'd miss Dad. He would come see us, right?"

"Certainly."

"I guess we could try it for a year, if you promise we can come back."

"Can't promise anything, but I'd try with everything in my power to reinstate you."

"It would be scary."

"Since when did anything scary stop you, Miss Determination?" Ally reached for her daughter's hand. "Just think about it. We can talk later."

*   *   *

At midnight, Ally heard a tap on her bedroom door.

"Mom, are you asleep?"

"Not now."

Kylie pushed open the door and bounced down on top of Ally's bed.

Ally yawned and sat up. "What's up, kiddo?"

"I've been thinking all night. I've always wanted to live on a lake and be where it snowed. Are you positive Dad will come to see us?"

Kylie twisted the hem of her tee shirt that read *Turner Junior High's Got Talent!* "So many of my friends' parents are getting divorced, and Katie is getting depressing to be around. I want to be by Aunt Nettie. She makes Benjie and me happy, and maybe you can be happy, too." Kylie shot her mother a pleading look.

Ally's mouth dropped open. Had her griping and her sullen attitude been so obvious?

"Aren't you going to miss your BFF?" Ally grabbed her daughter's hand and saw the steeled determination of an older person, mixed with sadness in Kylie's eyes.

"Her dad just got laid off too, and they are going to have to move in with their cousins in Modesto. I won't like school much without Katie."

"I didn't know that." She squeezed Kylie's hand. "You'll find new buddies wherever we go. You're such a friendly girl—who wouldn't want to hang out with you?"

"That's nice, Mom. You know, maybe we're *supposed* to be in Michigan. I've always wanted to live where it snowed."

Ally laughed. "Remember Lake Tahoe two years ago at Christmas vacation? Benjie went crazy over the snow. I had to pry him away from his snowball collection. He made forty-six balls and had lined them up on the deck from small to large." She pulled out a photo book from underneath her bedside table and flipped it open. "I love this one."

It was a photo of Kylie and Benjie sitting behind his line of frozen balls, grinning from ear to ear. Benjie's favorite pastime kept him busy for hours. He lined up buttons, sea shells, pebbles, blocks, even her earring collection. "Whatever keeps him occupied," she'd say to Bryan.

The next morning, Ally wrote Nettie a quick email confirming her plans:

Dear Aunt Nettie,

I am going to take you up on your generous offer of living with you. I can't believe we are moving. You are so kind to let us bunk with you until we find suitable housing. The kids, to my amazement, are excited about the move. Evidently, Kylie's best friend is leaving, so she's okay, and all Benjie can talk about is snow, snow, and snow!

It's a huge change for me and the kids, but I think it will be healthy. At least we can afford to live in the Midwest. Bryan's okay with the move. He's actually relieved that I don't have to deal with our huge mortgage payment anymore. With his job, he can travel and will probably see them often—he flies to Chicago a lot. He's so busy trying to keep his company afloat, he hardly has time for the kids, anyway.

How are the job prospects around Traverse City? I

figure I'd find a job to get on my feet and then look for more promising employment. I could do technical writing, or teach creative writing at the local junior college. I've never had a hard time nailing down a job.

This is all happening so fast. Am I dreaming? Kylie says she thinks we will be in a happier place. I hope so.

We'll be leaving next Tuesday, June 2nd. We'll probably arrive at your house by Saturday. Don't plan on us arriving in time for dinner.

Thanks for a chance at a new start. Thanks for loving my children.

Your niece,

Ally

She re-read the letter, held her breath, and hit *send*.

Had she just stepped off a cliff? Her mother had already called and given a three-point opinion on why she shouldn't move.

Mom and Dad, you have your routines, a house paid for, and Dad's retirement. You can afford this area. Yes, the weather's great in the Bay Area, but only if you have a life.

Ally shut down the computer. She looked down at a box where she stored old pictures. The first one was of her and Bryan as newlyweds. The next section showed the two of them holding baby Kylie, their starter home in Redwood City in the background. Consecutive photos featured little baby Benjie propped up against a soft pillow and big sister looking on. The last series of photos captured their vacation skiing at Heavenly Valley by Lake Tahoe. They had been happy, or maybe she had just imagined it. Bryan had mentally dropped out of the picture. How had she not realized?

That night she twisted the sheets in her bed until she finally got up at two a.m. and heated milk in the microwave.

She wrapped her fingers around the warm ceramic mug. *What am I doing moving?*

CHAPTER
SEVEN

Monday morning, Ally answered the front door to face a short mustachioed man with the words *Hefty Moving Company* on his shirt.

"It'll take the better part of the day to load the van," he assured her.

All morning she watched as a confused Benjie ran laps around his empty room. Part of her wanted to stand at the front door and block the dining room table that was about to go through. *Am I really moving cross country?* A twinge of guilt pinched at her heart as her son flapped his hands while surveying his empty room. Bewilderment clouded his eyes as the moving men dismantled his bed. She wished she could slip inside his head and convince him life would be okay.

Ally rubbed the back of her neck, trying to massage away a tension knot. A couple of times she'd found Benjie in her closet or coming right between two groups of movers on the stairs. After one of the men hollered for someone to "watch this kid," Ally put Kylie on shadow detail while she directed the movers.

Ember came over at noon, bringing turkey sandwiches, soft drinks, and cupcakes. Ally's parents showed up at two o'clock, and her mother took all the extra supplies from the freezer and refrigerator. "Just hate to have any good food go to waste. I'll take this to the food pantry tomorrow."

"I still can't believe you're leaving. It's so sudden. You know you can still call it off," her dad reminded her.

"Yeah, I guess I could have the movers unload my stuff at your house. How about a little company for a few months?" Ally said with a dry laugh. He just shrugged.

Ally's mother jumped up. "Bring out those two boxes from Macy's, Al. Thought these might come in handy when you move to the hinterlands."

Kylie and Benjie ripped open the boxes to find two brand new parkas and waterproof mittens. Benjie fingered the puffy coat and brought it to his mother to help him put it on. It stayed on all day, even 'til after dinner.

"Goodbye, dear," Ally's mother gave her a kiss after they had settled the kids down in sleeping bags on the living room floor. "You're in for an adventure."

Ally walked them out to the car and watched them drive off, swallowing the uncertainty that had haunted her all day.

* * *

Next morning, the movers left and the family waved goodbye to all their worldly goods. They wouldn't be reunited with them until they got to the storage unit Ally had rented in Traverse City. Unlike yesterday, her dread of the future had been replaced with a sense of buoyancy. She fastened her seat belt with a renewed sense of purpose. New wasn't always bad.

Kylie looked out her window, watching until the truck disappeared down the street. "Michigan is a long way away."

"Bye-bye, bed," said Benjie.

*　*　*

Five days later, Ally and the kids drove down the lane to Aunt Nettie's house. The leaves on the trees had fanned out, making the lane quite shady. It had been a grueling trip, and she wanted to forever forget the previous night.

They had stopped at her old college roommate's house in Glen Ellyn, Illinois, a western suburb of Chicago. Ally and Jen spent several hours catching up on old friends, and Ally felt like they'd picked up where they last met. But as they sat in Jen's sunny living room, she noticed Jen's two sons, Nate and Tyler, eyeing Benjie. One brother elbowed the other, and whispered words that made him laugh. Jen, who cast an irritated look toward the lingering kids listening to their moms' reminiscing, suggested the boys take Kylie and her brother to the park. Ally pushed her hair behind her ear. The last thing she wanted was unfamiliar boys supervising Kylie and Benjie.

Jen waved them out of the room. "Just come back in an hour." Kylie and Benjie were back in twenty minutes, he distressed and she scowling.

Ally bent to address Benjie—"What's wrong, honey?"—but he looked toward the door.

"Swing, swing, swing."

She glanced up.

Kylie shook her head. "I'll tell you later."

At dinner, Kylie refused to speak to Jen's boys or pass them any food. Ally frowned at her, not wanting to cause a scene, but her daughter clamped her mouth shut and thrust out her chin.

After an otherwise elegant dinner, everyone gathered outside on the deck for coffee and cocoa. The brothers soon went inside to play video games, but Ally's children stayed with the grownups, and Benjie pulled his chair close to hers.

At nine o'clock, she clapped her hands. "Okay, time for bed."

Ally herded them down the hall to the guest bedroom. Once in the room, she closed the door. "Why were you so nasty to those boys during dinner?"

"They're jerks!"

"Hush up."

"It's true."

Ally folded her arms. "Did something happen at the park?"

Kylie nodded.

"Swing, swing, swing," said Benjie, rocking side to side on one of the twin beds.

"So?" Ally raised her brows.

Kylie sat beside her brother. "When Benjie saw the playground swings, he flapped his hands. He seemed happy, so I let him choose a swing and started pushing him. The other boys were playing HORSE, but Benjie wouldn't stop squealing, so they came over and asked why he flapped his hands and talked funny. They called him a 'tard.'"

Ally rubbed a hand on Kylie's back. "And then what happened?"

"I told them my brother's autistic, and they said they didn't want to catch a disease. I told them I hoped they caught cancer. Then I grabbed Benjie and raced back to the house."

She enveloped her daughter in a hug. "You're the best big sister ever. I'm so proud of you."

"I never want to see those turds again."

Ally sighed. "We probably won't. I'd never put you and Benjie through that again. Unfortunately, honey, you will run into people like that your whole life, mean-spirited people who can't accept anyone different."

She settled Benjie in bed and Kylie in a sleeping bag on the floor. Ally crept into the clean sheets and closed her eyes.

My poor sweet Benjie. Some people don't know how good they've got it.

She was ready for this trip to be over.

CHAPTER
EIGHT

"You're here, you're here!" cried Aunt Nettie. The screen door smacked the side of the house as she charged out to greet them. She flung open the back passenger door and extracted Benjie from his car seat, enveloping him in a hug. "Welcome to Michigan."

Benjie put his head down and wouldn't look up.

"Say hi to Aunt Nettie," directed Ally.

Benjie took a quick glance up at his aunt's round face and flushed cheeks. "Hi," he said, and ducked his head again.

Aunt Nettie laughed and scooped him up in her arms. "You're going to love it here."

Kylie grabbed her overnight suitcase and tote bag of her brother's toys that had just tipped over in the back seat. "We're sick of being in the car," she said. "Do you have anything to eat?"

"Kylie!" admonished Ally, but Nettie only laughed. She grabbed another suitcase and beckoned the trio to follow her.

Once inside, they followed her upstairs to the bedrooms.

The first one on the left had a sign that said *Kylie's Room*. The room was almost all bed, a beautiful walnut frame, a cream canopy and a green-checkered bedspread. A large rocker held a gaggle of stuffed animals, an odd assortment of dolls from Ally's childhood, and a long full length mirror stood next to the bed.

Kylie deposited her suitcase on the floor and examined the toys. "Mom, Aunt Nettie said these were yours and Aunt Georgia's when you were kids. Cool." Down the hall, Benjie's room overlooked the lake and was paneled in knotty pine. He ran inside, jumped up and down on the blue denim bedspread, and pointed to a collection of plastic boxes on the floor—eight plastic bins full of different things. One bin contained coins; another, all sorts of dried beans.

"I know Benjie loves to sort and collect, so I thought I'd start him on a project."

Her aunt showed Ally her room across from Benjie's, the room with the daffodil quilt. She set her suitcase on the floor as her aunt trotted down the steps to answer the kitchen phone.

Ally went back to Benjie's room and put his clothes in the dresser while he checked out the bins. He'd be absorbed in his new venture for hours. *Bless that woman.*

Aunt Nettie came back, her brows pulled into a frown.

"Guess I should catch you up on the local news. Just got a phone call from that kids' camp down the road. There's been trouble brewing there."

*   *   *

"Enjoying the last quiet moments before the camping season starts and my life slips into high gear. By mid-summer, I usually feel like the lead car in an Indy 500 race. Don, how about you change jobs? You can be the director, and I fix things?"

The short, tanned man wearing the Tiger baseball hat laughed. "You'd destroy the camp in one week. Anyway, what are you fiddling with in your pocket?"

Will whipped his hand out of his windbreaker. "What do you mean?"

"You keep opening and closing something. You nervous?"

Will grinned wide, put his hand back into his pocket, and felt the nap of the velvet as he drew out a grey velvet box. He flipped open the cover to show a delicate silver band encrusted with tiny diamonds. "About to pop the question to Sarah."

"Wow, didn't know it was becoming so serious."

"Hey, I've waited for this woman for a long time."

"Think the answer will be affirmative?"

Will balled up his fist and punched the maintenance man in the arm. "Of course. Who would turn down yours truly?" He put both thumbs under his arm and did a little strut. Don laughed as he sat down.

The sun was beginning to set on Lake Surrender. Tangerine rays of sun shot through the remaining patches of blue sky. Will closed his eyes and drank in the earthy smell that only the lake could produce. And the sounds—from the *plink* of a neighbor's fishing pole dropping into the water near a boat dock to the haunting tremolo call of a loon traveling over the water as it warned its mate of danger. The native Michigander knew he'd never live anywhere else. He looked up. From a few cottages down the beach, kids splashed in the water for one last romp of the day.

"No tranquilizers can sooth like the sounds of a lake. It's my own piece of heaven," said Don.

Will nodded. "Yep, couldn't agree more. Hate to leave, but I need to attack a pile of paperwork tonight." He stood and turned to open the screen door to the camp lodge, but a gentle *kerplunk* of a canoe paddle being dipped into the quiet evening water caught his attention.

Don squinted into the sunset. A man pulled a canoe to shore and beached it down a few yards by the junior boys cabins, then removed a backpack from the stern.

"That's strange," said Don. "I know everyone who comes and goes on the lake this time of year."

"Must be a lost tourist. Let's take a look."

The man wore tan pants, a black sports coat, and light blue shirt underneath, nothing that looked like lake gear. Even his shoes— black shiny numbers—seemed out of place. The man turned his head, but didn't look toward Will and Don. Both men tried to catch up to the stranger to see if he was lost, but he disappeared into the brush. Will and Don headed back to the lodge.

"Keep an eye on that woods in the next day or two," Will told Don.

"You betcha. Hey, before I forget, it looks like we're going to need to put a roof on girls cabin number seven. I just went in there and found a big puddle of water by the south corner of the building."

Will sighed. They didn't have extra in the budget this year.

"Just patch it up the best you can. Maybe we can make it another summer."

"You betcha, Boss. Just don't say I didn't tell you when a little junior high girl comes knocking at the office door in the middle of the night, crying cause her sleeping bag is sopping wet and she wants to go home."

"Consider me warned. Although, according to you, every minor repair will turn into a lawsuit with one of the parents. We'll take a trip to Menard's tomorrow and pick up supplies. Which reminds me—the Native American Dads Club, you're meeting tomorrow night?"

Don lowered his voice. "Yes, we've got a couple of important things to discuss. You know I don't usually share these private matters."

"I'm as tight-lipped as a clam with lockjaw." Will raised his right hand in a pledge.

"Ha."

"I've heard the entire goings-on with tribal politics in the last few years, and have always sworn myself to secrecy."

"That's true. Anyway, we've been checking into the possibility of a new project, planting and growing wild rice.

I don't know if you've heard about the Manoomin Project? It's for young people starting to run with the wrong crowd. I think the professionals call these kids 'at risk'. You know I might have been one of them in my younger days. I was wild. But with three boys of my own, you might say I've got a heart for how tough it is for these kids growing up."

"I hear you. Economy's tough and not many jobs. With alcohol and drugs so easy to buy, kids can go down the wrong path pretty quickly."

Don leaned closer to Will. "The club has been looking at a particular parcel of land. We want to purchase it, and turn it into a wild rice planting site."

"Sounds like a great idea. Why so secretive?" Will shot him a questioning look.

"It's secretive because it's part of the parcel of land adjacent to Lake Surrender. Lots of people would give their eyeteeth for a chance to purchase it."

Will smiled. "Like a big-name developer?"

"You've got it. But our experts have looked over the property and say the lay of the land is perfect for the wild rice. We'd be putting back nutrients that had been taken out of the land many years ago." He swiped at a lone mosquito poised to drill into his arm.

Will zipped up his jacket; the day's warmth dissipated as the sun set. "I remember you telling me wild rice had been an important crop to the Native Americans who lived around here."

"Now, I'm no scientist, but experts say wild rice has medicinal uses from reducing blood serum cholesterol to slowing diabetes blindness. Think how great these kids will feel when they can contribute something useful to society." Don stood. "I'd better be heading home to take care of my brood before they become 'at risk', if you catch my drift." He picked up his keys and headed for his truck.

Will pulled out his phone to dial Sarah's number.

He heard a rustling around the bushes in front of the Frisbee golf course. He jogged toward the sound and saw a shadow dart out from a clump of trees.

"Hold on!" cried Will as he hot-footed it after the figure. He wove in and out of the woods, dodging poison ivy and low-growing vines, but couldn't find anyone. Puffing for air, he headed back to the lodge. Too late. The man and the red canoe had vanished.

Will dialed Don's number. "We've got prowlers. With camp starting up in a week, we're responsible for any person that sets foot on camp property."

"Got it."

The smell of fried chicken jerked Will's thoughts back to camp, reminding him he still didn't have a cook for the season. He grabbed his cell phone again and left a voice mail.

"Hey, Nettie, I'm in a jam. Still no cook for camp. Got any ideas? Call me. I'll have my phone on me all evening."

He put the phone on vibrate and walked into the kitchen.

"Fix me up a plate, Stew! I'm pulling a long shift tonight."

Stew shot him a frown, but grabbed a plate and piled it high. Will plopped down on a bench in the corner of the empty dining room, spending another evening thumbing a pile of applications. He looked up at the cavernous room, dimly lit by green hanging lights. *I love this time of year, but I'm tired of eating by myself.*

* * *

Tuesday morning, the first week in June, Hal Schwindleman sat at his desk. Being the number ten producer for an office of twelve meant he often pulled floor duty for Lakeshore Realty. In his early sixties, with a head of salt-and-pepper hair, Hal's lukewarm sales weren't setting the real estate industry on fire.

The office manager hated cigarette smoke, but Hal took a slow drag on his menthol cigarette as he scrolled through the new listings for downtown Lake Surrender.

"Hey, old Nancy isn't around to whine about my smoking, so what she doesn't know won't hurt her," he said out loud to Sandbar, the office cat.

The phone rang twice, and Hal picked it up. "Hello, Lakeshore Realty. Duh, it's slow. That's like saying Northern Michigan gets some snow in winter. Not many buyers but plenty of sellers. Most of those in the Detroit area own second homes and have listed their property at rock-bottom prices." He paused to take a final drag on his cigarette before smashing it into half a powder-sugar doughnut on a paper plate.

"If business slows down any more, I'll have to supplement my income by helping my brother on his truck farm this summer. 'Bout four more months to make good money, no more. I just clicked on lookforyourdreamhouse.com. Hope someone's looking for a weekend getaway. Be great if they had cash. What a concept in this state. We're the leading edge of the depression. Yeah, think I'll take an early break, but I'll be home for dinner. Hey, got to call you back. Customer just pulled up."

Hal pushed back from his desk as a short, small-framed man with shiny, slicked-backed hair opened the door.

"Hey, this where you sell lakefront property?"

Hal came around the desk to greet him. "We're the main game in town. Have a seat and let's talk." Hal handed him a Lake Surrender-area pamphlet. "Care for coffee?"

"No."

"Excuse me while I refill my mug."

When Hal returned, the man hadn't even opened the pamphlet. "I need a sweet little piece of property on Lake Surrender. Know anything available?"

Hal logged into the company website and clicked on *Listed Properties*.

"What is your price range?"

"Money's no object. Location's what I'm after." Hal scrolled through the listings and found the more expensive offerings. "I found a few that might look promising. Do you have a realtor yet?"

"Are you a realtor?" the man said, his voice dripping with unconcealed sarcasm.

"You betcha. I'll print up a few of these listings and let you look at them." He hit *print*, and then handed the sheets to the stranger.

"I'll just take them with me." The man stood.

"Hey, uh, wait a minute, what's your name?" Too late. The man slipped out the door. Hal punched in his home phone number. "How would ya like to spend winter in Boca Raton? Yep, think I got a hot one, as in B-I-N-G-O. Maybe I won't have to work at Bill's farm this year after all. Anyone who wears two pinky diamond rings ain't hurtin'. Yep, I tell you, they dripped of diamonds."

*   *   *

Aunt Nettie answered the phone hanging on the kitchen wall. "Hey, Will, relaxing before the storm hits?"

Ally opened the refrigerator and pulled out rice pudding for the kids. She ducked under the ancient extension phone cord stretched out from the wall. It hadn't been replaced since she was a kid and had lost a lot of its spring.

"No, I don't know anything more about the canoe. No one I know has that color. Yes, of course." Nettie paused again.

Ally spooned out helpings of the dessert into two bowls, and sprayed whipped cream on top. She put a little dollop of cream into J Bean's bowl.

"No I don't know of anyone right now … You don't have much time. Have you tried the college? I see. I'll send up a quick prayer. You're in a pickle … Okay … Talk to you later."

Aunt Nettie put the phone back in its cradle. "That was Will Grainger. He's the camp director at the kid's camp on the other side of the lake. You remember him, don't you?"

Ally tipped her head to the side as if to answer no. Last thing she wanted to do was run into him.

"Anyway, it seems the woman who was going to take the job as main cook this summer decided to stay in Saugatuck. She just got engaged, but it slipped her mind until today to call Will and tell him. The inconsideration of people. I told him I'd think of somebody who might need a job." Nettie's gaze drilled into her.

She can't be thinking of me? I can barely get dinner on for my family. "I'd think there's probably a college student looking for a summer job."

"The problem is the camp starts next week. He's running around like crazy, trying to finish up everything, and this comes up. I tell you *I* wouldn't want to run a camp."

"I went to camp once, that was enough. It was in the Santa Cruz Mountains, and I got so homesick and covered with mosquito bites—I even stepped on a banana slug. All in all, a miserable experience," said Ally.

"Wish I could go," said Kylie. She plucked the maraschino cherry from on top of the whipped cream, and popped it into her mouth. "I never have any fun anymore."

"Actually that's not a bad idea, Ally," Aunt Nettie chimed in. "Kylie might still be able to sign up for the first session next week."

"That'd be great if we had money. I had to use my Christmas bonus to pay off what I still owed on the mortgage." She took empty bowls and set them in the kitchen before running hot water for dishes. "Kylie, I'd love to sign you up for camp, but we can't right now."

Kylie's mouth drooped. She scrunched up her eyes, turning them into instant faucets.

Here come the prepubescent tears. Come on, I don't need this.

"It's not fair," said Kylie

"Not fair," said Benjie.

"Both of you stop!" Ally screeched, and then flinched at the sound of her voice. *I sound like a shrew.* In a measured tone, she said, "Look, if you haven't noticed, life's unfair."

Kylie looked down, used a spoon to draw an imaginary design on the tablecloth. "I never have any fun. My best friend moves, and then I have to move, and I will never see my dad."

"Listen, we've already been over that. I told you he'd be here in a couple of weeks. He has a meeting in Chicago, and is going to fly up here."

"How do I know he'll come?" Kylie peered straight up at her mother.

Ally gulped as her stomach took another nosedive. "He'll come."

CHAPTER
NINE

The next morning, Aunt Nettie took the children to town to buy new beach towels. Ally let out a long slow breath. Basking in the solitude, she sat on her bed and fired up her laptop to work on her résumé and check job websites for openings. Michigan's unemployment rate was fifteen percent. Had she been too impulsive?

Taking a break from the job search, she searched online for Camp Lake Surrender. The website read:

Remember those summers when you were growing up? Making that tree house? Hiking a trail in your backyard? Wading in a nearby creek? Would you love to give your children the gift of summers gone by? Leave the cell phone and video games at home, and let your child spend a week enjoying God's creation.

Camp Lake Surrender offers archery, canoeing, swimming, crafts, music, first aid training, and nature studies in the beautiful setting of Lake Surrender, twenty minutes from Traverse City, Michigan. Here your child will learn team-building, outdoor survival skills, and spiritual principles that will enhance your family's core values. Give us a call at 231-868-7758 to talk to our camp director. We'll give your child the summer of a lifetime.

Ally looked at the photos of smiling kids jumping off a swimming raft, bouncing on a trampoline, and sitting around a campfire. She had to admit, it looked fun. What child wouldn't want to spend a jam-packed week there?

She just wished the website had toned down the "spiritual values" part. The staff seemed to go overboard. Who knew what kind of religious jargon they'd be offering her child? It sounded a little too right-winged. Still, the kids in the photo seemed to be having the time of their life. She scrolled back down again on the website and copied down the phone number. She didn't have much to lose if she just called over there. She'd check it out later.

*   *   *

A new day dawned, and Ally tiptoed down the hall and peeked into Benjie's room. Sitting cross-legged on the carpet, he didn't even look up when she opened the door. All along the length of the room he had lined up a row of sea shells, from small to large. Next to that lay a long line of Skittles candy. He had about five projects on the floor.

"My, you've been busy!" said Ally. She stroked the top of his head. He jerked away.

There went the old wall of isolation again. She sighed. She knew there were days he pulled into his shell. Bryan used to call him Robinson Crusoe when he went to his mental island where family and friends weren't allowed. All the changes in his life had set him back.

Why is life so hard? She immediately chided herself for that thought. She wasn't a baby. She hated people who felt sorry for themselves—they bored her.

I'm strong. We'll make it.

She had two children who loved her (and, yes, she *knew* Benjie loved her in his own way). She'd sold her house, and had free room and board from a dear aunt who adored all of them. Things could be a lot worse. She could be living in a sub-par apartment in East Palo Alto, California, terrified for her children to play outside.

"Benjie, I'm going to go do a couple of errands. Benjie, are you listening to me?" Ally gently put her hands on the sides of his head and turned him toward her. She wouldn't let him look away. "Aunt Nettie will pour you your Cheerios and cut your banana in a little while. She will put twenty Cheerios in the red bowl and five slices of banana in the blue bowl. Did you hear what I said?"

Benjie nodded before sliding out of her grip.

At least he acknowledged me.

*   *   *

Sitting in her car several yards from the main building, Ally took in the camp. Made of thick hewn logs, the lodge was a wide expansive building with stairs in the middle that led up to a large friendly porch. A mish-mash of oak rocking chairs, old Adirondack chairs peeling white paint, and an assortment of plastic resin chairs sat scattered all over. Two wilted daisy plants drooped in their terracotta pots, a sad attempt to dress up the porch. A thirtyish man of medium height and sturdy build opened the screen door and stood on the porch. *He looks like he'd be comfortable chopping wood.*

The serious-looking man broke into a grin and waved a greeting. *Good grief, he must think I'm scoping him out.*

Ally grabbed her purse. *Here we go. I'm learning to grovel. No, learning to negotiate.* Whatever. She needed to find a way to sign up Kylie.

She walked toward the porch, fiddling with her cell phone that had just gone off, and didn't look up until she heard a soft "Hello" at the bottom of the steps.

Jerking her head up to meet his gaze, she felt the blood rush to her head, cheeks burning. Was this a crazy joke played on her by the déjà vu god of the universe? *That restaurant guy again— that guy I thought was someone from my past. Please, God, don't let him recognize me.* She stuck out her hand. *Get it together, Ally.*

"Hello to you, too. You must be Will Grainger." She looked for a flicker of recognition in his expression, but didn't see any. *Thank heaven.*

"Will, it is, and you must be Ally." He had a twinkle in his espresso-colored eyes.

He shook her hand, and Ally brushed against his pinky finger where the top joint was missing. A strange twinge of excitement and fear swept through her body. It was him. But what was going on here? Why did she have such a feeling of anticipation, while at the same time being flustered? For heaven's sakes, she was a grown woman.

She appraised him, the kind of hale-and-hearty outdoorsman one might expect to find in Northern Michigan. All that was missing was a plaid flannel shirt. He had a trustworthy look, and dark honest eyes that seemed to be sizing her up.

He smiled, and his whole face joined in.

Seems to be pouring on the charm. Probably a great marketer— used to schmoozing with the parents of potential campers. Hey, I know that gig. I can play that game too.

"Let's talk in here."

She followed him up the steps. Will gestured at the screen door that opened into the dining hall and put his hand out to open the door, but Ally had already grabbed the handle.

Will hesitated.

She went through the door, and he followed.

"Let's talk in my office."

They passed through the dining room with about twenty-five round tables covered with red vinyl tablecloths. On the left side of the room stretched a long horizontal opening. A piece of wood connected by chains on either side dropped down to form a shelf that held stainless steel water pitchers and red plastic baskets of sorted silverware. Lots of banging of pots and pans came through the opening, and Ally figured the kitchen lay beyond.

The director turned right, and they walked down a narrow, musty, wood-paneled hallway. Ally glanced at a wall of framed black and white photos of the camp over the years. She noted the modest one-piece bathing suits in one photo, and the Model T cars in another. *This camp has been around forever.*

Will paused before opening the door to his office. "After you."

Ally bit her lip and reminded herself why she was here.

He flipped on the light. "Sorry about the mess," Will said as he gestured at the desk covered in manila file folders. He shoved aside a candy bar wrapper and a McDonald's bag.

Behind the desk stood a floor-to-ceiling set of wooden shelves sagging under the weight of books on camp management, plants and flowers of Michigan, and cookbooks for institutional cooking. One whole section was full of Bibles and Bible commentaries. *Must be pretty religious. Better not have any plans to convert me.* Her motto was, "Rely on yourself—you have the power within."

"Have a seat." Will cleared off a pile of manuals lying on an old vinyl and plastic chair that looked like it came out of a doctor's waiting room. "We were planning to expand the office this year, but that got put on hold because of the economy." He handed Ally a brochure with a picture of two campers waterskiing the lake.

"What can I do for you, Ms. Cervantes? You know Cervantes is Spanish for servant."

"So I've been told." She flashed him her best smile. He returned it. "It's Ally. I've recently divorced, but kept the name. I'm interested in talking to you about enrolling my daughter Kylie at camp. She just turned twelve."

"I see." He leaned forward in his chair. "Has she ever attended camp?"

"No, but since we just moved here from Northern California, I thought it would be a good way for her to make friends." Why did she feel so flustered? It was just a camp application.

"Spent a few years out there. Quite a beautiful place. I was involved in an intern ministry, and worked at a grocery store called Jolly's for a while to supplement my income."

"Yes, I grew up there. But when I became single and had to support myself, I realized I couldn't afford to live in such an expensive area. After the real estate market tanked, I had to sell my house on a short sale. And, like many other people, I lost ninety percent of my 401k." Ally put her hand over her mouth. "Sorry, didn't mean to sound like a sob story. I just wanted to know if I could enroll my daughter Kylie?"

Will pulled out a clipboard and flipped a page in the camper rooster. "Yep, we do have openings in next week's session. I'd have to have a deposit, and the rest paid the beginning of camp next week."

Ally hadn't thought about how to pay for camp. An awkward silence filled the room. The only sound came from the low roar of a lawn mower as the maintenance man cut the grass outside the office window.

She flipped through the brochure, mentally adding up next week's expenses in her head. "After moving across country, I'm a little low on funds. I thought maybe I could pay for the camp in installments until I find a job."

"Doesn't your husband—um, your ex—help with expenses?"

Ally shifted in her chair. "Yes, when he can."

She felt his eyes scrutinize her, and that old lack-of-money humiliation crowded into her mind.

"I'm sorry." He grimaced. "I didn't mean to ask such personal questions." He picked up a pile of papers, reshuffled them, and put them down.

"I don't know why I'm telling you all this. I know we'll make it. I am living rent-free with my aunt until I find a permanent job. I've been in publishing for years, and have great credentials that will help me find a job in a couple of months."

Will smiled, and Ally thought he seemed condescending. "You know, the job market is pretty tight in this state. It may take a while to get your feet on the ground."

"Thanks, but I have the best references in the industry backing me." She glared at him.

"Sorry, I just wanted to give you a heads-up. This isn't Silicon Valley." He leaned back in his chair. "I debated whether or not I should tell you this, but your aunt called over here this morning."

Ally leaned forward, her eyes lowered. "What is this, a kind of Christian charity?"

"Hey, relax, it's not like you think. She called back in response to my phone call. You see, I'm in a bind. I lose my main cook next week, just as camp starts."

Ally crossed her arms. "What does that have to do with Kylie and me?"

"Your aunt thought maybe you could fill in until we find a permanent cook. I'd be able to pay you a small stipend, and pay for your daughter's time at camp." He grinned, and Ally again noticed the laugh lines around his eyes. "It works out for both of us."

What was Aunt Nettie thinking? To say Ally was domestically challenged would be an understatement. She wasn't like three fourths of the population of the Bay area who fancied themselves foodies. *Bryan always said I couldn't operate a microwave without an instruction book.*

"I'm not the greatest cook in the world. Anyway, what happened to your cook?"

Ally glanced at Will, but couldn't analyze his curious expression. He spoke carefully. "Well, let's just say he's lucky to be the assistant. He needs to reevaluate his values if he wants to remain in my employ."

"So"—Ally squinted—"is this a person I'd want to work with?"

Will leaned over and lowered his voice. "Stew is—well, between you and me, he's on probation. He's had a drinking problem and got a DUI, even though we've never caught him drinking on the job." Will stood, then paced behind his desk. "He came as part of the camp when I took the job, and the previous owner made me promise to keep him on." He looked out the window. "He's a great cook. Too bad his personal life is messed up." He turned back and cocked his head to one side. "Actually he's done a lot better lately. He comes to work, stays in the kitchen, and doesn't go anywhere else on the grounds. If I thought he'd be a detriment, I'd fire his butt, but he seems to be behaving himself."

Ally nodded. "I understand how people can mess up their personal lives. Seen it first hand in the last year. Anyway, I don't think I'd be the right person to be your cook. Honestly. I have trouble just putting dinner on the table. Let's just say we eat a lot of take-out."

Ally stood, and put out her hand. He shook it.

"Thanks anyway. I'll have to pass. I'm in the publishing biz, not food service." She picked up her purse and grabbed the door handle.

"Let me walk you out. If you change your mind, we'll be here. Stew has great recipes and would help you."

He followed her down the steps, opened her car door, then grabbed a card from his shirt pocket. "Let me give you this." As he handed her the card, their hands brushed. He looked up and studied her for a moment. "Say, are you positive we haven't met somewhere before? You look familiar."

"I doubt it." Ally smiled good-bye, and snapped the car door closed.

* * *

Back in Aunt Nettie's cottage, she found a note on the kitchen table: "Gone to the park with the kids, back in an hour."

Next to the note sat two piles of mail. Ally picked up her pile, yellow forwarding stickers slapped onto the front of the envelopes. She recognized Bryan's handwriting, and seeing it brought up the familiar twist in her stomach. Using a butter knife from the kitchen drawer, she ripped open the envelope. A check fell out of a note.

> *Dear Ally,*
>
> *I'm sorry this is all I can afford this month. I hope it will make your car payment at least. Things are tight. Business is sliding downhill. I'm trying to keep things afloat, traveling all the time.*
>
> *I hope you are happy at your aunt's house. You deserve happiness, and I guess I just couldn't be the one to give it to you. I miss the children, but I know you have to do what you have to do. I'll probably see them when I come to Chicago next month.*
>
> *Give the kids my love,*
> *Bryan*

Ally sighed. How odd to receive a note from the person she'd been married to for years. She picked up the check. Five hundred dollars. That would barely cover the Audi's payment.

Things must be pretty bad. Even though Bryan had decided to walk away from the marriage, he still took care of the kids. He was nothing if not generous. *We might have made it if you hadn't given up. People do have autistic children, and their marriages still survive.*

Ally added up what she needed for the month. By depositing the check, she would have about sixteen hundred eighty-five dollars. Four hundred went for the car payment, five hundred twenty dollars went toward health insurance, and six hundred was the minimum payment of her Visa and Nordstrom cards, hardly enough to pay for the camp fees. She thought about calling her sister, but Georgia and her husband were tight on money. Ally could ask her parents. Mom had called a week ago and reminded her that if she needed any money, they were good for a loan. *I refuse to take any money from Mom and Dad. It's bad enough I'm camping out at Aunt Nettie's.*

It wasn't as if her aunt acted like it was an imposition for them to be there, but Ally wanted to support her kids herself. She'd have to be out on the streets before she took Mom up on her offer. If she prided herself on anything, it was self-reliance. Maybe she'd receive a check for her IRA cash out. That would help her over the hump until she could find a decent job. She poured hot water into a tea cup and ripped open a packet of her favorite Peach Ginger tea, letting the bag steep for a minute. She then plopped down to read last Sunday's want ads. All she found was temporary office work, house cleaning, wallpapering, babysitting, waitressing, graphic designing, lawn maintenance, retail sales, but nothing in publishing or editing. All the jobs seemed to be minimum wage or temporary. What did a local tell her about the Traverse City area, the closest city? "View of the bay, low pay."

She scratched J Bean around the ears, and then he rolled over for a belly rub.

Did I make a mistake thinking I could find a job here? Maybe I should have stayed in California. But jobs were disappearing in San Francisco, too. At least she had a roof over her head. Every day, the evening news reported the economy slowing down a little more.

She decided not to dwell on it. *We're here, and we'd better make the best of it.*

Kylie staggered through the front door, carrying a large watermelon. "Hey, Mom, did you check out the camp? Was it cool? Can we afford to go?" She hefted the melon onto the counter then stood bouncing on her tiptoes, ready to launch.

"It's not in our budget, but I'm trying to work things out. I think the director wanted to give me a job as a cook. Imagine that?"

"Oh good! So if you cook there, I can go to camp. Yippee!"

"Hey now, just hold on. I have to find a real job. We can't live at Aunt Nettie's house forever."

Nettie walked in from the garage and plopped down a large bag of groceries. "You can't live *where* forever?"

"See what I mean? You can't afford groceries for us all.

You barely survive on your small pension and your furniture painting."

"Then, maybe you just might have to find a job sooner than later." Aunt Nettie opened the refrigerator and put away a carton of milk. "Honestly, Ally, you have to be realistic. Swallow your pride, sweetie. Times are tough."

Ally went out onto the porch and plunked down on the swing. Benjie followed and took a seat next to her. As she stroked Benjie's arm with his surgical sponge to calm him, she thought about what Nettie had said. Had she spent five years in school, earning her masters in English, just to throw it away for a menial job? Was this what her life had come to? Should she even consider taking the camp job? She knew nothing about cooking for groups, but how hard could it be? No harder than speaking to the board of directors of a publishing company, trying to explain why sales were down, right?

She looked down at Benjie. "I love you, Benjamin."

She knew not to wait for a response. He wouldn't say "Love you, Mommy" back to her, but she could always hope. Right now, it was enough for him to allow her to hold him on her lap.

Kylie came out to the porch, a popsicle dripping down her hand. "Mommy, I'm sorry I bugged you about camp. It's okay. I know you have to find a good job so we can have a house someday. I just always wanted to go to camp." She gave her mother a sticky kiss on the cheek. "Maybe I can go next year."

"You're such a good girl, Kylie." Ally wrapped her daughter into a hug. "I don't know how I could have gotten along without you the last few months. I know you want to go to that camp. I just don't know how we can afford it." *Never thought I'd have to say those words.*

"I'm just going to pray that you change your mind. Auntie Nettie says, 'We have not because we ask not.'"

Ally studied her daughter's determined look. *What on earth was she talking about?*

Ally walked back into the kitchen. She had always marveled how her aunt never left anything out of place. Her spices were always to the right of the stove, alphabetized, and she never left even clean dishes in her sink. The wooden floor shone. To the right of the sink, a large book lay open on the counter by the stove. Out of curiosity, Ally picked it up and looked at the name on the binding: *Cooking for Groups: Institutional Cooking 101.*

Chapter
Ten

On Sunday, Aunt Nettie took the kids to church in her ancient '85 Chevy station wagon, probably the only one in Michigan still sporting the fake wood paneling on the side. Ally, not up for a religious experience, said she'd meet them for lunch at Wendy's. She rattled around the family room, flipping through her aunt's art magazines, checking email, and finally clicking on the television.

The Cooking Network popped up. *Must have been Kylie—she loves watching that.* Ally flipped over to the History Channel. They had a segment on how the government created K-rations for the soldiers in World War II. On the next channel, a local newscaster sampled wedding cakes from bakeries in the Traverse City area. Ally clicked off the television and tossed the remote control onto the end table. Food, food, food. Couldn't she just find a no-brainer movie to watch?

She cracked open the front door. Maybe she'd just take a walk. No, she smelled that pungent ozone scent that predicts rain; on the lake, that could mean a heavy downpour and lightning. She'd seen storms gather on the lake in a manner of minutes.

Restless, Ally walked to the refrigerator and held the door open wide. She didn't find anything of interest, just spaghetti sauce and coleslaw. She went back to the living room and grabbed her phone, then pulled out a business card from her jeans pocket and studied it. Taking a big breath, she dialed the number.

"Camp Lake Surrender. How may I help you?"

It was him. She couldn't back down now. Ally picked at the cuticle on her thumb. "Uh, Will—"

"That's what my mother named me. What can I do for you?"

"This is Ally Cervantes. I think we might be able to help each other out."

"How's that?"

Geez, he wasn't making things easy. "Is that cook job still open?"

"Depends on who wants to know."

Am I sure I want to work with this guy? She took a big breath. "I'd like to throw my hat into the ring, if the job is still open."

"I thought you weren't interested."

"I'm interested in enrolling my daughter in camp next week. Now, can I apply or not?"

Will chuckled. "You drive your little green Audi over here tomorrow afternoon, and we'll push your interview up to the top of the pile. One o'clock sharp."

Ally almost blurted out, "Yes, sir!" but caught herself. What was this, the army?

*   *   *

"Come on back," a deep voice hollered from the kitchen.

She followed the sound to the kitchen where Stew chopped onions for dinner.

"Hear you're the new cook." His face belied the forced cheerfulness in his voice.

In a grease-splattered wife-beater shirt and five days' worth of beard, he hardly looked like a poster boy for the Michigan Health Department. He motioned for her to sit down on a stool across from the stainless steel counter where he stood.

"Looks like you're going to be my boss. Ever done much cooking before?"

"Oh plenty," Ally answered and hoped her tone sounded convincing. His eyes narrowed a bit as he gave the onions one last whack. "What's your specialty?"

"What's yours?" she countered.

"I do a mean chili, and the kids love my pot roast, but my cinnamon rolls are legendary." He paused as he put down his knife. "You know, darlin', cooking for a crowd is a lot different than home-cooking."

Ally gritted her teeth. "I'm aware of that."

"I'll be training you this week. We need to hustle, since

the camp staff comes in Tuesday to start training. They work up pretty big appetites. By the way, my real name is Stan, but they call me Stew—get it?"

She smiled. *If only Mom could see me now, working at a camp, with a guy every inch a northern redneck.* She looked at Stew. *Even your shaving lotion reeks of a Family Dollar Store weekend special.*

"Grab you an apron and wash up. Remember, you need to lather for ten seconds. That would be like the length of the song, *Happy Birthday*. Next, you grab yourself a long chef's knife. Now watch me chop this baby." Magically, the onion disintegrated into a hundred tiny pieces. "Now you try."

Will walked in and flashed a thumbs up at both of them. "Stew, not so fast. We still have to interview this lady before we start her into the kitchen."

He motioned to Ally, and she followed him to his office, manila folders everywhere. A half-eaten ham sandwich and a dill pickle on a paper plate sat on the credenza.

"Let's talk about the job. It starts immediately. Does that work?"

"If it means letting my daughter into camp next week, I'm on board."

"Great." He leaned over and gave her a handshake, his grip surprisingly strong. "Welcome aboard. We're glad to have you. Your aunt tells me you come highly recommended. She says you are a quick study and have a high energy level. Believe me, both will help you in this job."

So that's what's been going on.

"Anyone parenting an autistic child needs to keep ahead of the game," Ally said.

"I didn't know. How old is your child?"

"He's six. My aunt watches him, but there will be a lot of times I might have to bring him to work. Are you okay with that?"

"As long as you finish your work, there's no problem. We have a great staff here. We can keep him busy. Alicia, our senior staff counselor, is majoring in Special Education." He jotted notes on a legal pad, and then the phone rang.

"Yes, I can make the meeting at the County Health Department. Make it about two o'clock today. Thanks, Betty." He turned back to Ally. "Sorry. Let me go over our camp policies, and then I can spell out the job in more detail."

A half an hour later, Ally walked out, following Will. Her head spun. *How does this guy keep all the balls up in the air at once?* There was more to running a camp than she originally envisioned.

"Okay, Ally, now you can officially put on your apron." He handed it to her. "Stew, fill her in on the agenda for dinner, and take it easy with the knife tricks."

She sighed as she put on the apron and started to peel another onion to add to tonight's dinner of hamburger stroganoff.

Stew stirred the hamburger browning in a pan. "Will, I'm whipping a delicacy up for the year-round staff tonight. Can you stay?"

"No, I've got a previous engagement."

"Oh, *that* previous engagement. She hogs a lot of your time lately."

Will's face turned a little red, but he just waved good-bye and left.

"Hey, greenhorn, we best start frying up the hamburg."

"Hamburg?"

"Yeah, we drop the -er up here. Take out a couple of those packages out of the walk-in." Stew glanced around to see if anyone else was in hearing distance before lowering his voice.

"Just want to say one thing. This is my kitchen, and I'm getting it back. I'll teach you anything you want about cooking, but don't you start throwing your weight around. You are only *technically* the camp cook. If you want to survive this job, you won't forget that. I can make your life easy or a living hell."

He winked at Ally.

What have I gotten into?

*   *   *

Ally dropped her purse on the kitchen counter. "You're looking at the new cook at Camp Lake Surrender."

A cheer went up, and Kylie dashed over to hug her mother. "Thanks, Mom. I'm proud of you."

Don't be too proud yet. I've only lasted one afternoon working next to Stew. Ally turned to her aunt. "Did you have anything to do with me being hired?"

Nettie bent over to study a recipe in an open cookbook, and didn't reply.

*   *   *

The second week of June, on a Monday morning, Ally walked into the camp kitchen at six-thirty. Stew, already at his post, had six dozen homemade cinnamon rolls rising on the counter. The pallid dough had a dark cinnamon ribbon running through the middle. He motioned for her to grab a mug of coffee and sit at the wooden table where the kitchen staff ate their meals.

"I've got the menu planned out for the rest of the week. Tonight, burgers and fries. Tuesday night, lasagna. Wednesday, chili. Thursday, teriyaki chicken. Friday, pizza, and then we start serious cooking on Saturday. That's when our first session of two hundred and fifty kids hits. Believe me, it will be a zoo. Ever tried frying five hundred pieces of bacon and flipping about eight hundred flapjacks?" His eyes glinted with sadistic pleasure as he rubbed his hands together. "You'll earn your keep then."

They spent another half-hour tweaking the menu and making grocery lists for the week. Stew told her where the camp had accounts and drew a couple of maps.

"I'll do the shopping this week because I need to know where everything is located. Next week, you'll do the shopping, Stew."

"Just to let you know, the main cook always does the

shopping. You do want to be the main cook, right?"

Ally wondered how long she'd last. She grabbed onto all the self-control she could muster; everything in her wanted to lob one back at him.

His phone rang. Stew sauntered out to the small porch off the kitchen, talking in short whispers.

"I didn't plan on eavesdropping on your phone call," she said, half to herself.

He came back. The phone call had downgraded his disposition from unpleasant to lousy.

This could be a fun few weeks.

He tossed a credit card onto the counter—"Better hop to it"—and left before she could answer.

Will pushed open the door. "How's it going?"

"Okay, I guess. I'm headed off to the store."

"Want me to drive you? I know you're still finding your way around."

Ally picked up the card and slipped it into her wallet. "That would be awesome. I do need to stop by the house. My aunt needs a break. She loves Benjie, but he can be a handful."

"I'm flattered that Mr. Benjie wants to accompany us on our grocery trip. And, by the way, your aunt is a saint. She's always one to pick up any slack for anybody in town. I don't know what this town would do without her."

* * *

Will's ancient Suburban rumbled in Aunt Nettie's

driveway, waiting as Ally dropped off her car and scooped up Benjie inside the house. The boy stiffened. He was in the middle of watching *Toy Story* for the thirteenth time that day and hated being interrupted.

She grabbed his car seat and snapped him securely into the back seat. "Benjie, say hello to Mr. Will."

Benjie looked up and studied the Camp Lake Surrender emblem on the pocket of Will's white golf shirt, but said nothing.

Ally shut the rear passenger door then climbed into the seat next to Will. "It takes him a while to warm up to anyone, so don't be offended. He loves grocery shopping because he knows when it's over he can have a ride on the penny horse."

Benjie nodded. "Horse, horse."

"We'll just have to find extra pennies for our cowboy."

They drove a couple of blocks, the silence occasionally interrupted by Benjie's motor sounds.

Will turned and winked at the boy. "Looks like this car is being moved by Benjie Power."

Benjie responded by making the vibrations louder.

"He loves making motor sounds. He must feel comfortable here if he's making his favorite noises."

"What other noises does he like?"

"He clicks his tongue on the roof of his mouth when he's upset, and when he's excited, he whistles." She paused. "He does a lot of clicking when he talks to his dad on the phone."

"Maybe he misses his father?"

Ally blew the air from her puffed-out cheeks. "It's been a hard year." She looked out the window at the deep woods flying by.

They drove a few more miles past Beyer's Dairy Farm, black and white cows dotting its pasture, and past the KOA campground, full for the first session.

Will kept his eyes on the road. "I hope I'm not prying, but how long were you married?"

"Almost thirteen years. He's not a bad guy, but his company was deteriorating, and then Benjie—" She paused. "Bryan's pretty lost right now."

"I'm sorry." Ally bowed her head as she hunted for something in her purse.

"Enough about me." She made work of pulling a breath mint from her purse and placing it on the tip of her tongue. "Did you grow up here?" she queried, even though she knew the answer.

"I'm a native Michigander. Except for a five-year gig in Northern California, I've been here. God's country."

"What were you doing in California?"

"Had a stint interning in a church. A great experience."

Ally groaned inwardly. Oh, no, one of those ultra-conservative types. He seemed so normal. *Keep the conversation on Michigan.* "What brought you back here?"

"A woman." Will chuckled as if sharing a joke with himself. "But she left Michigan, called to be a missionary, so I found the camp job and have been here ever since. I love it."

*　　*　　*

Back at camp, Will pulled out his key to unlock the back door of the kitchen only to find it already open.

"Dang that Stew, he needs to keep this locked." He propped open the door while Ally led Benjie inside.

Her son, all eyes, looked around at the large camp kitchen. In his excitement, he ran laps around the perimeter of the room until Ally intervened. She grabbed him in a hug.

"Sit down at the table, and I'll find you a toy." She turned to Will. "Trying to remember where the large measuring cup and spoons live."

Will hunted around, opening drawers until he found the items. Ally took the measuring cup and filled it full of water. She found a bowl and put all the items on the table.

"This will keep him busy. Benjie loves water, don't you?"

Benjie didn't answer. He had already become engrossed with the toys.

Will yanked open the mammoth handle on the walk-in refrigerator and put away milk, cheese, butter, and hamburger. He didn't waste any movements as he grabbed milk cartons and reached to put them away on the shelves. Ally pulled all the canned goods out of the sacks, and arranged the #10 cans in the pantry.

"We keep an inventory of all our food in the pantry and the walk-in. When you use up an item, double check that you cross off one from the list. It makes ordering easier, especially when things go crazy in the middle of the summer. Also, I need to show you how to use the gas oven. Occasionally the flame needs to be lit. It's ancient."

He opened the oven to demonstrate where and how to light the flame. Then he pointed to the large butcher block counter. "Over here is the institutional can opener. Ever use one?" She shook her head as she watched Will drop the top down on #10 can of soup and crank the mammoth handle 'round and 'round. He then took her over to the warming ovens. "Keep these on two hundred degrees, or dinner rolls dry out. These ovens are a lifesaver when we serve large groups."

"Let me check on Benjie." Ally walked back to the kitchen table, hidden in an alcove next to the screened porch. No little blonde-head on the porch.

"Benjie," Ally yelled. She turned to Will. "He's taken off!" She ran out of the kitchen and to the dining room, calling his name.

Will followed. "Maybe he's in the game room."

No Benjie.

They slid open the sliding door to the back porch. No sign of him.

"I'll bring the golf cart," Will gave her shoulder a reassuring squeeze before trotting down the road behind the lodge.

"Benjie, Benjie!" Ally called, frantically weaving in and out of the camper's cabins. Campers had all headed out for swimming so she could easily check them. Her call echoed throughout the bathrooms as she peeked in. She opened each stall, and found them all empty. Will swung by in the cart—"I think we'd better check the beach and the volleyball court"—and she hopped on. They turned left toward the beach. No Benjie.

Ally wiped her clammy palms on her jeans. He had to be close. Will turned the golf cart down a dirt pathway past the baseball field and the swimming pool. Ally shielded her eyes to see any sign of Benjie.

Finally, after a frantic twenty-minute tour of the camp, Will stopped the cart. "How could he move so quickly?"

"Story of my life. He's a bolter, as they called the runners in his class. Those teachers had to be in great physical shape, always flying after kids." She cupped her hands and called, "Benjamin, you answer me right now!"

Silence.

"Can you think of any place he likes to hide?"

Ally had an idea. She slid off of the cart, and sprinted back to the lodge. Down the hall from the dining room, she knocked and then pushed open the boys restroom. There stood Benjie, the faucet turned on full blast, splashing in the sink to his heart's content.

"Benjie!" she snapped. "You are not supposed to take off like that."

He didn't even look up.

She sat beside him and took a few deep breaths. "He does this a lot when he's in a new place. Scares me to death."

"Hey, buddy, you worried us." Will patted him on the head. "You need to stick around. We like your company."

Benjie turned his head a fraction of a degree toward Will. No one would have noticed but Ally. She knew even that small movement showed Benjie had responded to Will's voice. It surprised her. Her son rarely acknowledged anyone new.

"I think your perseverance is amazing," Will blurted, and then looked down. "Sorry, I didn't mean to—"

"Embarrass me? No, you didn't. I guess it's nice to have somebody appreciate the challenges of raising a special-needs child."

"Challenge is an understatement." Will grinned at Benjie and tried to catch his eye, but he was focused on the makeshift toys.

Will cleared his throat. "Stew's not the easiest person to get along with. Are you up for it?"

"Just try me." She sounded surer than she felt.

CHAPTER
ELEVEN

The alarm insisted she act, but Ally wanted to do nothing but put the pillow over her head. She was dreaming of being back in school and late for a class.

Run fast or I'll be marked tardy!

Then she woke, and discovered the school bell was the alarm clock. How she'd love to hop back into her world of high school days and stay there where life was simple and uncomplicated, a place where she had fun. She'd been editor of the school paper. Jason Crew, the "Most Likely to Become a Hollywood Star", was her boyfriend. *Didn't know how good I had it.*

She threw on a pair of jeans, a white tank top, and tennis shoes. Remembering Michigan mornings were chilly, she also snagged a periwinkle-blue hoodie from the hall closet, then paused, remembering how Bryan loved that color on her. She wrote a quick note for her aunt, and poured herself a small cup of coffee from the ancient carafe. Aunt Nettie never liked to spend money on anything frivolous like a new coffeemaker. *Note to self: buy a new one with first paycheck.*

Then she crept into Benjie's room and gave him a gentle kiss. Kylie stirred in the next room.

Ally cracked open her door. "I'm going to work. I'll be home by two o'clock."

Kylie nodded, eyes still closed. Ally planted a kiss on her cheek and raced to the door.

Breakfast was cranked up when Ally hung up her jacket on the hook by the door and turned on the faucet to wash her hands. Stew had already rolled out dough, and was cutting biscuits and arranging them in a baking pan.

"Wash up and throw your West Coast butt in gear," he said, barely glancing up from his project. "You'd better start showing up earlier. We want breakfast on the table by seven o'clock. Camp days start early." He put the first batch of biscuits in the oven. "When you've got your apron, turn on the grill and start frying the bacon."

And a "good morning" to you, too. Ally reminded herself she'd only have to do this job a month or so. She'd send out résumés later this summer. *I can outlast you, buddy.*

After feeding the staff, washing the oatmeal pots, and running the dishwasher, she and Stew sat down to discuss lunch.

"I thought we'd have tuna fish salad sandwiches, potato salad, fresh fruit salad, and granola bars," Ally said.

"No can do. The tuna fish is for the casserole tonight.

We'll have to have grilled cheese."

"Seems to me, *I* am the menu planner here. We're having lasagna tonight."

"Too labor intensive. Do the tuna casserole."

"Lasagna is what we're eating tonight," Ally said through gritted teeth.

Stew responded by heading to the walk-in freezer. He grabbed thirty pounds of solid hamburger and slammed it on the counter.

I hope this is worth it, Kylie.

By two o'clock, Ally's legs began to give out. She hadn't worked this hard physically in years. She'd gotten soft sitting in front of a computer in her corporate office, even with performing her daily ballet aerobics. *If Frank could see me now, he'd have a good laugh.*

Will pulled up a chair to the kitchen table after ladling a bowl of vegetable soup from the stove and helping himself to a grilled ham-and-cheese sandwich. He wolfed down the meal, poured himself a fresh cup of coffee, and then left. His furrowed brow probably meant he had camper cabin assignments on his brain as he'd barely nodded to her.

Stew had stepped out a few times for smoking breaks. He also seemed to be on the cell phone a lot. *He must have a wife who needs him to check in.* Maybe Ally would take advantage of his absence and make a couple of phone calls of her own. She called Aunt Nettie about the kids, and then listened to voice mails about a couple of jobs where she'd applied. A children's book company, Sleeping Bear Publishing, seemed tailor-made for her. Both companies left messages saying they'd received her résumé and they'd let her know if they were interested.

She wrote final notes on the week's menu, put several large pans of lasagna into the oven, and went down the hall. She stood in the doorway of the camp office.

"You look nice," she commented. Will had changed into a light yellow dress shirt and a deep navy and yellow striped tie. He stood under a ceiling light that enhanced the slight wave in his dark hair. He was singing "Tonight" from *Westside Story* when she walked into the musky cologne-filled air.

"'Tonight, tonight, won't be just any night …'"

"Hey, Josh Groban—"

"I made reservations for Sarah and myself at our favorite Italian restaurant, Spumoni's."

"Big plans, eh?"

"You might say that. I even washed the outside of the Suburban and detailed the interior."

His cell phone rang. "Hey, babe, I'm on my way. Plan to have an evening you won't forget," he said before closing it. He looked in a little cracked mirror hanging off the end of a bookcase. "You old devil, you've got the charm."

Ally snorted, put her hands on her hips, and flashed him a grin. "Pride goeth before a fall—isn't that what your Bible says?"

* * *

At lunch in the kitchen the next day, Betty, Will's administrative assistant, came up from behind Will and rested her hands on his shoulders. "So tell me details."

Will sipped a spoonful of tomato soup. "Not much. Just went to pick her up at her parents' house. They were pretty glad to see me. Always liked me. Then we went to Spumoni's in Elk Rapids and had rigatoni. Then I drove her home."

"You're skipping a lot here," said Betty.

Ally had heard Betty could pry information out of the head of Homeland Security if she had a mind to do it.

"Fill in the missing information." Betty plunked down next to Will and grabbed his sleeve playfully.

"Details about what?" asked Ally, putting her plate on the table.

"He got engaged last night!" replied Don.

Will took a bite of sandwich and grinned. "Wow, information travels around Lake Surrender faster than the speed of light." All eyes on him, he took another bite and swallowed. "You know I've had this on my mind ever since Sarah came home on medical furlough. I'm almost glad she got sick."

"Will!" yelled Betty. She smacked the top of his head with a notebook she'd brought to lunch.

"Just kidding. But it gave us a chance to reconnect after all these years apart. I've known her since high school. Anyway,

I did the knight in shining armor routine, and knelt down at the table to ask her to marry me. She was pretty surprised."

"And what did she say?"

Will wore an inscrutable look that gave no clue to his feelings. "She opened the box and stared at it. Think I surprised her. Then she put the ring on a necklace around her neck. I guess that's almost as good as putting it on her finger."

"Why would she put it on her necklace?" asked Don.

"She told me she had a lot of loose ends to take care of and wasn't ready to make it official."

"But you *are* engaged, right?" Betty leaned over to pour herself another glass of ice tea.

"Yes, pretty much. I'm letting her take her time. She doesn't like to be pressed for an answer. She told me when the time was right she'd put the ring on her finger."

"Never heard that before," said Betty. "Either you want to get married or you don't, and at your age you'd think—" Betty shook her head and took a sip of coffee.

Maybe Betty should keep her opinions to herself.

"Back to the office." He stood, leaving behind the half-eaten sandwich. "I've a ton of phone calls to return."

"Don't get these modern romances," muttered Betty.

* * *

"If I can have your attention." Will used a spoon to clank on the side of a coffee cup to silence the group for the morning meeting. He looked around at the staff: Jordan the swim director, Jeannette the camp nurse, Stew, Don, Betty, and all the summer counselors. "We have a new cook, Ally. Please welcome her and her son, Benjie, who will sometimes come to work."

Ally shook hands with several smiling staff members.

Will passed out the meeting minutes. "We've got a lot to cover. Let's begin." Flipping open a yellow legal pad, he called on Don for an update on the progress of the new girls cabin being built. Betty, his administrative assistant, gave the head count for all twelve weeks of camp, and Jeanette, camp nurse, reported on two campers that needed to be monitored for diabetes and epilepsy.

He nodded to Ally. "How's the kitchen shaping up?"

She flipped open her notebook and rattled off the menu for the next few weeks. "We're trying to keep on budget. If we don't have a repair on the walk-in freezer, we'll be okay." She turned to Stew, who had an immoveable frown chiseled all over his face, his gaze peering at a water spot on the ceiling.

"Sounds like you're catching on pretty quickly," said Will. He put down his written agenda and paused. "There is one thing I'd like to say to you guys before you go back to work. I want to see us as a team pulling together. We've got a great group of kids, and I want to keep the vision of Camp Lake Surrender alive so these children understand the love of Christ. We, as staff, can reflect that daily in our actions. I, for one, need to daily depend on Him to keep my attitude good.

We all know that can be hard when the stress of running a camp kicks in. I'm grateful to work with a great bunch of people, and I just wanted to tell you guys that. Any other comments?"

Ally looked at Will. *He sincerely believes this Jesus stuff.* She had to give him credit for that. So many people just gave lip service to religion.

Will spoke a short prayer to end the meeting. Ally gathered she'd probably need to bow her head while he was talking. As she closed her eyes, she caught a glimpse of Benjie, his head bowed.

Afterward, the camp director leaned over the table. "Hey, Benjie, come to help your mom cook?"

Benjie didn't respond.

Will ruffled his hair. "Say, I've got a surprise for you." He pulled out a Matchbox car. "It's a 1969 Mustang."

Benjie grinned, and opened up his hand to receive it. He fingered the toy and made the sign for "thank you" in sign language. Ally had taught him signing before he started to talk.

"How did you know he loves cars?" Ally tilted her head. "He collects them." She turned to her son. "Benjie, why don't you ask Mr. Will what kind of a Suburban he drives?"

Benjie closed his eyes. "What?"

Will laughed. "A 1999 Suburban."

Benjie looked up and stared at Will's shirt. "What license number?"

Will frowned, pretending to concentrate. "Hmm, let me see if I can remember it. It's JJJ345."

"JJJ345," Benjie repeated.

"It's now in his computer. He'll never forget that number *or* the car you drive," said Ally. "One of his more remarkable gifts."

"Amazing." Will shook his head. "I can hardly remember my phone number, Benjie. You must be smart!"

The boy grinned, rocking back and forth in his seat, clasping the car to his chest.

Dripping wet in her swimming suit, Kylie sprinted into the room with a blonde-headed boy about her age. "I got tested by the lifeguard, and I'm an *intermediate* swimmer!"

Ally laughed. Kylie was all grins having earned her new status.

"Fantastic, sweetie, you've always been a fish!" Ally gave her daughter a high-five, and wrapped a beach towel tighter around Kylie's shivering body. "Who's your friend?"

"His name is Carson. He's from Wolverine Hill, two towns away, and he is an awesome runner."

"Nice to meet you, Carson."

Carson nodded, and produced a shy smile.

"Why don't you two follow me into the kitchen and watch me make pizza."

Kylie and Carson giggled, and Benjie's hands flapped. Pizza was the way to his heart.

CHAPTER

TWELVE

Last thing I want to do is put money in that old car.

Ally dumped the pile of wet denim into the basement dryer. The car needed new brakes, so Betty had brought her home, and she planned to whittle down a few things on her to-do list before Betty picked her up for the dinner shift.

Bryan had sent five hundred dollars last month, but he was late again sending this month's payment. *Money, it's always about money. Will I ever get ahead?*

Ally had left the basement door ajar. As she stood folding a dry pile of jeans, she heard Kylie's voice floating down from upstairs. Must have just come back from hanging out with her new friend, Jess.

"Do you know my dad very well?" Kylie asked Aunt Nettie.

Ally heard mumbling and then Kylie's voice again. "He's pretty cool, but he used to work too much. I overheard Mom saying he was always at the office so he didn't have to be a family man. Do you think that's true?"

More mumbling, and then Aunt Nettie walked closer to the basement steps. "Of course not. I know he loves you. Dads are busy a lot."

"Mom told her friend Ember she didn't think he wanted to be a father to an autistic son. Maybe he didn't want to be a father to me, too."

Ally cringed, remembering the phone conversation. She had no idea Kylie had been awake that night.

She placed the pile of jeans in an empty basket and kept eavesdropping.

"I know your father loves you, honey, just like he loves your brother. I remember how happy he was when you were born. He called me from the delivery room at midnight to tell me about his new daughter."

"He used to love me, but maybe he changed his mind just like he did to Mom."

Why, oh, why hadn't she shut the basement door? This was one conversation she'd never wanted to hear. Here came the little achy feeling that started in her heart and slid down to her stomach. Ally longed to fly up the stairs and reassure her daughter that she'd never leave her, and wasn't that enough? But it wasn't. She could never replace Kylie's father. She could only hope the wounds would heal in time.

Ally started the washer, threw in a load of T-shirts, and then stood hypnotized by the agitator that swished the clothes back and forth. *It reminds me of my life. Me and the kids, yanked around by life, spun, hung out to dry, or dumped into an overheated dryer.*

What could she possibly say to Kylie? She listened as Aunt Nettie's voice filtered down amongst the rhythmic thuds of the dryer's drum.

"I know he loves you. He's troubled with his business and misses you kids. He hurts too. Maybe we should pray for your father?"

"Why? He doesn't care." Kylie's voice got softer.

"He may care more than you think. We all screw up at times."

"My dad doesn't think he needs Jesus."

"Life has a way of coming back and hitting us upside the head if we miss the message the first time. God hasn't forgotten him, and we can't forget him either."

Kylie sighed. "I guess you're right, Aunt Nettie. I'm going to try to pray for him every day."

Nettie chuckled.

With a laundry basket on her hip, Ally headed upstairs. Her aunt turned around. "Hey, didn't know you were down there."

"Mom, Aunt Nettie had a great idea. She said we should pray for Dad. Don't you think we should?"

Ally used her foot to close the basement door. "Hey, as long as I don't hear it," she replied over her shoulder as she headed upstairs.

"Honestly, Ally," said Aunt Nettie, "You take after your mother."

*   *   *

Don knocked at the open office door. "Can I talk to you a minute?"

Will put down his sandwich, and motioned for him to have a seat in the extra chair.

"Just got a call from the president of the local tribal Dads Club. You know we've been trying to purchase that land adjacent to the camp."

Will nodded, and then swallowed a mouthful of tuna sandwich.

Don continued, "We just talked to our treasurer, and it looks like we'll have enough money to put a down payment for that land by the end of summer. Our treasurer says we have forty-five hundred dollars, but we need another couple thousand."

"That's fantastic, Don. Don't worry, we'll find the money. Give me the paperwork, and I'll bring it up at the next board meeting." Will brushed crumbs from his hands and shook his friend's hand. "We'd planned on a craft and flea market after camp, during the Harvest Festival. That's still a go, right?" He flipped through his calendar.

"You betcha. The guys at the club can't wait to start. Just wanted to let you know the plan." Don stood to leave. "Oh, and by the way, there's no hot water in junior girls cabin five. Looks like I'll have to get a new hot water tank installed, pronto."

Will scratched the side of his head. "Once we fix one thing, another thing wears out."

"That's why you need me." Don grinned. "Great job security."

"If I didn't know you better, I'd think you were fishing for a raise."

Don gave a thumbs-up, and then waved as he left the office. "Going to check out the new tanks at Brown's Plumbing."

*　　*　　*

As he gunned his truck, the driver zoomed past a dark-skinned man carrying a tool box. *Must be the maintenance man. Hope he didn't see me. I don't need no trouble.*

He shoved his tripod over to the window of the passenger's side. *No more surveying these "off the record" properties. After this deal I'm going to go straight and get a regular gig. Tired of answering to those thugs in Grand Rapids and Detroit. Just going to get my money and get out.*

He opened the glove compartment to see if the gun was still there. Only gun he wanted to operate was the surveying gun.

*　　*　　*

A cool breeze caught the opening of the kitchen curtains and lifted them playfully as Aunt Nettie set a plate of grilled hamburgers on the kitchen table. She had all the fixings, including Big Boy tomatoes bought at the Farmer's Market on Saturday, potato salad, baked beans, and string beans. Everyone stuffed themselves. Even Benjie ate more than his usual two bites of hamburger.

Must be the fresh air and running around at camp today that gave them such an appetite.

Benjie, to Ally's amazement, wasn't freaked-out by all the staff members he'd had to meet. He especially liked wearing his swimmies and splashing around in the pool at camp. The swim director had taken a liking to him and gave him a paddle board to use.

Ally yawned. Maybe she should chill on the job search and enjoy the summer. These Michiganders definitely did. They loved their stretched-out summer days, when the sun lingered long past supper. She still wasn't used to the long evenings. She'd drive by the local golf course on her way back from camp and see men and women playing at eight in the evening. The sun didn't set until ten in midsummer, which meant she could never put Benjie to bed when she should. Aunt Nettie said it was because they were extremely far north and west on the Eastern Standard Time zone.

Ally dipped her spoon into the saucy berries and the sponge cake covered in whipped cream. She'd quit buying desserts years ago because Bryan watched every calorie he ate. He rarely had anything sweet. She relished this summery treat, a food for the gods. She could eat this for breakfast, lunch, and dinner! Maybe it was the sweet northern berries that made the dessert so heavenly.

They all laughed as she caught Benjie, berry juice coming out of both sides of his mouth. He looked like he had grown a scarlet Fu Manchu mustache.

After helping her aunt wash up dishes, Ally sat down at the kitchen table and flipped through the mail. A letter from Ember but still no check from Bryan, and it was already July. He did send a postcard to the kids from Carmel, California, a beautiful shot of a cypress tree hanging off of a cliff. She ripped open an envelope from her mother and read:

> *Dear Ally,*
>
> *Things here still move at a hectic speed. I know when we finish the fundraising dinner and silent auction for the humane shelter, I will have more time. Your dad is painting the family room, and we just had new thermal windows replaced in the kitchen and living room. Always stuff to take care of. Even the pool seems to be a lot of work this year.*
>
> *We miss you and the kids. How long do you think you'll want to be in Michigan? You know, their summers are great, but you are not used to the snow, and my sister always reminds me how many feet of snow they average each winter.*
>
> *Have you found anything in your field? I know someone will want a gifted editor like you. Keep looking.*

You probably won't want to stay at that camp much longer.

Bryan came by to pick up his mail you left at my house. He wasn't here long and looked strained. I will say he's not my favorite person now. Imagine leaving your family because you can't cope with a child. Isn't that what family is all about, taking care of each other?

We're off for a short weekend in wine country. I love the off season when it's a bit hotter and fewer tourists. Let me know if you want a bottle of your favorite Pinot Noir, and I'll send it to you. You do need to take care of yourself, and treat yourself once in a while.

Best of luck. Your father sends his love. Please use this check for yourself.

Love, Mom

Ally looked at the check, seventy-five dollars. It would help buy a week's groceries. When she and a client had gone out to lunch in San Francisco at The Redwoods, a trendy seafood eatery, this check wouldn't have even started to cover it. Now, though, it seemed like a lot of money.

Kylie was engrossed in her book when Ally kissed her goodnight. "We already said our prayers with Aunt Nettie so you can just kiss me goodnight."

Ally laughed. "That must be a great book if you don't want to talk to your old mom."

"Sorry, Mom, I just have to see what happens to the zombie ballerina dog that ran away."

"You're kidding, right?" Frank would have gone nuts seeing a book like that.

Ally slipped into Benjie's room. Aunt Nettie had left a nightlight on the table next to his bed. Benjie had already slipped into a deep sleep. He clutched an object, bright red in his hand. Ally looked closer. It was the Matchbox car Will had given him.

In his other hand he had a picture book, A Child's Bible Stories. Maybe it helped him to fall asleep. Aunt Nettie always tried to sneak a little Bible in wherever she could.

Ally kissed Benjie on the forehead. He turned his head but didn't wake up. She loved this time of day, watching her children fall off to sleep. Benjie slept peacefully. She almost wished she knew a prayer to say for him, but she'd leave that up to Aunt Nettie.

Ally headed to the back deck that was covered with newspapers for Aunt Nettie's latest project. It was a balmy night, and a full moon hung low in the sky. The bright light illuminated short rows of corn and the bean hills. Sunflowers edged the plot of land, and had closed their leaves to rest.

Aunt Nettie had tucked her gray curls into her predictable bandana as she slaved over her newest creation. She dipped a brush into mint-colored enamel, then added curlicues, leaves, and vines onto a small bedside table. The most recent pieces of furniture she had painted were slated to be sold at the Harvest Festival in November. Many of the high-income families in town had also put in orders for her creations, and lately she often had a paint brush in her hand.

"This isn't for the festival. I'm painting this one for Kylie." She waved her hand at the wooden chair covered with tiny flowers that trailed across the back of the chair. The legs sported a black and white checkered pattern. "Think she'll like it?"

"She'll love it."

"How are things at camp?" Aunt Nettie put down her brush, balancing it on the edge of the paint can and looked up at her niece.

"Pretty good. Will's been easy."

"I've known Will for years, before his mother died. He's the real deal. I remember how you and your sister played for hours in his fort house."

"Yeah, I know. I'm just not letting on yet that he knew me when. But that's not what's worrying me. It's the guy whose place I'm taking. Stew. I don't trust him, Aunt Nettie."

"Why?"

"He's always on time at work, but he steps out a lot to take phone calls and is careful he closes the door behind him. Can't all be from a girlfriend. He seems sneaky, not to mention angry at me for taking his job."

The next few days flew by, marked by mounds of chopped onions, buckets of pancake batter, and dozens of grilled cheese sandwiches. Her once-smooth hands became chapped and red. Ally thought she'd be washing dishes in her sleep. She was proud of one accomplishment: she'd learned to clean the grill—no easy process. She used the carbon brick to scrub the top of the grill, then she swabbed out the oil and grease from the side gutters. It was a nasty job, but Ally felt an odd sense of satisfaction when she finished.

Will stopped by the kitchen the second week of camp to check up on her and to make certain Stew was giving her complete instructions on all aspects of the job. Will always had a funny story about a crazy parent who called to see if their little Travis was eating his vegetables, or of a staff member who got lost on a trail and had to be led back to camp by one of the veteran ten-year-old campers. He entertained her as she swirled vanilla icing on cupcakes to be served that evening.

As he picked up a paper plate to carry a couple of cupcakes, his phone rang. He looked at the number.

"Hello, babe."

He lowered his voice and stepped outside into the hallway, but his words carried right back to Ally. She didn't like to eavesdrop but, honestly, how could she help it? She turned off the sink faucet to hear.

He listened for a minute and then said, "You need to give it a chance. Yes, I know, but there are other ways to serve. Are you married to it?"

Ally wondered what "it" was.

Will's voice, normally calm and steady, took on a tense tone as he walked over to the corner. "Don't give up on us," he whispered.

Wow, now she needed to stop snooping. She suspected Sarah, his fiancé, was the girl she'd seen when she had come to the writing conference in spring.

Ally still hadn't let on she knew him when he was a kid. She couldn't figure out why, but she wanted it that way for now. Ally busied herself scraping the leftover frosting from a stainless steel bowl then glanced up. Will had finished his call, but his demeanor had changed, and when she caught his glance, she saw hurt seared in his deep-set eyes. A momentary wave of tenderness she hadn't experienced for a while swept through her heart. She'd never seen this happy-go-lucky man depressed. Should she say anything? *No, Ally, butt out.*

His phone rang again, and Will answered it as he poured himself a glass of tea from the small beverage refrigerator. After a few terse sentences, he stuffed the phone back into his pocket.

CHAPTER
THIRTEEN

On Friday afternoon, after the first two-week session in July, Don raced into the kitchen where Ally, Stew, Betty, and Will were planning the food budget for the rest of the summer, waving his hands in the air. He talked so fast no one could understand him.

"Hey, slow down," Will said. "What's the big crisis?"

Don took a deep breath. "I did my weekly plumbing check of all the camper bathrooms. Cabin five was still having hot water problems. I cleared out the bathroom and put an orange caution cone in the entrance—all I need is a bunch of squealing girls hollering about a guy in their bathroom. I unlocked the utility closet located behind the stall showers, and turned on my flashlight to look at the heat gauge. The arrow had moved all the way to the right, registering 'high', which is normal. Then I noticed there was no water coming through the pipe to fill the hot water storage tank." Don gulped and continued. "Can you imagine? A container that should have been filled with fifty plus gallons of water heating up for camper showers was completely empty. I took out my wrench and worked fast to release the pressure, wanting to avert an explosion."

Betty put her red manicured hands on her head. "Had you come an hour later the whole thing might have blown up like a bomb! Dear God in heaven."

"Yeah, I turned off the heat and slowly watched the gauge come down. How on earth it happened, I don't know. I just installed the water heater last week, and remembered watching the water heater fill up to capacity. I even checked the cement floor around the heater for leaks. The floor was bone dry. It doesn't add up."

"Do you think any of the girls would play around with the heater?" Will asked

"I doubt any of them would even know where the water heater was located. Obviously someone's done some tampering—but who? And why?" Don's hands shook as he reached for the water pitcher on the table.

*   *   *

Aunt Nettie drew herself up off the porch floor and away from her new project, a child's rocking chair, and went into the family room to sit in her easy chair. Closing her eyes, she settled into a silent prayer. She felt a gentle nudge so she asked protection for Ally and the kids, for her niece in Baltimore, and her sister and husband in California. She figured she'd covered all the bases. Then she looked at the camp brochure

Kylie had shown her, and felt a need to pray for the camp. She prayed for each staff member and all the campers, and did not let up until she felt God's peace. Satisfied, she went back to her project.

That night at Nettie's kitchen table, Benjie entertained them all. "Tell us all the names of the cars that the staff members drive." Ally nodded at her son. "Okay, Stew's."

"2001 Camaro, license GRR877

"Miss Betty."

"Toyota Camry 2005, license ABG223."

"Miss Jeanette the nurse."

"2005 Saturn Vue, license NMB341

"Jamie the lifeguard."

"2008 BMW, license KKL898."

Aunt Nettie clapped her hands, and Benjie looked straight at her and smiled before taking another brownie from the plate in the middle of the table.

"Child, you are truly one of a kind. I think the FBI might have a job for you down the road!"

While they were cheering, a knock sounded at the kitchen door.

"Come on in, Will." Aunt Nettie waved him inside. "We were just talking about Benjie's abilities to memorize anything related to cars."

"I can't stay. I just came to drop off a couple pints of extra paint the camp didn't need. I know you've been painting your little arm off all summer. Figure you could use this stuff."

"Didn't need to make a special trip." Aunt Nettie motioned to a chair, but he shook his head.

"I'd like to, but I just need to talk to your niece."

Ally went out on the porch where Will had put down a cardboard box full of paint cans. "What's up?"

"Just wanted to run a question by you. Have you seen anyone strange at camp lately? I mean an adult other than staff members?"

"Why?" Ally studied the intensity in his brown eyes.

Will wiped the sweat off of his forehead with his forearm. He wore a nicer shirt than earlier. "I'm concerned about what Don discovered today." His rolled-up sleeves showed forearms that had gotten tanner and stronger during the summer. "I'm not telling anyone outside of camp, Ally. It's got me rattled."

Ally nodded

"By the way, I think I know where I might have met you. Were you in a certain restaurant on Mission Point when you came back in the spring? I think I remember you sitting across the aisle from us."

Ally felt like she'd just stuck her head in a sauna. She gulped. "Hmmm, I don't remember that." She lowered her brows, hoping to appear confused.

I'll quit on the spot if he ever figures out we knew each other as kids. She still had memories of the cocky Willy she knew from the past. And the whole tripping incident—she'd never admit to that.

She sneaked a long look at the stocky figure in front of her as he looked out on the front lawn. His dark brown eyes had a more guarded look. Gone was any resemblance of the show-off of years ago. What bumps and bruises had knocked him down to make him a little more vulnerable? She didn't know that person behind those brooding eyes, but his expression grabbed her and made her want to know his whole story.

Will turned back to Ally. "Try to keep on Stew's good side. We don't want him quitting in the middle of the summer," he said as Ally walked him out to his car.

"Yeah, you might need to hire a legitimate cook."

"I didn't mean it like that. You're doing okay."

"Thanks for the compliment."

"Hey, look, I took a risk hiring a newbie. I hope you appreciate it."

"Yeah, I'm grateful but what do you think I am, a welfare mother? I'm doing this until I can jumpstart my career, thank you very much." Ally heard her voice ratcheting up a few decibels as she concluded her speech. *I take back my revised opinion of you.*

Will winced. "I didn't mean for it to come out that way."

"What way did you mean for it to come out?" she shot back, digging her nails into the palms of her hand.

"Looks like I hit a sore spot, sorry. Hey, let's just forget this whole conversation. Sure don't know how to talk to women. I'm striking out today."

Ally placed her hands on her hips. "It's just that I'm sick of men either dumping on me or thinking I can't handle things on my own. I'm fine."

His miffed expression morphed into a sardonic smile. "Hmm. Joining the Man-Haters Club tonight?" He hopped into his truck.

Some things never change. "He's still as annoying as he was as a kid," she mumbled to herself.

Note to self: Send out five more copies of résumé tonight. A new job couldn't come soon enough.

"See ya." Will slammed the Suburban door and sped off.

*   *   *

Ally and Don hopped into the camp truck and went to town to pick up supplies at Sam's Club.

"If you've got a minute, I need to swing by Lakeshore Realty," said Don.

"Fine." She'd go anywhere to stall going back into that kitchen for a while. Even with a ceiling fan, the temperature was uncomfortable. Hair stuck to her cheeks, and she used the sleeve of her shirt to wipe sweat off her forehead.

"I'll just be a minute. I have to check on the Moomin Rice project. You know we're close to having enough to start the program. Just need the land deal finalized."

Ally grinned at Don. He might be her favorite person at camp. His enthusiasm for anything from fixing a broken water pipe to finding a sale on grass seed made her giggle.

"I'll keep my fingers crossed. I'm excited for your group—such a great concept," said Ally, relishing the cloudless day and the sun on her arm she slung outside the truck window. Don had contacted the schools for names of the kids who needed a job and extra responsibility. She liked the down-to-earth way he related to the kids and other staff members.

He came back in a couple of minutes, his eye bulging out in fear.

"What gives?"

"Let's vamoose out of here, and I'll tell you." He backed up the car and started talking. "I waited around and didn't see anyone, but I heard muffled voices in the back. I hollered and heard the back door slam. I've been around this town long enough to learn you need to snoop a little, so I went back to the rear of the building and looked through the window overlooking the parking lot. I swear I saw three men in a car. Two in the front, one in the back. The one in the back seat was holding a knife to the driver, and it looked like Hal Schwindleman. I just called the chief of police."

Ally laughed. She knew Don's penchant for the melodramatic, but deep down she wondered if he did see a crime. "Betty said the last time there was a robbery, they traced the culprit to a local dog who stole food out of people's garages," she said, more to reassure herself than anything else. "Still, you'd better report."

"Already done." Don pulled a bandana out of his bib overall pocket and wiped the sweat off his face. "It's weird."

*   *   *

Back at the camp kitchen, Ally checked outside and saw Benjie still playing with his button and rock collection. As long as he stayed on the back porch, she could keep bringing him to work. The camp atmosphere seemed to influence Benjie. He had been coming out of his shell a bit. Ally was thankful for any little progress. She smiled to herself, thinking about Julie, one of the counselors who had been babysitting him and had made him a special board game where he could stack tokens to win a game. The staff had taken to Benjie, bringing him little treats, and crayons and paper for drawing. Betty and Will would take him for rides on the golf cart. She loved hearing Benjie giggling as the cart drove past. Her heart soared to hear her boy having fun and connecting to people.

She pulled a pan of cornbread out of the oven and set it on the counter to cool. Stew had taken the weekend off, so she had to hustle to prepare dinner for two hundred kids and staff. Kylie and Betty would be coming in to give a hand, but she still had a lot to do.

Hauling out a large box of powdered sugar, Ally dumped it into the industrial mixer, threw in a couple of sticks of butter, and cranked up the machine. A small blizzard of white sugar flew up, covering the counter. Hmm, maybe she should have mixed the butter first. What a mess.

Ally turned off the mixer and grabbed a rag to clean off the snowy white counter. Then she put the beater's paddle on low, mashing the butter and sugar. She poured a cup of milk into the mix before noticing she'd put in too much liquid. The whole thing was a gooey, runny mess. She wanted to kick an inanimate object, anything would do. Turning on the hot water, she dumped the whole sloppy mess down the sink. What made her think she could cook anyway?

She glanced up from the sink aware that she hadn't seen a blonde head lately. Ally breathed a sigh of relief when she saw him in a far corner, cross-legged and playing with his Mustang. She looked closer, and saw a lollipop hanging out of his mouth.

"Where did you find that candy?" she asked him.

"JJJ345."

"What are you talking about?"

He took another lick off of the lollipop. "The man."

"What man, honey?" she quizzed him, trying to take the exasperation out of her voice.

But Benjie returned to his own world, savoring the lollipop. Ally pulled it out of his mouth and smelled it. It seemed okay, but she threw it away anyway. Before Benjie could pitch a fit, she produced a small Kit Kat bar from her apron pocket as a substitute. She peeled away the wrapper and popped a piece of it in his mouth.

She wanted to search the grounds, but fear kept her glued to Benjie, and responsibility kept her tied to dinner. She called Will's number, but he didn't answer. She left a message to find out if he knew where Benjie got the candy, then called Don and left him a message, too.

Calm down, you're overacting, but she couldn't shake off the queasy feeling in her gut.

The next day, Don showed up carrying a large roll of screening and his tool box. He clipped and hammered, creating a three-foot-high screen around the porch. He built a gate, and secured it with a child-proof lock.

"That should keep our little guy in, and strangers out." Don had a soft spot for kids; he had five of his own. "I've alerted the police chief. He's going to send out a few patrol cars to keep an eye on the camp for a while. Looks like me and the sheriff are becoming buddies. This is the second time I've called him in the last twenty-four hours."

"What did you find out about the car incident in the real estate parking lot?"

"It probably wasn't a knife, and it probably wasn't Hal Schwindleman in the car. The chief said I've been watching too many CSI shows on television."

Will strolled into the kitchen, reached for a glass, and poured some iced tea. "What on earth are you talking about?"

Don looked down, intently studying the top of his work boots.

"Anyway, nice job on the porch. I heard about our escapee."

Will had a faraway look in his eyes as he stared absently out at the screened porch. She studied him as he gripped the frosted glass of ice tea and took a big gulp. He had shaved off his beard earlier in the summer, but a lack of shaving that morning had left a shadowy chin, defining his jaw and giving him a rugged outdoorsy look. He reminded her of an old-time cowboy just off the range. He'd been gone for a long lunch in town, rare for him. When camp was in session, he never left the grounds except for an occasional day off. *Probably saw Sarah, but that's his business.* He was her boss, and that was that. That was enough after last night's conversation.

"Got a minute?" Will asked.

Ally looked down, her fingers grasping the vegetable peeler. The peelings flew into the sink. "I guess, but I've got to peel potatoes, and Stew is off all afternoon."

"No problem." Will turned, iced tea in hand. She heard the rhythmical *thump, thump, thump* of his boots as he headed off to his office. The door snapped shut.

Hmm, he never closes the door. A pang of guilt nibbled at her conscience. *Maybe I could have been kinder. But, hey, I had a bad day too.*

The rest of the afternoon, she checked on Benjie every ten minutes. She wasn't taking any chances.

After draining large vats of boiled potatoes to be mashed, Ally dragged herself to ring the dinner bell outside, in front of the dining hall. What a day. She watched the campers file in, singing the Camp Lake Surrender song. They were quite wound up from the scavenger hunt that afternoon. Will halted two boys who decided to take off their camp scarves and snap each other while waiting in line to eat.

Each day before dinner, two of the senior campers picked

up their guitars and led the campers, singing their lungs out. The silly hand-motion songs she remembered from her childhood had the kids jumping up and down like members of a pep squad at a homecoming rally. She loved hearing the campers singing. Offkey or not, it always gave a lift to her day. What was it about music that made one joyful?

Ally set out trays of baked chicken and bowls of mashed potatoes and tossed salad. As she brought out the pitchers of punch to put on the buffet, the songs became slower as campers sang:

All to Jesus, I surrender;
All to Him I freely give;
I will ever love and trust Him,
In His presence daily live.

She looked at the sea of kids standing around the round tables, regular kids of all shapes and sizes, from all kinds of backgrounds and places: little towns, farms, suburbs, and big cities in Michigan. She had heard them yelling and horsing around before dinner, but now she perceived a change, a sort of magic among them. Were these the same rambunctious kids who twenty-five minutes before stood in line for dinner?

She spotted her daughter sitting among a group of friends at a table. Kylie had done cartwheels when she found out she could continue at camp for two more sessions. She looked like an angel as she sang along with the others. At that moment,

Ally wanted to climb back into her own childhood, into those innocent, uncaring years. Childhood, carefree and full of promise. She closed her eyes and listened to the chorus of voices. These kids seemed intent on the words they sang.

"'Taste and see that the Lord is good', Psalm 34:8," Will started his nightly talk. "Tonight I have a story about a little girl. She grew up in China where her parents were missionaries. She became very sick. She had lost a lot of weight because she had a disease called tuberculosis, which made her cough a lot. Her clothes hung on her, and her mother had to constantly take in the seams so they would fit. She had no appetite, and couldn't eat much at all. Her mother tried everything to encourage her to eat, but she just kept becoming thinner and thinner. One day, her mother brought her an avocado." Will picked up a shiny avocado on the table in front of him. "Who has ever eaten one of these?"

A handful of campers raised their hands.

"Have you ever eaten guacamole? It's mashed up avocados. Anyway, the mother didn't say anything. She just held the fruit that had the shiny green skin in front of her daughter for her to look at. Taking a sharp knife, she peeled the skin off of half the avocado. 'Look what a beautiful piece of fruit I have in front of me,' she said to her daughter. In a quick, smooth motion of her hand, she sliced a thin piece of the creamy fruit. 'Hmmm, this is delicious', she said, and popped it into her mouth. Her daughter watched her chew and swallow it. 'Would you like to try a little piece?' her mother asked.

The little girl nodded. Her mother sliced off a tiny section and popped it into the little girl's mouth. It was smooth and delicious and easy to swallow. Each day, the mother gave her daughter a little more avocado until one day she could eat almost a whole one by herself. The mother knew that the avocado would bring back her daughter's appetite and help her grow into a healthy girl. Learning to love God is a lot like eating a new food, like an avocado. We need to taste and see God's goodness." Will paused to take a chug out of his water bottle before continuing. "Did the mother stuff the whole avocado down her daughter's throat?"

The kids laughed and answered, "No!"

"And just like the mother didn't force the little girl to eat the avocado, but demonstrated how delicious the fruit was, we at camp hope that you will all have a chance to 'taste and see that the Lord is good.' I want to encourage all of you to seek a relationship with Jesus during this week. Now let's bless the food."

Ally bowed her head out of respect for Will and the campers. Even if she wasn't buying into the entire Christian lingo, she experienced a great sense of peace here. *Peace— what I've been grasping at for the last few months. I didn't think I could ever have peace again.*

The campers scraped their chairs up to the table and sat down to dinner. As each table was called, one at a time, the kids approached the buffet table. The cabin that had won the "Clean White Glove" inspection that day were served first. Ally watched the kids load up their plates, devouring her day's work. All her afternoon work disappeared in a few minutes. These kids were burning a ton of calories.

In the kitchen, Ally dished up a plate for her and Benjie. She pulled a few pieces of meat from a drumstick, and added a couple of spoonfuls of potatoes and beans.

"Taste and see that the food is good, Benjie," she said.

"I think that's 'Taste and see that the *Lord* is good', but glad you are listening."

Ally felt her face burn and knew it probably matched the table's red-checkered tablecloth as Will pulled up a chair at the kitchen table and sat down next to Betty and Don. For once, she didn't have a snappy comeback.

"Anyway, your cooking skills have improved vastly from the first few meals a month ago. Remember the baked beans we had to chew 'cause they didn't cook long enough? Or how about—"

Ally grinned, and held up her hand. "Okay, stop."

Will winked, and leaned close enough for her to smell a whiff of lime-scented aftershave. "No, seriously, how did you make this coating on the chicken?

"Old family recipe, stolen off of the Bisquick box. I just added paprika, garlic powder, salt, and thyme."

"Miracles do happen. Look at this hardened career woman cooking like she's the new Rachael Ray. I probably should warn her she's got competition."

"I love it, keep it coming." Ally giggled, thinking how

absurd her world had become. Six months ago, she never would have pictured herself balanced on a tiny wooden stool in a rundown camp kitchen, basking in a culinary compliment from a rugged backwoodsman.

Will ripped a piece off a steaming roll, buttered it, and popped it into his mouth. "Now, before you run off to attend to another gourmet project, I want to talk to you."

Ally sighed inwardly. Now what?

"Humble pie has a bitter aftertaste, but occasionally I need to eat it. I want to apologize for last night, what I said about hiring a 'newbie.' Granted, you're new, but you're doing a great job." He paused and looked right into her eyes.

Ally blinked, and almost looked away from his intense stare. The faraway look was gone.

"And Stew should be glad he has a job, especially in this economy. He's a little shaky, and I've had to watch him, but I do appreciate the job you're doing. Isn't that right, Benjie?" He broke off another part of his roll and put it on Benjie's plate. Benjie gobbled it up.

"Apology received," said Ally. "I guess I overreacted, too."

"Oh, a woman who overreacts? You're kidding me!"

"Ha, ha, you must have experienced that."

"Actually, she's rather calm and together. She rarely flies off the handle, but she is hard to read."

"And you've set a date?"

"Rather a personal question." He flicked a piece of roll at

Ally as he raised an eyebrow.

"I love to get up close and personal."

"Hey, I'd just rather leave my personal life personal, if you know what I mean. But I'll bring Sarah around. You'll like her."

"Ah, the mystery woman." Betty inserted her voice into the banter. "Does she walk through the woods at midnight, carrying a candle and wearing a long white gown?"

He laughed. "All right, if you all must know, Sarah and I are close to setting a date."

Betty put her hands on her hips. "I've already given Sarah a pile of old *Bride* magazines."

"Enough, enough!" Will yelled in mock horror. "Change the subject."

"Okay, here's one," said Ally, "does JJJ345 mean anything to you?"

Will raised his eyebrows, searching for a moment. "Sounds familiar. Oh, wait a minute, duh, it's my license plate. Why?"

"Do you keep suckers in your office?"

"Why, yes, I give kids one when they visit my office. Why?"

"No reason."

That little rascal had me so worried. She frowned at her son, but secretly breathed a sigh of relief.

CHAPTER
FOURTEEN

"Are you positive you want to do this?" Ally set down her coffee cup for the waitress to refill. She just had breakfast with Will at Linda's Café to go over the plans for the rest of the summer menus. Linda's, known for its bacon pecan pancakes and spicy breakfast burritos, won hands-down for the locals when it came to early morning chow. "It's a big step, and once you own a house, you've got permanent roots."

"That's exactly what I'm hoping for. I'm tired of calling a 12-by-12-foot room behind the camp office my home." Will shook his head, and Ally caught a momentary slice of loneliness in his eyes. She'd never thought of him as being lonely; he was always surrounded by people.

"My heart is always going to be in Michigan. I love the camp life. It suits me perfectly. I'll never be an accountant like my dad." Will grinned his wide grin and gulped the last drops of his coffee. He leaned back in his chair and sighed, patting his stomach. Then he pulled out his wallet and set down two ten-dollar bills on top of the table. "Follow me over there," he said as he headed out to his car.

Driving her own car, Ally followed him in his Suburban as they drove past Snowfall Park, Lake Surrender High School, and an abandoned gas station. After turning right onto a gravel road that vibrated her Audi so badly that Ally thought the axle might fall off, Will slowed to enter the driveway near a huge grove of pine trees.

She stepped out of her car and took in the view of the hundred-year-old dwelling with the gray-stone exterior. It reminded her of an English cottage. The left side of the home had a magnificent chimney, and the high-pitched roof had been replaced only a couple years ago. The house stood alone, no trees surrounding it. Behind, five acres of meadow spanned to meet the edge of thick woods. Ally breathed in the stillness. Deer grazed in the meadow, and squirrels romped. Flanked by a split-rail fence twined with crimson floribunda roses, a cement walkway led up to the front door.

Will took a deep breath as if absorbing the serenity, then turned to Ally. "Let me show it to you."

They walked into the cozy living room. A bright shaft of mid-morning sunlight beamed through the large picture window. On an adjacent wall, the same stone as on the front of the house adorned a massive fireplace that climbed to the ceiling. On the raised hearth stood a stack of firewood that had been left by the previous owner.

"Across from the living room is a dining room I'm turning

into my office," Will told Ally before motioning her to the kitchen behind the dining room. The old owner had left a round pine table and two chairs. A red teapot sat on top of a chipped enamel stove circa 1950. Glossy white cabinets surrounded the cooking area.

Ally followed Will to the master bedroom as he dramatically flung open the door for her to walk through. "'Come into my den, said the spider to the fly.'" He twirled the ends of an invisible comic-villain mustache as Ally walked past him. She turned and batted her eyes back at him.

For a house this small, the room was quite generous, plenty of room for a king-size bed, one or two dressers, and even a comfy chair. And the view, straight out of a decorator's magazine, showed off an expansive meadow lined with towering maple and ash trees. She almost expected Bambi to trot out from behind one of them and walk up to the window.

Will pressed the back of his head against the picture window that overlooked the meadow, closed his eyes, and let out a sigh. "Thank You, God, for this piece of heaven. You are good to me."

On impulse, Ally sauntered over and threw her arms around him. He returned the hug, and she felt his solid torso press against her. It felt good to have a man's body close again.

What am I thinking? Ally pulled away. "I'm sorry, I'm just happy for you." She locked eyes with Will, and realized she'd never noticed what dark eyes he had. She dropped her gaze.

He jerked out his cell phone and dialed Sarah's number. "Get a piece of paper and pencil and take down these directions." After the person on the other end repeated back the directions, Will clicked off his phone. "Think Sarah will like it?"

"What's not to like? It's sweet and cozy."

Will caught her eye. "Hey, sorry, I imagine you miss your home."

"A home's where your family resides." Ally looked out the picture window and wondered what it would be like to wake up to such a bucolic view.

Will leaned toward her and squeezed her shoulder. "You'll have your own home again, someday."

Honk. Honk. Will sprinted to the front door and waved at Sarah, and Ally followed him outside. Sarah jumped out of the driver's seat, tossed back her golden blonde tresses held back with a thin tortoise shell headband, and flashed Ally a friendly quizzical look.

"Sarah, this is Ally." Will strode down the walkway to meet her. "She took Stew's job."

Sarah nodded and stuck out her hand.

"I needed a woman's opinion before I showed you this, so I brought her out here." He put his finger to his lips in a hush motion. "No questions yet. Close your eyes and take my hand." He led her through the front door. "Okay, open your eyes."

"It's an empty house. Whose?"

Will laughed. "Well, you know how I like to surprise people. I guess I got impulsive and bought a house. Maybe I got a little ahead of myself. I don't want to pressure you." He combed his fingers through his hair as if searching for the perfect words. "I thought this might help you picture yourself back in Lake Surrender."

Did his grin look a little sheepish?

He put his arm around Sarah. "Come see the kitchen, you'll like it."

She hesitated.

"Don't you remember this house?"

Sarah tilted her head.

"Senior year, after grad night, we drove by it."

Sarah's mouth dropped open. "Gosh, Will, that was eons ago." Her brow furrowed. "Can't believe you remember that. How sweet."

Ally pulled her car keys from her jeans pocket. "Hey, folks, I need to head back to camp. Have fun reminiscing."

The last thing she felt like doing was going down memory lane.

*   *   *

"Hold on there," said Will. Lounging on a bench with a second cup of coffee, feet propped up against the porch railing of the lodge, he stuck out his hand as Ally and Benjie breezed by him.

"Hey to you, too," said Ally.

"Got a minute?"

"Perfect timing. I have an easy breakfast today." She plunked Benjie down on a nearby rocking chair, and sat next to Will on the bench. "Sounds serious."

"I just wanted to talk to you alone about the petty cash. Did you have a chance to go through your purse and wallet to find the receipts?"

"Believe me, I hunted all evening. I only found one little one for $3.78 from when I bought birthday napkins." A worry groove etched her forehead. "I don't know what to say. I'm positive I put the receipts in the petty cash box."

She looked directly at Will. For the first time, he saw her startling sea foam-colored eyes pool with tears. Why did she have to have such a helpless look? He hadn't seen that coming. Great, that's the last thing he needed—a single mom breaking down in front of him.

"Well," Will took the tone of his voice down a notch or two, "just keep looking."

He decided to change the subject. "What's for breakfast?"

"Egg McMuffin casserole. I made it yesterday afternoon. Listen, I've got to turn the oven on." She placed her hand on the screen door latch.

Will reached out and grabbed her other wrist, and then dropped it. "Hey, please don't run off. I'm not angry with you. I've got a lot I'm juggling."

"Wouldn't have to do with Sarah, would it?" She shot Will a sympathetic smile.

"That's part of it." Will exhaled. "Sarah's a missionary in Mexico, and she's on medical furlough."

He stood and emptied the rest of his coffee mug into the bushes, letting the last drops drain out. "She and I were high school sweethearts. After college, she left Michigan and began working at an orphanage in Guadalajara. It was only going to be a short-term project. She came back for three years, but now she's been there several years. I visited her a few months ago and begged her to come home for a while. She said she had too much responsibility to leave. But then she contracted hepatitis from something she ate from a street vendor's cart. While she's home, we've been seeing each other again, and I picked up the dream of marrying her."

"That's great. When is the wedding?"

Will put his hand on his forehead. *How did I get into this conversation?* "Soon. She needs to get used to the idea of working at a camp."

"Well, I don't understand this foreign missionary stuff. From what I've heard you talk about at camp, you can be a missionary anywhere. You're sort of a missionary yourself at camp, right?"

Will shaded his eyes as he took in the lake with its tiny waves lapping onto the beach, a perfect day for sailing. "It's a question of calling, figuring out where God wants you, but, yes there are plenty of kids right here at camp who could use her love."

"I'll say."

Will turned toward her.

"Look at Brianna Olsen." Ally cocked her head to the side, and the waterfall of red hair followed. "She lost both parents this year, and is having a terrible time adjusting to living with her grandparents. She's just as needy and full of potential as any kid around."

"You're right. The staff has been great with her this week. She's starting to come out of her shell. I'll tell you, that's what's gratifying about my work. I love seeing God change hearts and heal these kids' hurts. I just hope Sarah can share my excitement about camping someday. Hey, didn't mean to dump on you. Guess I like having a woman's viewpoint."

Will looked away and then glanced at her again. *And, yeah, she's definitely a woman. The curves give that away.*

Benjie rocked in his chair, and she ruffled his hair. "She's got a great setup here to do any ministering, or however you describe it. And she's oblivious not to see a great guy standing right in front of her. Trust me, there aren't many around."

"Thanks. Would you like to call her and tell her that?" He reached into his jeans pocket and started to hand her his cell phone.

"I'm sure that would go over big. 'Please do me a favor, and marry my boss so I can have a secure job.' Ha, ha, ha."

"Ha, ha, ha," repeated Benjie.

CHAPTER
FIFTEEN

The next day, Will sauntered in to the kitchen and picked up some paperwork from the kitchen desk. Ally's eyes widened. Freshly shaven, he wore a navy blue blazer and yellow tie, ready for the board meeting. Ally never remembered seeing him so dressed up before.

"Just going over the food budget." He leaned down in front of her, and she saw dark circles under his eyes. He waved the papers and left.

An hour later, Will scraped a chair up to the kitchen table and motioned for Ally and Stew to sit down. "We've got a big discrepancy here."

*   *   *

Ally opened the door to Lakeshore Realty office and saw Hal Schwindleman with his feet up on his desk, buried in brochures of Florida, from Disneyworld to the Everglades.

"This winter is going to be sweetest." He leaned down to talk to his old striped tabby cat. She meowed in agreement.

"Guess I'll have to take you, but hey, I can pay the extra pet deposits on hotels now. Heck, I'll even buy you a pound or two of fresh salmon. When I get this deal sewn up, I'm taking you and the missus for a month's vacation, no expense spared. Several acres of Lake Surrender real estate with lakefront will land me a great commission."

He leaned forward, and flipped his daily calendar open to February. "Wonder if I should go ahead and start making reservations early. This year *I'll* have the bragging rights about my winter get-away. Might even get Melba a new swimsuit. 'Course, she'll want to drop about thirty pounds before she leaves."

Ally cleared her throat. "Uh, hello."

Hank looked up. "Hey, there, you need some help?"

"I'm just here to drop off some papers from Camp Lake Surrender."

The phone rang. "I'll be with you in a minute." He motioned to Ally to have a seat. "Lakeshore Realty, where the water is as clear as the sky, and stress and worry are left to die—"

An angry voice came through the receiver: "Cut the crap, Schwindleman. Looks like we'll have to go to plan B."

*　　*　　*

Aunt Nettie waved to Ally as she pulled into the driveway. "I ordered pizza for us tonight. Kylie's at her friend's house."

"I'll eat anything I don't have to cook," said Ally. She

160

unfastened Benjie's car seat, and he hopped out. "Not a great day at camp."

"You just sit on the picnic bench out back, and I'll bring us both some ice tea." Aunt Nettie tightened her pink bandana before grabbing the screen door. She came back with a tray of ice tea and the carton of pizza.

"Now, let's have a relaxing meal, and you can tell me about your day." She set the tray on the table and passed out napkins and plates, putting a slice of pizza on each plate.

Ally chewed in silence for a few moments, savoring the gooey cheese and crisp crust. No better comfort food. Swallowing a sip of tea, she started her story. "Well, as you know the bigwigs came in today, the board of directors. I overslept—"

"I remember."

"—and Stew didn't let me forget it. Then, Betty comes in and compliments me on the cinnamon rolls Stew made."

"Oh, my."

"Yeah. It's only his trademark recipe. He was furious and got pretty nasty. Well, I tried to blow him off, and then Will came in. He had just met with the Board of Directors, and they'd been looking over the budget. He sat down with us and showed us the receipts, and then showed us how much was in petty cash. I couldn't believe it. Over seventy-six dollars unaccountable. I was stunned. I've been careful to save my receipts so this wouldn't happen."

"Check your pockets to see if you might have misplaced

a receipt?" Aunt Nettie frowned as she closed the pizza container and shooed away the flies.

"I plan to tonight. I don't know, but something's a little fishy. I've been so careful." Ally took another sip of tea. "You know, sometimes I can't believe the last few months. I'm reduced to a common thief accused of taking money from petty cash from my employer. It's almost too much to take in—my going from a successful editor and married, to divorced, living in Michigan, and working as camp cook. My life's been crazy. Sometimes it seems like there's no logic to my universe." Ally stared at a shadowy bat swooping around the top of a blue spruce. It touched the top and took off for the night sky. She hated bats.

"Well, if it helps, you've made this old lady very happy by keeping her company. Not having any children of my own, I've always felt like you and your sister were my children." Nettie reached across the table and squeezed Ally's hand. "Things are bound to get better. Just hang in there. You know everything has an end to it."

"You've been wonderful, Aunt Nettie. What would we have done without you, right, Benjie?"

Benjie looked up from chewing a piece of pizza, and Ally dabbed some sauce off of his chin.

"I just need to keep job hunting so I can find something substantial to support us."

"All in good time. Meanwhile, you're welcome here as long as you need to stay. Are you feeling okay about settling here?"

Ally nodded. As difficult as finding a job had been, she wondered about going back to the chaotic life she'd left. She loved the peace of Northern Michigan; its quiet serenity had grown on her in the last few months. Being by the periwinkle-blue water, the wildlife, and even the camp job had, in a strange way, given her a new outlook on life. She especially cherished her time with Aunt Nettie. Talking to her gave Ally the reassurance that life would someday straighten out. Maybe it was Nettie's faith. Whatever it was, Ally wished she had it.

She brought the empty pizza carton inside the house. As she headed back outside, Ally stopped in the family room and picked up a sterling silver picture frame with a photo of her aunt and uncle on an end table. The camera had caught them sitting in their swimsuits on a dock, arms around each other. They had not been married long, and her uncle had a look of pure contentment on his face. They must have been terribly in love.

Her aunt walked in and took the frame Ally handed her. She studied it a minute. "That's one of my favorites."

"How did you cope when Uncle Charlie died? I know he went fast. Massive heart attack."

Her aunt fingered the edges of the frame. "I'm afraid I didn't cope well. I felt like I'd lost my footing when he left this life. You see, your mother and I weren't taught to deal with life in spiritual terms. Your grandmother had a lot of bitterness toward religion, and she decided your mother and

I didn't need any church upbringing. When my Charlie left me, I didn't have much comfort and found myself wishing I'd die too." She looked out the window. "I'd get up in the morning and feel I had no purpose in life. I'd wander around the house in my old bathrobe for half the day and camp in front of the television, watching old reruns of *The Price is Right* and *Jeopardy*. Friends would come by to get me to go out and eat or play Skip Bo, but I just shooed them away. Even teaching, which I loved, didn't fill the gap. Wherever I turned, I had reminders of forty years of marriage. Photos of our trips framed on the walls, his shirts still hanging in the closet, his chipped blue coffee mug in the cabinet. I'd pull a shirt out of the closet and sleep with it. I just needed to smell his aftershave lotion."

"Something happened. You're one of the happiest people I know."

"It's not something—it's someone. I met Jesus."

She picked up Benjie, who had followed her inside, and put him on her lap. He sat contentedly, still chewing a piece of crust.

"Met Jesus," repeated Benjie.

They laughed.

"What exactly does that mean, you 'met Jesus?'" asked Ally.

Aunt Nettie's cell phone jingled. "Hold that thought."

While her aunt left to talk, Ally thought about a marriage that lasted forty years. She couldn't even imagine a love that would last that long. Maybe marriage was like the garden Aunt Nettie had put in, filled with tall pole beans, staked-up tomatoes, short bell pepper plants, and overflowing vines of zucchini. The warmer August weather helped the harvest to be abundant and early this year, but her aunt always said good gardens begin with fertile soil and fertilizer.

Had she and Bryan lacked good soil?

Aunt Nettie came back with an empty paper bag. "That was Sally—wants some tomatoes."

She was known for her garden, and had a full yield. "Always pray for a good crop," she'd say. Ally thought she shouldn't bother God about the little things, but her aunt persisted. Well, it must work—at least for her gardening. Mom would laugh if she heard how Nettie talked about praying. Not one for sentimentality, Ally's mother, even more than her father, held the opinion that life is what you make of it. She labeled prayer a crutch, saying people should be strong enough to handle life themselves. "Look within and find your strength," she would tell her daughter. "I'm raising you girls to be strong women who can take care of yourselves. Don't ever fall for that religious junk your aunt relies on." Dad never had much of an opinion either way, but Mom stressed self-reliance.

Some of Ally's happiest memories were those few weeks the family spent here in Lake Surrender. Did she just want to retrieve those happier times for her and the children? She couldn't live in the past. Still, the longer she lived in Michigan, the less she wanted to return to the competitive world of publishing. Living in Lake Surrender made her question her true identity. She wasn't a mover and shaker in children's publishing anymore. Now she grilled hundreds of hamburgers and frosted dozens of cupcakes for a living. Funny, though, she didn't care anymore. Something in the camp atmosphere had gotten to her.

Aunt Nettie plopped down again and took a sip of her ice tea. "Now, where were we?"

"You were telling me something about 'meeting Jesus'. I always thought that was an expression people used when they were about to be killed."

Aunt Nettie laughed. "Actually, that's not the best time."

"So He shows up at your door and wants to have tea." Ally didn't mean it, but somehow she couldn't keep the sarcasm out of her voice.

"No, silly, but He does show up at the door of your heart. You see, we were created with a large void inside. It's the part of us God created for fellowship with Him. Unfortunately, our selfish nature has separated us from God. The Bible labels it sin. It's the normal human condition—selfishness." Nettie rose and pulled a plate of cut lemons from the refrigerator.

Ally reached for a slice of lemon and squeezed the juice into her tea. "You don't have to convince me of that, with all I've been through in the last couple of years. Before my life crashed and burned, I thought people were good at heart. If you worked hard and kept a positive attitude, life and people would treat you fairly. Boy was I wrong."

"I understand. We always were taught that knowledge was the answer to the human dilemma."

"Kylie's school kept talking about self-esteem. The teachers seemed to think that raising esteem would fix anything."

"Exactly. Humans always want to find an alternative to mending their relationship with God. But God already fixed it."

"You mean the part about Jesus? I'm still not understanding it. Even if He were God's Son, why would God want Him killed?"

"Well, to take a thought out of the Bible, 'What greater love has a man than to lay down his life for someone?' In my mind, it proves God's love for us. Jesus was quite capable of hopping off of the cross and finding another way, but He didn't. He created wine from water, healed the blind, and even brought Lazarus back from the dead. He certainly could have evaded the cross."

"I never thought about it that way. I guess I've never looked into Christianity. I've always been wary of born-again Christians. Thought they were either prissy do-gooders or gun-toting members of some military militia group."

"I understand. Often Christians don't represent the true character of Christ. All of us are works in progress. Only Christ is perfect."

Ally finished her tea and poured another glassful. New ideas were coming at her fast.

*　　*　　*

"I tell you, it's a done deal. Don, the Indian guy—his club is buying it. They're going to turn it into a wild rice harvesting area, some sort of do-gooders project for juvenile delinquents. Can you believe that? How insane. I say lock them up. It's a waste of a primo piece of property, makes me sick," said the thin man with the dark tan and gray goatee

"Sounds like something you might have needed as a teenager," Hal joked but wiped the smile off his face when he saw the joke had failed. Ted pulled out a pack of cigarettes, tapped it on the side of the desk, and slid one out. Putting it in his mouth, he flicked his lighter and lit it.

"Mind if I smoke?" said Ted as he looked around for an empty coffee mug to use as an ashtray.

"Of course not," said Hal flipping over the *Please Don't Smoke* sign on his desk. "There's not a lot of lakefront property left in this area. Why, think what kind of contribution you'll make with your plans. You'll be bringing all kinds of money and jobs into the community."

"Yeah, we're so noble, the guys coming in on the white horses. Won't be able to do that if we don't get the property— buddy." Ted sneered. "What are you doing to help us? You're slated to earn a big commission on this, and part of earning that is softening up the sellers to sell to us."

"I've got some ideas, just hold on. These things take time. We'll have to let a few things play out first."

"Play out?"

"Let me handle this, Ted. I know how to motivate the seller."

"Schwindleman, you better know how. Time's getting short." He smashed out his cigarette in a yellow ceramic coffee mug printed with the slogan *Hal Sells Houses!* and walked out the door.

*　　*　　*

Will and Betty stood cheering the Summer Olympics on the soccer field. A cool breeze had kicked up off of the lake, so Ally zipped up her hoodie as she approached with a sack full of letters. She'd be very popular for mail call.

"Big day at the post office." She waved the bag of mail.

"Uh huh," said Will, absently.

Betty elbowed Ally. "He's got big decisions on his mind." She handed him a pile of bills. He grabbed them and flipped through them. "We're running at a deficit each consecutive week. I'd hoped we'd make up for it during the fall conference season, but so far we don't have many bookings."

His frown line deepened. Will wasn't a big worrier, so the stress vibes she picked up from him surprised her.

"Isn't there any way of marketing the camp? You know, I've got some background in that area."

"I appreciate that, and I do have a project for you, but we have an immediate solution that's just come up. Thing is, I don't know if it's a good idea."

Betty leaned toward Ally and said in a stage whisper, "We've got a fabulous offer for the land adjacent to the camp."

"That's great, isn't it?"

"That depends." Betty shrugged. "It's the same property that Don's group is looking at, but a second party is offering quite a large amount."

"If it was just the money, you and the Board of Directors would take it in a flash, if I understand your thinking," said Ally.

Will nodded. "It's a terrific offer. If we hadn't gotten involved with Don's group, I would feel free to pursue it. I love this camp, and God knows I'd do anything to keep it going."

"Who exactly is this other party, and what are they planning to do with the land?"

"It's a property development company. They told me they plan to build a few modest cabins to rent to summer tourists. It would work great with our overflow during Family Week."

Betty patted his arm. "I know this camp is your life, Will, and you're torn. Heaven knows we've put the budget under the microscope this summer and examined every expense we could."

Will handed the mail back to Ally, put his hands in his back pockets, and leaned back on his heels. "Think of the kids like Juan Garcia whose family works in the fields in Texas. They move back here each winter. There wasn't a dry eye at campfire last year after he spoke about what camp had meant to him. If we closed down, how could we help the Juan Garcias of the world?"

Betty gestured at him. "What about Jenny from Birmingham? From an affluent family. Everything given to her—ballet lessons, trips to Europe, that girl had anything she wanted, except a reason for living. She got into some serious drugs in high school, and her parents sent her here out of desperation. It was a wild two weeks, but I've never seen a kid change so drastically."

Will turned to Ally. "You know Jenny. She's a swim instructor at camp."

"You're kidding?" said Ally.

Betty continued, "The first week, the camp was in an uproar. She stole clothes from her cabin mates, threw up half her meals, and smoked pot behind the dining room lodge with a guy she'd met in town. The second week, well, never seen such a dramatic change in a kid's heart. She took a step forward to serve God and never looked back. Her last few summers as a camper, she spent her vacation with ten-year-old girls, being a role model."

Will closed his eyes and breathed a quiet prayer. "Oh, God, don't shut this camp down. We need it for Your kingdom."

"Amen to that," said Betty.

She glanced at her watch. "Oops, got to meet with some parents about a scholarship. I'm off."

Ally shaded her eyes as she waved to Kylie out on the field. Kylie waved back, and then turned back to join a bunch of giggling girls before jogging up to the makeshift judges' platform to accept a second-place ribbon for the broad jump.

"She's pretty athletic," said Will.

"Takes after her father."

He fixed his gaze on her. "You look pretty athletic."

"Ex-ballerina. Got too tall."

They watched for a few minutes as the judges awarded the rest of the ribbons.

"Where's your sidekick?" Will asked.

"He's home with his aunt. What's up with your sidekick?"

"Sarah? Doing fine." Will gave a high-five to one of the older campers running by who had just won the fifty-yard dash. "Seriously, how are Kylie and Benjie? Don't want to pry, but I imagine they must miss their father a lot."

"Kylie talks to him a lot on the phone. Benjie occasionally says 'Daddy?' but that's it. Bryan came into town a couple of weeks ago, and was supposed to come back in August, but had to cancel as he's just trying to keep his company afloat. I thought Kylie would have problems settling in here, but it's been better than I could have hoped." Ally took a final swallow of her diet pop before pitching it into the trash can.

"Glad to hear that. You have great kids. Must have done something right."

Ally looked down at her chewed fingernails. "I try. Actually I'm trying harder now. I think I was too wrapped up in my job. Now that I'm out of the corporate merry go round, I have more time to spend with them."

*   *   *

Down-home music streamed out of the Activity Barn. The square dance started out with the caller telling the campers and staff to square their squares, grab their partners, and do the do-si-do. The dance was open to all of the town of Lake Surrender, and always brought in extra money and support for the camp. The building had been cleared out, and bales of hay had been stashed around the room. Against one wall, bleachers were filled with townspeople who looked forward to the summer event. A popcorn stand, fudge counter, and a table of local baked goods lined up against another wall, where the camp would be fundraising during intermission. The sound of fiddlers echoed throughout the building, two men and a woman each trying to outplay each other.

Will perched on the top of the bleachers, with Don and his wife, Wilma. Although not much of a dancer, Will loved to watch the campers and members of the community. He scanned the crowd and saw Ally dancing with Dr. Ernest, his arm wrapped a little too tightly around her waist, her auburn hair flipping back and forth in time with the music. *Ernest moves pretty fast—when did he meet her?* They circled around past the bench, and she passed under a hanging light that reflected the reddish-gold highlights in her hair, as if it were lit by dozens of fireflies.

"Come on and dance," she hollered up to Will, Don, and Wilma as she sashayed past.

"Want to see a five-person collision on the dance floor?" shouted Don. "It ain't pretty."

Wilma nodded in agreement. "My short legs can't move that fast." Then she elbowed Will. "Where's our missionary girl?"

"She had a family wedding out of town."

"I'll bet," said Wilma under her breath. She leaned over and cupped her hands around his ear so only he could hear her message. "Get out there and dance with her, you fool," she whispered.

Will felt his ears do a slow burn 'til the heat reached his entire face. Why did everyone care so much about his personal life?

He turned to answer her, but Wilma just shook her head and put up her hand. "Women's intuition."

On the other hand, I'm the director here, and if I want to jump in and swing a partner, I darn well will do that. He leaped out of his seat. Striding like a man with purpose, he leaped down the bleacher aisle and walked over to the side of Ally's square, waiting for the song to finish. When the music stopped, he watched, waiting until Doc Ernest let go of Ally's hand. In one smooth move, Will stepped forward, grabbed her by the wrist, and drew her close.

"You don't mind letting me take a turn, do you, Doc?" he asked over his shoulder. But before the doctor could answer, Will reached his hand around her waist. "Let me show you how real Michiganders dance," he breathed in her ear, his heartbeat going from trot to a full gallop.

When the last dance ended, Will escorted Ally back to her seat. He gave her shoulder a squeeze and sent her a wink before striding back out to the lodge's front porch.

The stars glistened with their summer brilliance. He barely noticed. All he could think about was the lingering perfume Ally had been wearing.

*   *   *

The next morning, Will passed Ally in the back hallway and gave her shoulder a squeeze, the second time in twenty-four hours. "You do a mean do-si-do, missy."

"Ah, yeah." Ally felt the roots of her hair turning hot, and hoped her face didn't match. "Fun time."

Betty waved Ally into the office. "Got your paycheck somewhere in this mess." she rifled through papers. "Hey, how's it going with Stew?"

Ally blew a few stray hairs off of her forehead before plopping down in a rickety folding chair. "He's a great cook, but he can be a bit hard to work with."

"Hang in there. He'll come around."

She shrugged. "I just get the feeling he's watching my moves. He doesn't like me much." She debated mentioning she smelled beer on his breath the other morning.

Betty flipped through two more piles before opening her desk drawer. "Oh, here it is." She handed her an envelope. "Stew has been around here a long time. He probably hated to be demoted. He's gruff, but harmless."

Will walked back into the office. He leaned over to Benjie and balled up his fist. Benjie gave him a fist bump.

"Any more of that Texas sheet cake leftover from last night, Ally? I need something with my coffee."

"Looked like you had a lot of Texas two-step in your blood last night," Betty remarked as she turned to answer the phone on her desk.

"I'll check the walk-in." Ally lowered her gaze and scooted back to the kitchen with Benjie.

She hauled out a large baking pan, and plunked it down on the counter to cut the cake. Stew watched her put a large square on a paper plate. "Kissing up to the boss again?"

Ally just rolled her eyes at him.

"Nothing like schmoozing for job security," hollered Stew as she walked down the hall to the office to deliver the cake. *Keep your cool.*

When Ally came back, she grabbed several milk pitchers from the walk-in refrigerator to set out for lunch.

Stew stuck out his forefinger wrapped with a bandage and waggled it in front of her. "Don't stick those out so soon. We need to keep them cold. Ever hear of food poisoning, honey? Those county health inspectors could show up any time this week, and they'll have your head on a platter. They have no problem shutting down a camp for non-compliance with the health code." His taunting grin almost seemed to hope for an inspection.

Ally threw open the walk-in, grabbed the pitchers left on

the counter, put them back on the shelf, and slammed the mammoth steel door. Stew looked up for a minute, a smirk scrawled across the beginnings of a scraggly beard.

She charged across the kitchen 'til she was standing inches from his face. "Look here. If you want a showdown, we'll have a showdown."

Stew's finger recoiled to join the rest of his hand, and his grin morphed into a glob of sheepishness. "Hey, just trying to help. Quit getting your britches in a wad. You do know what britches are, or is that too backwoodsy a word for ya, darling?"

Ally planted her hands firmly on her hips, entering a staring contest with the ugliest pair of red-lidded eyes she'd ever seen. "I'll get my britches in any kind of configuration I want them to get in. I'm your boss, and don't you forget it. I don't want to lord it over you, but if you don't start treating me with a little bit more respect, there'll be you-know-what to pay. I refuse to swear at a Christian camp."

Stew let out a loud guffaw. "Oh, so now you've got religion? Wow, looks like they're finally getting to you." Chuckling, he turned to squirt more dish detergent into the sink to finish washing some pots. "Just watch you don't go over the edge, like a lot of them have around here." He started to scrub on a large chili pot, and then reached up to turn up the volume on an ancient radio on a shelf above the sink.

Ally reached her arm over Stew and flicked the lever on the radio to off. "It's staying off from now on."

His face turned purple, and his eyes bugged out. "So when did Hitler start to wear skirts and shave his legs? You better watch your step if you want to last the summer. I can make things miserable around here. And you've never seen miserable like I do miserable."

This guy is nuts. She turned on her heel, grabbed Benjie's hand and a small makeup bag she left in a kitchen drawer, and fled down the hall. Pushing the restroom door open, she raced to a stall and locked herself in.

"Don't you go anywhere, Benjie," she yelled through an explosion of tears, hoping he would stay put by the sink. She grabbed some toilet paper and wiped her dripping nose. *Miserable job—*

Pulling herself together, Ally opened the door and walked to the sink where she ran cold water on a paper towel. Putting it over her red eyes, she took a deep breath. She wouldn't give Stew the pleasure of knowing he'd made her cry. She opened the makeup bag and reapplied foundation, a little eye liner, and mascara. *There, the outside looks normal.* But what about her inside? Who was she? She didn't know anymore. She did know she didn't deserve working with this creep. In fact, she didn't deserve anything that had happened to her in the last seven months. Where was this great God everyone kept talking about?

"Why, God, why? I haven't thought much about You in the past, but I keep hearing how You love me. Well, where's that love? It looks like You're just torturing me."

Enormous swells of anger welled up inside of her like an

ugly summer storm. She had always been independent, taking care of herself, but this year she'd crashed, and nothing had worked. She needed something.

"Why should I serve a God who stands off, not lifting a hand to help me? Is that a God of love?" She was almost shouting at the mirror as she pounded the white porcelain sink in frustration. She looked down. Benjie had grabbed her leg and hung on hard.

"Does a God of love allow a woman's husband to give up on a marriage? Does a God of love take away a job that can feed three mouths? Does a God of love make a woman lose her house?" Her voice rose with each question. Her legs wobbled then gave way, tumbling her to the tile floor, Benjie still hanging onto her. She could feel the pressure of tears. Her body shook as the hammered-down emotions ripped free.

Finally, the tears spent, the room grew silent except the *drip, drip, drip* of the water faucet.

As she stood and picked up Benjie, her arms weak and shaky, a calmness permeated her insides. Even with her body spent with the outburst of emotion, a strange serenity replaced the anger, filling her body with peace. She felt scrubbed inside. She stared at the bathroom stalls, enjoying this feeling of well-being.

Nothing had changed, and yet it had. Something told her she would get through this summer. Benjie raised his hand and patted the top of her head, something she'd done to him many times. Normally, he'd be rocking back and forth at any outburst in the family, but now he was patting her head.

CHAPTER
SIXTEEN

The next day started out with a literal bang. Heavy storm clouds hovered over the camp since daybreak, and by eight o'clock in the morning, they grew vengeful. Thunder and lightning evacuated all boats and swimmers off the lake. The camp staff kept their eyes on the growing ugliness in the sky. Every once in a while, the threatening cloud dipped lower as it developed a long straggly tail. Ally heard staff members mumble "mare's tale." No one liked the looks of it. The tail could turn into a tornado. If it made contact with the ground, it could become a natural buzz saw, destroying much in its path. The Weather Channel announced a tornado watch. Most of the staff who lived in Lake Surrender looked on edge. The town had survived a vicious tornado touchdown a few years ago. The town hall roof had been ripped off, and several people were killed.

Groups of campers, cooped up inside of the dining hall and craft cottage, were restless. The Boat Regatta, a favorite event with toy boats, had been cancelled; Will had used the loudspeaker and told the lifeguards to pull any stray swimmers out of the water. Wrapped in beach towels, diehard swimmers ran into the dining hall whining and complaining as they shivered to get dry. No one was in a good mood.

Ally sat in the dining hall, playing a game of Hearts with Kylie and her friends, when Will marched past her and out on the back deck, checking the sky.

"Things okay?" she asked as he passed by again. He shook his head absently. He carried the burden of keeping two hundred campers safe. Ally had learned to respect his instincts.

"I've got a great idea, Mr. Grainger," said Jason, the hiking instructor, leaning over Will and outlining his alternative plan for the day.

"Go for it," Will said.

Pushing back tables and chairs into the daylight of the plate glass windows that looked out onto the lake, the camp counselors made a makeshift stage at the end of the room. From a dusty storage closet came a drum set, guitars, costumes, a spotlight and a couple of tropical palms to decorate the stage. In an hour, grownups and kids laughed and clapped at the spontaneous show as staff members played a banjo solo, did a mime act, put on an impromptu skit. One of the girls' counselors juggled dinner plates and whistled the camp song at the same time. While the entertainment was going on, Ally saw out of the corner of her eye Kylie turning around in her seat and sneaking looks at one of the counselors who had taught her to dive, the sign of a full-blown crush reflected in her face. Ally's mouth went dry. *She's way too young to notice boys.*

But Kylie didn't take her gaze off of Travis when he walked up front to perform, and she was the first to jump up and give him a standing ovation. Ally stifled a frustrated sigh. *Why can't she just be my little girl a little longer?*

Ally left to check the lunch menu. They had an easy lunch today: tomato soup, chips, and brownies. Brownies were already started.

Stew sidled up to her. "Hey, just forgot I had a doctor's appointment. Do you mind finishing up the brownies?"

Ally said a silent *hallelujah* to have him gone for a full afternoon.

"It's the chocolate syrup that makes them. I've got one can already open you can use."

That's odd. He usually guards his recipe file with his life. Well, maybe he and I are finally mending some fences.

He had apologized for calling her Hitler, and Ally would take the olive branch as a sign he wanted to make peace.

Things had been less stressful in the kitchen after their big blowup, and she noticed he kept the radio off. *Thank God. I can't take one more tenor drawl reminding me how my life has become a bad country song.* She scolded herself for that last thought. She wasn't going down the self-pity trail that she'd seen her other divorced friends hike.

Outside, the thunder grew louder, and Benjie curled up on Ally's lap while studying the clouds outside the kitchen window. She smoothed his hair off of his forehead, and wondered what he was thinking. Thunderstorms were new to him. Northern California had calmer and more temperate summers. Mid-west Michigan thunderstorms, straight off of Lake Michigan, were the stuff of Hollywood movies. The sheer power and force of the lightning and thunder would almost make a believer out of an atheist.

By eleven, the sky had a demonic gray look to it as loud clouds rumbled by. The lights flickered, and then just as if a giant candle snuffer had passed by, the camp went dead— no lights, no music, and no electricity. Ally's heart sunk as she rummaged around the darkened kitchen for a candle to light, but no such luck.

How was she going to heat up soup and make grilled cheese sandwiches now? They didn't even have cold cuts, as Will had insisted they economize on the food budget, so she had bought on the meager side this week. Maybe she'd get creative and choose a special lunch theme. *Hmm, how about Thunderous Desert Lunch? That would work.* At least she had put in the brownies before the camp lost power.

She opened a drawer and found a flashlight. For once, the kids wouldn't have to eat regular food. They could have desserts and fruit. She'd made five huge institutional pans of brownies, and that would probably be enough to tide them over. Normally they'd have peanut butter or cheese to make sandwiches, but the bread truck hadn't come that morning, so why not make it a decadent meal?

The parents might kill me, but who cares? I won't ever be back.

The brownies went fast. Some kids had three. "It's our sandwich for today." Then for dessert, watermelon and more brownies.

"If any parents get wind of this, we'd probably be sued by the American Dietetic Association," said Betty as she swished by to grab a banana on the kitchen table. She rarely stepped out of the office, always overwhelmed by paperwork. Ally liked the large-framed, fiftyish camp admin. Betty's standard uniform of capris and an untucked Hawaiian shirt gave deference to the time she and her husband, Ralph, spent living in Hawaii.

Ally giggled. "My lips are sealed. It's a kid's dream, a total sugar meal!"

Staff members had propped up flashlights and lit candles to put on the tables. The pans of brownies disappeared as the talent show took down the house.

The storm passed a couple of hours later, but the camp still had no power. Ally put the finishing touches on hobo stew that would be cooked outside tonight in the campfire pit. Hopefully, they'd have power by tomorrow. *How do you operate a camp of two hundred kids with no power?* Even the alternative generator wasn't working.

She and Betty bussed the pans and bowls back to the dishwashing area of the kitchen. As she had the afternoon off, Ally thought she'd take her kids to a movie before she had to get back to camp. She had heard Traverse City still had power, and not all the houses on the lake had lost their electricity. She'd take a chance.

Ally drove downtown with the kids and bought three tickets for a summer Pixar movie, then stocked up on popcorn and bottled water. After putting the phone on vibrate and closing her purse, she sighed, luxuriating in a few hours to just enjoy her kids and the show.

A couple of times the picture flickered on the screen, but the power stayed on. She and the kids giggled throughout the movie. She slid off her sandals and thought of nothing except the silly hamster on the screen. Three times the cell phone vibrated, but she ignored it. She had the afternoon off, and she was determined to enjoy it.

Kylie took a handful of buttered popcorn and leaned over to whisper, "Mom, it's just like the old days, except for Daddy. Do you think he'll visit soon?"

Bryan was low on travel money, but that didn't matter to a kid. Kylie needed to see her father. Ally turned to her daughter, took the renegade strand of hair hanging down from Kylie's face, and tucked it behind her ear. Just when Ally was enjoying herself, reality smacked her in the face. No physical slap could ever sting this much.

Since Aunt Nettie had her knitting club that night and wouldn't be home for dinner, Ally suggested pizza. They still could squeeze in an early dinner before she scooted back to the camp for tomorrow's prep time.

They took the long way back, passing Grand Traverse Bay. The sun had come out, and the bay looked like Hawaii, the soft sand beach and aquamarine water now calm and beckoning. Tourists watching the waves coming on shore might swear they were looking out to the Pacific Ocean instead of Lake Michigan. What a deceiving body of water. She'd read three thousand ships had been wrecked in this wickedly beautiful inland ocean. Don had told her the West Michigan coastline was one of the deadliest shores of all the Great Lakes. Between undertows and sinking ships, many had died on the lake. Still, being around the big lake helped her not miss the California coastline so much. To Ally, the lake's serenity restored her soul. She rolled down the windows, and the kids stuck their heads out like little puppies to catch the gentle early evening breeze. Perfect weather, now that the storm had passed and taken the humidity with it.

Maybe I'm starting to heal and get my life going again. She drove through downtown Traverse to pick up a coffee. At Cherrio Coffee, she ordered a caramel latte and two hot chocolates. While the kids sipped their drinks, she wrote down her plan for job hunting.

I'll have to work on getting out more résumés, and following up on those I've already sent out. One company seemed promising, although they offered much less pay than she'd received before. No matter. The cost of living, much lower here, made a salary go farther. If she could count on Bryan's regular checks, and get a good job back in her industry, they could move out of Aunt Nettie's house and rent somewhere for a year.

A part of her thought about staying in Lake Surrender. Each week she logged made it seem more and more like home. She liked how she could go to the local grocery store and say hi to half a dozen people. The owner and his wife always asked about the camp and how her job search was going. The hometown feel of Lake Surrender gave the kids a sense of belonging. If she could keep working at camp through the conference season, she could save up money and take her time getting a job in the publishing field. She'd talked to Frank last week, and he had given her some leads.

Ally lifted the nozzle on the gas pump at Gas 'n Go. Her phone buzzed again.

"Keep pumping, Kylie," she yelled, motioning her daughter to take her place at the pump. She extracted her cell phone from her purse, walked a short distance away, and saw Will's number.

"Don't you ever check your messages?" he yelled into the phone.

"Wow, chill out!"

"We've got big problems. You've got to get here right away."

"What on earth?"

"I'll tell you when you get here."

Ally dropped the kids off at home with her aunt then gunned the car as she rushed to the camp, dodging puddles as the storm decided to do a repeat performance. She had just stopped in the parking lot when Will ran out to the car and yanked her door open.

"We've got a mess on our hands. About three-fourths of the kids have come down with some strange intestinal sickness. They have horrible diarrhea."

"That's awful. What are you doing about it?" she asked as she stepped out of her car and into the rain.

Will chewed on his lower lip as they returned to the lodge. "Because of the number of campers sick, we had to report it to the Michigan Department of Health. They could either find influenza or worse—food poisoning. They're coming first thing tomorrow morning."

"What can I do to help?" She tried to keep up with Will's loping strides.

In the kitchen, he threw down a list onto the counter. "We're doing some major cleaning. First step, the grill. We're completely taking it apart. After that's been cleaned, the electric beater and the milkshake machine will be dismantled and disinfected. I've got a list of what we will be cleaning tonight. Every nook and cranny of this kitchen will be disinfected."

He turned and hung the list up on a corkboard that held the weekly menu and shopping list. He clamped his lips together and then took another breath. The color had drained from his face, emphasizing the dark circles under his eyes. "When we're finished with the kitchen, we'll take on the bathrooms, which are not in the greatest shape right now. And by the way, where is Stew?"

As if to answer his question, a car crunched the gravel on the road. She looked out the back window. Stew hopped out of a black Camaro and kissed the driver, a brassy blonde wearing enough Red Slashed lipstick to keep one cosmetic company in business. The only reason Ally knew the name was that his babe had once left a tube in the kitchen.

Stew's frown announced he wasn't happy about interrupting his plans for a fun-filled weekend. "What's up?"

"Finally," Will said. "Where you been?"

Stew didn't answer, but hung his jacket on the coat hook on the back of the screened-in porch's door.

Will's eyes narrowed. "Just get busy, Stew. We've got a lot to get done."

Don stuck his head in the door. "I've got three of the bathrooms cleaned. Wow, what a stinking mess. You should have—"

Will held up his hand to avoid hearing the blow-by-blow details.

Don tried again. "You know we got to get this place shining. We don't want to get shut down by the health department. All we need is some bad publicity and—"

He scrambled out the kitchen when Will shot him a deadly look Ally'd never seen. He usually portrayed an even keel, but now his gritty demeanor reminded her of the commander of a sinking ship.

Don and Ally finished up the rest of the bathrooms about midnight. Stew scrubbed off the plastic tablecloths and chairs in the dining hall. After several hours, they all met back in Will's office.

"Tomorrow's inspection is very important to keeping this camp running. I will expect you to be here at seven." He took off his ball cap, and wiped his forehead. "I'm sorry to have you all work so hard tonight. You're a great staff, and I don't tell you that nearly enough."

Ally looked at Stew, who had a vacant look on his face.

"Now, get on home and sleep while you can."

"I'll say a prayer for you," Ally said.

Will managed a grateful smile as he turned to lock the office.

The inspection took two hours with the inspector, an elderly gentleman with a buzz haircut. He examined the water source and every inch of the kitchen, and collected water samples to take back to the lab. While he checked off items on his list, the line at the nurse's office grew. The health official also took feces samples that the nurse had obtained. After a couple of hours, he left with the promise to get right back to them with the test results.

The rest of the day, the staff and campers limped along, but by dinner that evening, most campers and staff members seemed to be recovering. The power was back on, so Ally put out chicken noodle soup and crackers for dinner.

Will hoped it might be twenty-four hour flu, but he

couldn't take any chances with the camp's reputation.

"This could ruin us," said Don.

"Shut up," said Stew, and for once Ally agreed with him.

*   *   *

"Morning, Ally." Don greeted her as he passed through the kitchen for his morning cup of caffeine. He lifted his hand in an anemic wave. He felt the results of the cleaning marathon last night in every muscle of his body.

As he bent over to tie the ends of the white plastic trash bag sitting outside on the porch, he saw something odd. A couple of large plastic bottles were wedged in the side of the bag. Don leaned over and inspected the bottles. His hunch had been right.

He called Will. "Hey, boss, I've got something you need to see."

CHAPTER
SEVENTEEN

Ally turned over in bed and looked at the clock. No, it couldn't say ten o'clock. But the bright mid-morning rays that slipped through the old lace curtains told her otherwise. She jumped out of bed, shoved her feet into her slippers, and headed out to the kitchen, almost colliding with Aunt Nettie and Benjie. They sat cross-legged on the linoleum floor, pushing cars back and forth on a race track. Benjie, a big grin on his face, seemed to be passing up Aunt Nettie's green sports car.

He cheered, "Yay, I winning."

"Guess you saw the note about last night," Ally said to Nettie. "I didn't get in until about two o'clock."

"Benjie and I just recreated the Indy 500. He's quite the racecar driver."

"No signs of sickness?" Ally felt Benjie's forehead.

Kylie popped out from around the refrigerator door. "We're both fine, but we didn't eat any lunch yesterday. I think that's what made everyone else sick."

She headed towards the family room and sat down on the rug. Ally followed her and plopped onto the sofa.

"Well, the health department will report back to us today or tomorrow. Kylie, get me the bottle of half-and-half."

Kylie stayed on the rug.

"Hey, what's wrong?" When her daughter decided to pull the stubborn routine and act like she didn't hear, it was time for a probe. "Look, I know you're mad about something. Would you please just tell me what's going on?"

"It's just that you're gone all the time, and I don't ever get to see you. Benjie gets to be with you all the time. He's always with you. He gets to be in the kitchen, and goes with you on every errand. How come I don't get to do those things? You love him more than me."

"Kylie, I didn't even have your brother with me last night."

Ally walked over to her daughter. Kylie's tanned face was drenched by angry tears. She slapped down Ally's attempt to give her a hug. Ally threw up her hands. For a minute no one spoke. Then Kylie dabbed her eyes with a tissue. "I'm so sick of Benjie hogging your time. I'm just the babysitter."

"What?" cried Ally. "Why would you say that?"

"You know it's true. All you do is work, work, and work, just like you did in California. You never have time for us."

"I just took you and your brother to the movies—"

"Wow, first time this summer. Guess you were feeling guilty. Dad said he never saw you. And he was right," she shot over her shoulder before she raced upstairs and gave her bedroom door a slam that would have split a more flimsy door in half. Ally, stunned, dashed upstairs and pounded on the door. "Let me in right now, young lady." Kylie's music cranked up loud.

She pounded on the door again, and Kylie peered through the crack in the door. "Go away."

"Listen, Kylie, I'm tired. I was up half the night, cleaning the camp. Please don't rag on me right now. You've been so helpful by taking care of your brother. I didn't realize you felt neglected."

Kylie shoved the door closed and turned the volume even louder. Ally swore her dangly earrings were doing back flips in time to the music.

I'm holding my ground on this one. But after a few minutes of standing in the hallway feeling foolish, she headed back downstairs in defeat. She sighed. *I feel like I'm cut up in a million pieces and can't please anyone.*

Aunt Nettie handed her a mug, and she stirred cream into her coffee. "I think I'll need about four cups today."

"Hey, it'll blow over. Hormones kicking in. By the way, this might wake you up. I just got a message from a member of the board for the camp. He had an interesting tidbit to share." Aunt Nettie readjusted her bandana. "Bill Clancy told me that the camp is just about to get into a real-estate deal where it will sell off a lot of adjacent land. Seems some anonymous businessman has offered the camp a deal they can't refuse." She cocked her head sideways as if she had the low-down on something for the *Traverse City Record-Eagle* front page headlines.

"So it's been rumored. I didn't know it was a done deal." Ally reached for a box of cereal. "Please tell me you're kidding—that it didn't go through."

"Not what I heard."

"But I thought the camp wanted to expand. Will told me about the plans he had for building more cabins and developing nature trails for the camp. What's the rush?"

She put the cereal on the table and went back for a spoon and bowl. Yuck, eating cold cereal at 11:00 in the morning.

Aunt Nettie pulled two glasses out of the top rack of the dishwasher and then turned around to face her niece. "Ally, you of all people know that times are tough. This year, the camper numbers are way down and the budget is in trouble. They might even have to close the camp."

A dry cornflake stuck in the back of her throat, and she coughed until her eyes watered. Was it the choking or something more that brought her to tears? Was this backwater camp in a remote part of the country starting to seep into her blood?

Half an hour later, Kylie waltzed downstairs, a huge smile painted on her face and her mother's cell phone held to her ear. The most recent version of Ally's daughter had been replaced by the older, sweeter one. *One thing about Kylie, she blows and then bounces back.*

"How about we do something, just you and me today?" Ally said while handing her a box of granola for breakfast.

"Oh, that's okay, Mom. I just need someone to take me to Danielle's house. She wants me to go swimming, and anyway I'm not hungry." She pushed open the front door to the porch, letting a couple of hungry mosquitoes zoom into the house, looking for dinner. Kylie kept talking on the phone, not missing a beat.

Ally cupped her hands and hollered, not sure if Kylie heard her—"I'll take you later, but bring back my phone"— and then turned to swat the blood-sucking insect that had just landed on her arm. "What's gotten into her, anyway?"

Aunt Nettie mixed lime juice, hot pepper flakes, garlic, and sesame oil to concoct a marinade for chicken she'd be grilling later on. She leaned over and whispered, "You know, Kylie just found out that the counselor she has a crush on just started going with another counselor, Meaghan."

"That explains the meltdown. You can usually trace it to a boy or her best friend." Ally looked up at the ceiling, remembering back to her junior high years. "It's so hard to be young."

She stuck her finger in the marinade. "Hmm, interesting flavor." She wiped a spot off the counter where the sauce had dripped.

"Hey, keep your dirty digits out of my marinade." Aunt Nettie slapped the back of her hand.

"I thought Will said the camp would be selling Don that land? You know, his project with the Dads Club where they were going to get local at-risk kids and start a wild rice planting and harvesting project."

"Boy, do I know. Whenever I get within ten yards of Don, he fills me in on the latest. It's a big dream for him. If you ask me, someone got to Will. He's had a huge change of heart." Aunt Nettie pulled a watermelon the size of Texas out of the refrigerator and started hacking it into slices. "I have several board members coming for dinner tonight, so maybe I'll find out more."

Kylie walked back into the kitchen, her phone call complete. "Hey, Mom, I want to show you something I taught Benjie. Benjie, come over here."

He grinned a toothy grin in anticipation of showing off a new trick.

"What did I teach you yesterday? Remember what I learned at camp? Okay, if you ever see a fire, what do you do?"

Benjie looked at his sister, frowning. "Staaaa," he tried.

She nodded. "That's right, 'stop.'"

Benjie opened his mouth: "Staaap, dwop, and wowol."

"You said it, Benjie! Stop, drop and roll!" Kylie jumped up and down and clapped her hands. Benjie flapped his hands, unable to contain his excitement.

"Now let's show Mom and Auntie Nettie how to do it. Ready?"

Kylie took his hands and put them down by his side.

"Now, stand real still. That's stop. Okay, now drop down."

She pushed on his shoulder, and they both dropped to the floor.

"Now roll."

Kylie maneuvered her brother's arms so they were stiff by his side and his legs were together and straight. She gave him a push, and he rolled as smooth as a rolling pin across the linoleum kitchen floor.

"I worked all last week teaching him that," said Kylie.

Benjie, overcome with success, started doing laps around the kitchen table.

"Come on over and give me a hug. You're a natural-born teacher!" said Aunt Nettie. "A chip off of the old block." She winked at Ally. "Oh, almost forgot, you got some mail yesterday." She pulled a few envelopes out of the pocket of her threadbare apron, a garment that had seen many good meals.

Ally sorted the pile. She had a letter from her mother telling her how well the Legal Aid auction went. Mom had enclosed a check for fifty dollars to "get the kids some school supplies." The second letter contained Bryan's scrawl, and caused Ally's heart to jump a bit. Even a divorce hadn't changed that. Would it always be that way?

> *Dear Ally,*
>
> *I can't believe you've been back in Michigan for almost four months. I've missed the kids a lot, but think about how much fun they are having with Aunt Nettie. She was*

always one of my favorites, quaint little Bible sayings and all. Just hope Kylie doesn't go overboard on that religious stuff. She needs to be grounded in the real world.

I feel awful that I haven't been back more. Looks like I might make it back in September. Got a possible client in Chicago. In fact, he might even buy my company and give me a job. I think I'm ready to get out of the Bay Area and try somewhere new.

I've been thinking a lot about us. I sort of flipped out on you, and I feel badly. Pressure got to me. I do love my son—I just don't know how to relate to him. I guess I'm not cut out to be a father of a special-needs child. I know what you're thinking—I had no choice. That's true. I know I had to deal a lot with my own ego, knowing I wouldn't ever have a son I could mentor in the business or shoot hoops with.

Ally put down the letter, unfinished, her eyes blurred. *You don't know if you could ever shoot hoops with him. You never even tried.*

"What does Dad say?" Kylie asked.

"He sends his love, and thinks he'll probably be here next month to visit." Ally turned her head the other way so she could hide the sorrow. Kylie didn't have to know everything.

But Kylie saw. "Mom, I'm sorry. I love you."

"I love you, too." Ally squeezed her daughter's shoulder. "Now, didn't you want to go swimming at Danielle's house?

Go get your suit and towel. I'll drop you off on my way to work."

Kylie darted up the stairs.

"Benjie, pick up your cars and put them in your backpack. We're going to work in a few minutes."

He grunted but didn't move.

"Now!" Ally got in his face. "Do you want to go with us to the beach this weekend?"

He looked at her out of the corner of his eye, but otherwise didn't react. Ally had learned to read his body language, watching for a possible temper tantrum in the works. She saw the foot start to stamp. *Please, not today, I'm too tired.*

"Dear Lord, just help him cooperate."

Benjie, startled, looked up with a quizzical expression on his face. He stared at Ally for a few seconds, and then leaned over to pick up two of his racecars and put them in his backpack. In three minutes, he had packed up all the cars and racetrack.

What did I just see? He's never gotten in gear so fast before.

* * *

Ally pulled a box of hamburger patties out of the walk-in freezer to start them defrosting. As she pried the frozen patties apart, Will walked in. He didn't say a thing, but grabbed a cup of coffee and walked right out again.

"Guess we got a good report from the health department." Stew took the bowl of peeled potatoes and rinsed them off in the sink. "Still wondering why all those kids got sick. Almost all recovered by this morning."

He dumped the washed potatoes onto the chopping board and selected a knife. As usual, he hummed one of his most annoying country tunes. Since the radio fight, he'd kept the radio off, choosing to hum in his off-key way.

"What do they think happened?"

"They're puzzled." He wore an odd little grin that looked like something was squashing down one side of his mouth. He knew more than he was letting on.

Why wouldn't he tell her if he knew something? The instant she thought that, she knew the answer. He loved having "one over" on her. Well, she'd just act like she didn't care.

"We'll get to the bottom of it sooner or later." She worked to have her voice sound nonchalant as she assembled the frozen burgers on a tray.

"They'll figure it out," he replied, whacking a potato in half with a vengeance.

Ally put the hamburger patties back in the refrigerator. She had extra time, so she thought she'd go out on the back deck and phone some of her job leads. One small publishing company had read her résumé and left her a voice mail. Yahoo. She could hardly wait to trade in her apron for a briefcase.

Out on the deck, she dialed the number. After a few rings, someone picked up the phone.

"Black Bear Stories for Children, Helen speaking."

"This is Ally Cervantes, returning Kyle Duncan's call." Ally combed a wisp of hair behind one ear.

The receptionist put the call through, but all she got was his voice mail. Ally left a message then turned off the phone. This was the first time this summer anyone had responded to the résumé she'd sent out. She thought, even with the high unemployment, she'd be able to find a job. She should be snapped up for her experience working at one of the top children's publishing companies on the West Coast. Hadn't a top New York publisher, Ed Reese, christened her a "rising star" on his monthly blog?

Ally dialed her sister's number. After catching up on the goings-on at her house, Georgia asked how Ally liked Michigan.

"It's been great. I've had time to think about some things like why my marriage fell apart. Bryan's not a bad guy, he just worked too much."

"I'll say. He may be the consummate businessman, but you're the stable one."

"I always tried to encourage him not to give up on his business. I was there to buck him up when he lost key accounts."

"Hey, lots of men are workaholics. You two just had a very tough kid thrown into the mix."

"Well, he could have tried more. It's not that he doesn't love Benjie—he just couldn't fit into Benjie's world. He never came to his I.E.P. conference."

"His what?"

"Oh, that's just what the teachers label his individual educational plan. They wanted parental input, but Bryan couldn't seem to ever show up. Somehow he always had a meeting planned at the same time."

"You sound bitter."

"A little. I keep thinking about when Benjie turned four. I invited the kids and parents from his class for a barbecue. Bryan promised he'd be there to grill hamburgers, but no Bryan. He showed up about two hours later with some crummy excuse about a client golf outing he'd forgotten about. One of his customers could only get together with him that afternoon, and he couldn't cancel."

"That's lame. I kinda remember you telling me."

"I should have known things weren't working out, but I'm incredibly dense. We had our worst fight that night when I accused him of putting his business before family time. He asked how I thought we could afford to live in the Bay Area if he couldn't keep his business going—it's one of the most expensive places on the planet. Ever since that night, he started to pull away. He never was a great communicator, and it just got worse."

"Oh, Ally, I feel so horrible for you. I just wish we lived closer. At least you have Aunt Nettie. She's the perfect person to have to ride out a crisis. Give her a big hug from me."

Ally hung up the phone and went to check on Benjie. A staff member's college-age daughter was majoring in special education, and had been babysitting him without pay all week, hoping to gain experience invaluable for her field. The two of them were playing on the back porch.

"I'll have my cell phone on if you need me," Ally said, then headed for the path behind the lodge. Don had been working on it as a nature trail for the kids. He had labeled many of the trees and bushes with the scientific and common names. One section had all the pine trees native to the area. In another section of the trail, Don had planted a variety of wildflowers—the late spring trillium, Jack in the Pulpit, and Black-Eyed Susans. Ally loved to walk by the rustic garden and plop down on a log bench donated by the alumni club. It became her thinking spot. But today she needed motion, so she kept walking past the birch trees and sugar maples. She started up a gradual incline to a hill appropriately named Overlook Point. Ally could see the complete lake. A gentle southern breeze played with her bangs and cooled her forehead. The late summer sun felt comforting on her bare arms.

A hawk soared overhead in the soft blue sky. Her heart filled with a gentle calm and a sense of well-being. Funny, how even with the turmoil of the last few days, she should feel more stressed than she did. Could she be experiencing something in another realm, something she'd not known even existed before? Was she becoming a free bird, like her tattoo?

She had never thought much about anything that extended farther than her five senses. And yet, in this remote area of the north woods, she had begun to think about He

Who created her. She had never glanced at a Bible verse but now, over her morning coffee, she occasionally opened the Bible her aunt had given her. Just hearing bits and pieces of Will's dining room and campfire talks had opened up her mind to a different point of view.

Was it possible for God to be interested in her life? And who was Jesus? The talks always revolved around Jesus. She remembered being embarrassed to say his name, it sounded so, well, religious and corny. Anyway, she had never considered him anything but a good teacher. Was she wrong? Even forming the question in her mind amazed her. She didn't want to turn into one of those narrow-minded, right-wing Bible-thumpers, but if she was honest, she hadn't met anyone this summer that fit the stereotype. She didn't have the answers yet, but something told her she was asking the right questions.

She watched two sailboats racing against each other in the middle of the lake and, on her right, Don wearing his Detroit Tigers baseball hat and taking a fishing break off of the camp pier. Farther down the shore, tiny white tips of water glided onto the edge of the swimming beach as a toddler and his mother cut into the waves while they walked parallel to the shore.

Ally sighed. Back to work. She turned to head back to camp. Lost in thought, her head down, she almost collided with Will.

"Just coming to find you," he said.

Something in his expression stopped her short.

"What's up, boss?"

"You and I need to talk."

They walked in silence until they arrived back at the lodge. He gestured at a picnic table behind the dining room and put down the Coke can he had in his hand. Ally had the same feeling in the pit of her stomach as when she had been summoned to the principal's office for forging a doctor's note in high school. This is silly, she told herself. Nevertheless she sat down on the edge of the bench.

"I don't even know how to start this conversation so I'll just jump in. The good news is that I found the missing money from the petty cash box stashed in an envelope that held the receipts."

"Glad to hear that. I knew it would show up."

"That's the good news. Now for the bad. Don found something strange in the trash bin in the kitchen this morning." Will paused, and let out a breath of air. "He found four empty Milk of Magnesia bottles. They were stuffed around the perimeter of the trash can."

"Looks like my cooking doesn't settle well with someone," Ally joked.

Will put his lips together as he ran his hands up and down the side of his jeans. His eyebrows lowered, he hesitated before he continued. "The health department gave us a clean bill of health this morning. Do you see what I'm trying to say? The only explanation for the outbreak of diarrhea would be some kind of food tampering."

Ally put her hands on both sides of her head. "Food tampering! Who in their right mind would do that?"

"That's what I thought. But the evidence of the bottles leads to that conclusion. I had every food item that came out of the kitchen yesterday analyzed."

"And—?" Ally wasn't sure she even wanted to hear the results.

"And the brownies baked yesterday were full of Milk of Magnesia." He looked straight at her. "The campers consumed high levels of a laxative. I hesitate to even ask you this, but—did you bake those brownies yesterday?"

"Well, uh yes, sort of. I put the stuff in the Mixmaster and mixed it. I left the pans on the counter because I wanted to see the talent show. You're not thinking that—"

"I'm not thinking anything yet. I'm just trying to get at the facts."

"Why would I ever do anything to harm the kids?" Ally's pitch rose higher and higher. She bit her lip and felt her body quiver with rage. How dare he think that. Oh, how she'd love to take her kids in her car and drive far away from this crazy place. *Give me the insane pace of the Bay Area anytime.*

Will patted her on the back. "Hey, calm down. I'm not accusing you of anything. I'm just trying to recreate what happened yesterday. Was anyone else in the kitchen?"

"No." She hid her face in her hands. *Think, Ally, think.* "Stew took off with his girlfriend, and I don't know anyone else who came through the kitchen."

Will nodded. "I don't want to come across as the bad guy. I know you've had a tough year." He looked directly into her eyes, and she saw he meant business. "I have a camp to run, and the board is forcing me to take some action." Will dug his thumbnail into the palm of his hand. "Ally, I tried and tried to argue with the board, but they wanted to show parents they're being responsible. I hate like thunder to tell you this, but I've been asked to suspend you for a week."

"You're kidding. I didn't do it!"

"I know. Looks like you were the scapegoat for some sick joke. I'll get ahold of you next week, and we can talk again."

Ally took the can of Coke and chucked it against a nearby tree. "Life sucks, you know that? Life sucks."

Will wiped the splattered pop off of his face.

CHAPTER
EIGHTEEN

Don pulled into Lakeshore Realty, next to a shiny BMW sedan and an old Ford Taurus with a bumper sticker that read *Vacation at Lake Surrender!* He was a couple of minutes early for his five o'clock meeting. Something in his gut told him not to go inside. But what could possibly go wrong with meeting a realtor? He had told the Dads Club members he'd get the deal solidified. He wanted to see the rice project move ahead, and he wasn't going to let them down.

Don locked the car door and walked into the Lakeshore Realty's office. Hal should be expecting him. As he entered the room, he met three men with stony eyes ready for a stare-down, sitting around the conference table in the outer office.

"Sit down, Don." Hal Schwindleman pointed to the chair.

"And a howdy-do to you. Is this some police interrogation?" Don flashed a grin and put his notebook on the table.

"We want to talk to you about the Lake Surrender property

your Dads Club is trying to buy. It seems we have a bit of a conflict with the land your organization has opted to buy."

"I thought this meeting was about finalizing the deal. Will was supposed to be here. Our Dads Club has collected the down payment, and we're ready to buy."

"Well, something has come up. It seems that these two gentlemen have also had an option to buy the land adjacent to the camp."

"That's not true. You know I've been talking to you for weeks about this."

"Hey, calm down. We're here to make a deal with you. How would you like to make a cool five thousand dollars for your club?" said Hal. "Free and clear."

He pulled an envelope out of his jacket pocket and slid it across the desk to Don.

Don picked up the envelope and looked inside to see a certified check with the club's name on it. "What's this all about?"

"Let's just say it's a donation to your Dads Club," said the short dark-haired man with the gold chains.

"A donation? Oh, I get it, a bribe." Don slammed his hands on the table and stood up.

"Now, let's talk about this like gentlemen," the man with gold chains said. "You could do a lot of good with that money. Don't be stupid. All we are asking is that you talk to your boss. Kind of grease the skids so that he'd be open to selling that property to us."

"Will's not going to go back on his promise. He cares about the kids in the community as much as I do, and he supports the Wild Rice Project."

"I guess you don't know him as well as you think," said the rotund middle-aged man with the bulbous nose. He sneered at Don. "Are you aware that several parents have complained about the camp this year? We heard you had a health inspector come to visit. With this economy, you guys can't afford to lose any more paying customers. If you don't believe me, ask your boss. He may be holding some information from you."

"This meeting is over, fellas. You can have your bribe money. Dads Club is buying that piece of land, and you'd better just back off unless you want to see this Indian on the warpath." Don took the envelope, ripped the check into pieces and dumped it onto the floor.

"You'll live to regret that, redman." The gold-wearing guy stood up to meet Don's glare.

"American Indian to you, and by the way, I love challenges." Don clenched his fist and turned his back as he walked to the door. "Good day, gentlemen."

"We're experts at getting our way."

"So am I," said Don and jerked the door closed.

* * *

In the bathroom mirror, her face looked like an overripe tomato, and her eyes were tiny slits after a major flood of tears. She couldn't go home yet. Besides, Kylie was still at her friend's house, and Aunt Nettie had gone to Traverse— she had a big project she had to get done for the store. Ally had done her errands: the post office to pick up mail, the hardware store, and the paint store to pick up paint. Maybe she and Benjie could drive out to Mission Point and watch the sunset. She loved the view from there, with the old mission log cabin and the lighthouse perched at the edge of the point. From the tip, she felt as if she were looking at the end of the earth—and wasn't that where she lived, anyway?

Headed north on M-37, she passed the you-pick apple orchard and a trendy French eatery with a patio full of end-of-the summer tourists sitting under yellow slashes of umbrella tables, parents chasing young children, and college kids getting their last summer beer before school starts. Ally flew down the road past a general store. The cottages thinned out, and the road narrowed. Her car sped past the cherry orchards stripped of their brilliant ruby-colored fruit by this time in the season. Finally, she approached the end of the road, the Mission Point Lighthouse tower beckoning to her. She found the structure oddly comforting.

She parked, and then she and Benjie hiked the wooden pathway past the lighthouse toward the beach. As they plopped down in the sand, a light breeze cooled her swollen face. The only energy Ally could muster was spent watching the waves ebb and flow on the white sandy shore. *Wish the lighthouse could guide me like it did with so many ships.*

Ally looked over at her son, already busy sifting sand with his sand screen and pail. As long as Benjie had dirt or sand to play in, he was content.

She set out two cups. Unscrewing a liter of pop, she poured the bubbly liquid into the plastic glasses, then pulled out the two tuna fish salad sandwiches she'd picked up at Down by the Bay Deli in Traverse. After a few bites, Benjie slid off the bench and ran back to playing in the sand.

Ally raked her naked toes through the soft sand, thinking how much fun it would be to be a beach bum. The simple life. She could pitch a tent, read the books in her reading pile, and exist on anything she could grill over hot flames. She couldn't imagine sleeping 'til noon and not worrying about what to cook for two hundred campers and counselors. Oh well, back to real life. She should probably start calling a couple of job leads, but she didn't have the energy.

She checked her phone. Will had telephoned. *Now what? Did he find arsenic in the potato salad?*

Turning over onto her stomach, Ally lowered her weary body down in the sand and readjusted her beach umbrella to a different angle as she smoothed out her blanket. Benjie played with his pail and shovel, making sand mountains. As she lay prone, catching the last rays of the afternoon, curiosity got the better of her, and she returned Will's call.

"Where are you?" he answered. "I need to talk."

"I'm a free agent, remember?"

"That's what I want to talk to you about."

"I'm keeping office hours at Mission Point."

"Seems that Stew left on his weekend trip with the keys to the kitchen and storeroom. This is embarrassing, but I can't find my keys, and I forgot to get yours from you. Would you mind stopping by, or I can swing by to get them?" He paused, his embarrassment seeping through the phone. "Look, I'm in a bind."

"Me, too, buddy," Ally said and ended the call. Whatever had possessed her to take the job at the camp? Oh. Yeah. She was desperate.

Her phone rang again—Will's number.

"Now what?" she yelled into the phone. Benjie jerked his head up at her strident voice.

"Listen, I know you're angry. I tried to plead for your job, and I was trying to tell you that when you took off. I don't think you did it. I think you've been set up, but I can't prove it."

Ally sighed as she looked down at the coral nail polish chipping off of her big toenail. "The only thing I've been trying to do this summer is to keep my family afloat. I'm not a whack job!"

"I know you aren't. Maybe a little high strung, but—"

"Ha! You try juggling what I've been doing, and see how you come out."

"Just inserting some humor. Ally, I know the hand you've been dealt is unfair. I've said this before and I'll say it again—I think you're a remarkable person. Most women in your shoes would have become bitter and vindictive. I commend your attitude. You've shown me true grace under pressure this summer."

Will paused, and for a moment Ally heard nothing but the methodical slap of the waves against the shore and the cry of a pair of seagulls flying overhead. Did he just give her a compliment?

Then the sobs began. Uncontrollable sobs, sobs not meant to be shared but to be hidden in the deep recesses of her bedroom with the door locked. But she couldn't stop. She rolled over onto her stomach and dropped the cell phone onto her beach towel.

"Ally, Ally— Are you there? Are you okay?"

Ally opened her mouth but nothing came out.

*　　*　　*

Will made the turnoff to Mission Point and pushed down on the accelerator going well past the speed limit. The road had cleared of most pokey tourists, and he could make good time. He slammed on the brakes, and the two hot drinks he was juggling slopped onto the passenger's side.

"Hope she's still at the beach," he said out loud to himself.

Will then jumped out of the car. He scanned the horizon. In the last flitter of sunlight, he saw two figures—one little, one bigger—sitting on a blanket and facing the sunset. He ran toward them.

"I've been worried about you two. I texted, but you didn't respond, so I came to check on you." He dropped down on the blanket next to Benjie. "You okay?" Will handed Ally a warm caramel latte. "Sort of a peace offering. Coffee always cheers me up."

After a couple seconds—"Thanks"—Ally took the cup from him and took a few sips.

Will handed Benjie a cup of hot chocolate. "Be careful, it's sort of hot." He cupped his hands around the boy's hands and helped Benjie sip.

They sat in silence for several moments, the quiet interrupted by the motors of a few cars pulling out of the parking lot. Will looked out toward the sunset and then back into Ally's swollen face. *She's not as tough as she makes herself out to be.*

"I guess you need the keys." Ally struggled up off of the blanket.

Will offered her his hand, and then watched her root around in her voluminous straw purse. He coughed, and cleared his throat. "I've been thinking a lot about this brownie incident. I didn't stand up to the board and make a good case for your keeping your job. I've always had the final say with staff hirings and firings, and I know you've been very responsible in the kitchen. My problem is the board needs to show the community they've done something until they can nail down some solid evidence. It's a PR problem. And we can't finger Stew."

Ally lifted her eyebrows in a high arch.

"He was off for most of lunch that day. Have you seen

anyone else hanging around the kitchen?"

"Just some of the senior staff. Sometimes they come in to raid the walk-in for ice cream bars if they have a few hours off in the evening. They aren't supposed to have a key, but one of them snuck one. They know we keep the kitchen locked up when we aren't in there."

Will thought a minute. "I plan to quiz the staff tomorrow. We're going to get to the bottom of this. Meanwhile I'm planning to throw my enormous weight and authority around—"

"Meaning?"

"Meaning I am still the director of this camp, and I need a cook. Stew is still not ready to fly on his own." Will paused a moment and looked directly into her eyes. "Will you come back? I'll take the heat for my decision to let you back."

Ally's jaw dropped open. "You're reinstating me? Why? I thought the entire town thought I poisoned the campers."

"I never did, and I didn't do you right. I should have stood up to the board. You've been a great cook this summer, and I probably haven't told you that enough. You took on an enormous challenge—"

"Not to mention a huge pain-in-the-butt assistant cook."

"Not to mention the pain-in-the-butt assistant cook."

"Who plays the worst country music north of Nashville."

"Okay, who plays the worst country music north of Nashville? Hey, wait a minute, I like country music."

"Me too, just not from the 1920s."

"I see you've got your sense of humor back. Anyway, I'm going to challenge the board to look deeper into the incident. From this moment on, you are reinstated as Camp Lake Surrender's head cook. The board will just have to have a hissy fit."

"Don't do me any favors."

"You need a few favors, ma'am. Anyway, you'd be helping me out of a jam, 'cause I'd be taking over the job."

Ally put down her drink, and leaned over to pick up the beach towel and shake out the sand. "This is a strange turn of events."

"You got to admit, making spaghetti for two hundred campers is your kind of fun. I'll even throw in a modest raise if you stay through November, our conference season." She closed her eyes to mull over the offer and then nodded slightly.

"So you'll come back?"

"There'll be a thorough investigation?"

Will thought he saw a trace of a smile pass across her lips.

"You have my word. If I have to drag in every last detective in the Lake Surrender police force, we will get to the bottom of it." He raised his right hand as if taking an oath.

Ally giggled, thinking how minute the Lake Surrender police force was. The biggest case they had recently solved was the theft of a stolen bike parked at the Gas-and-Go station. "Okay, let's shake on it, especially the part about the raise."

Will put out his hand, and they shook. He took Benjie's

hand after the two of them gathered sand toys into a plastic basket. As they walked to the parking lot, Will hit his forehead with the palm of his hand. "I forgot to tell you some big news."

Ally opened the trunk of her car and stowed the beach blanket and basket of toys. "What's that?"

"I'm officially engaged. Sarah finally decided to wear the ring I bought her."

"Oh, uh, congratulations." She blinked. "So—when's the wedding?"

"We haven't gotten that far. Sarah has a lot to do when she goes back to Mexico. She takes her time with important decisions."

CHAPTER
NINETEEN

Ally sloshed the mop back and forth on the painted cement floor outside the office. She hadn't planned on eavesdropping, but couldn't help but hear Will's voice vibrate through the office door. She reminded herself she was just doing her job in a timely matter.

"Yeah, Dad, she accepted the ring. It's official. Not completely—still trying to decide about Mexico." A pause and then, "I know, I don't want to talk her out of her calling."

Ally opened her ponytail holder and re-did her hair before dipping the mop back into the bucket and wringing it out. She knew she should go back to the kitchen but, well, she did have to finish the floor before dinner. She'd missed a few days, and already it was smeared with muddy footprints.

"Thanks—I need your prayers. Looks like I'm going to have to go do battle with the board. Yeah … could lose it. But Dad, you always said to fight for something if you know you're right, and I know I am." Ally heard a short pause. "It's been a tough year. Thanks for your ear."

Will hung up the office phone. Ally picked up her bucket and mop, and high-tailed it out of the hallway to the kitchen.

*   *   *

That evening, the board of Camp Lake Surrender congregated in the dining room. Packey Taylor presided over the meeting.

"As the president of the camp board, I felt the need to request an emergency meeting. I don't like dealing with some of the things we've encountered this year. Here's an agenda for members to review." He passed out the schedule to those sitting around the board table. "I don't have to stress the importance of some of these items, and the privacy surrounding this meeting." He sounded just like the retired football coach he was, giving a half-time butt-chewing to players in the locker room.

Will looked down at the agenda.

I. Current Problems
    A. Immediate repairs:
        1. Water heater for Cabin 2
        2. Roof repair
        3. New compressor for walk-in freezer.
    B. Budget concerns
        1. Deficit for summer camp
        2. Income for upcoming conference season
    C. Sale of property

1. Update on sale
    a. Report from Will
D. Personnel problems:
    1. Tammy in office going on maternity leave 9/12.
    2. Disciplinary action:
        a. Stew: reinstate as cook next year?
        b. Ally's employment status

The agenda held many potentially explosive issues, especially the last item regarding Ally's continued employment. Don spoke for a few minutes, offering three estimates for the water heater and two for the roof. The board okayed Wilcox Plumbing and Quality Roofing. Don left, and the board members moved onto the next item.

Sally Garza, financial officer, read her report. "We are running in the red this summer. As we know, the recession has hit all segments of our economy. Parents have cut extras, such as recreational activities for their families, in hopes of balancing the family budget. As the season is ending, we are thirty-two thousand dollars in the hole. We've made all the budget tweaking we can, but we still need more income to pay bills and keep the doors open in years to come."

Sally passed around her report for the six members to see.

Brad Smith, a new member of the board and an ex-counselor, spoke up. "I love this place, and don't want to see it fail. This camp helped me through several rough years as a teenager, and was an anchor when I didn't have family to depend upon." Brad's voice shook. "I'll vote for anything to keep this open."

"No one has said anything about closing, Brad." Will surveyed the group. "I think we need to calm down."

"Thanks, Will, I'll take it from here." Packey hitched up his belt and stood.

"The next item of business doesn't leave this room." He cleared his throat. "We have been presented with an unbelievable opportunity to get this camp back in the black. The board has met over the summer, and we've decided to pursue selling the adjacent fifteen acres of land we own. We have had two parties pursuing the purchase. The first party, the Native American Dads Club of Lake Surrender, has shown interest in owning the property for their Manoomin Rice program for at-risk teens."

Upbeat murmuring shot through the group.

"I've heard about the program. Around Marquette, they've had fantastic results with the kids. Some end up choosing community service over jail time. I've even heard a couple of kids decided to go into farming after their stint," said Brenda Hiyata. "Coming from a Native American background myself, I'd like to throw my vote that way—"

"However, we have another offer on the table," injected Packey. "An undisclosed party has also shown interest in purchasing the land. They would like to build five to six small cabins on the back part of the parcel for rental purposes. It would be strictly low-key, and might even fit nicely with our camp plans if we ever needed overflow accommodations in Family Week."

"What kind of offers do we have on the property?" asked Cathy Henderson, oldest member of the board.

"The Dads Club wants to offer forty thousand. It's fairly close to fair market value," answered Will, a little defensively.

"And the private investment company?" asked Sally.

Packey looked down at the table for a few seconds then up at the group, grinning like a kid at Disneyworld. "Would you believe eighty-five thousand? It's a no-brainer to me."

A low whistle greeted his statement. Several people nodded in agreement, but others waved their hands in disagreement.

"I'd like to have a little more discussion before we sign off on the matter," said Will.

"Of course. Anyone care to comment?"

Gerald Turner, a local high school math teacher and a soft-spoken man who rarely entered into the discussions, stood up. "It seems to me that we're moving too quickly on this matter. Can't we find out more about this private party?"

"We could dink around for a few more months, and then they'd decide to pull the plug on their offer. Hal Schwindleman alerted me they had two other lakes they were considering," Packey said. "I don't want to be a pessimist, but with this economy, I suggest we take a hard look at the second offer."

He took a marker to the white board at the front of the room. Within a few minutes, he had outlined the facts regarding both offers.

Will pinched the bridge of his nose to collect his thoughts. "I believe we, as trustees of this wonderful camp, have a sacred responsibility to take care of this camp." He stood. "I know we can all agree on that. We all love what this camp has meant to the kids of Lake Surrender and, for that matter, all of Northern Michigan. We've seen changed lives each week this summer. I guess the reason I am a bit wary of the second offer would be my fear of losing the special work God has done here in the last twenty years. The Enemy could tempt us to go down the easier route and take the larger offer. But we need to know more about these new neighbors. One thing about Don's group, they have the same goals of helping kids that we have. It would be a great addition."

"That's great, Will—if we could afford it. Right now, we have a deficit to make up. I think we need to put the financial future of the camp as top priority," answered Packey.

"But what do we know about this group of investors?"

"They claim they will only put up six or seven modest cabins, and will leave a two-hundred-yard buffer between their property and the camp," said Sally. She put the letter from the investment company on the table in front of her. "You're welcome to look at the offer. They've also included the environmental impact statement."

"We gave our commitment to Don," Will said. "We would be letting him down. Plus, with his group, we know what kind of neighbors we'll have. Rice." He grinned, and gained back some momentum as he saw a couple of people nod. "I've thought a lot about this, and I've changed my mind. We shouldn't be money-driven when we make plans. God will provide."

"Unfortunately, money makes the world go around, son," answered Packey. "If we're given the provision to get out of debt, I think we should take it. Campers for years to come will thank us for keeping the doors open."

Sally raised her hand. "I'd like to make a motion to take a vote on it."

"Okay, all in favor of accepting Don's offer, I'd like a show of hands."

Four hands went up.

"Those opposed."

Three hands went up.

"Looks like we'll accept Don's offer," said Packey. "I'll notify the president of the club."

The rest of the meeting went quickly. As Will started to pack up his briefcase and papers, Packey came over to him. Will's heart began to race.

"I need to talk to you a minute, in your office."

Will glanced up at his boss, and saw a look on his face that could have curdled cream.

Chapter

Twenty

Packey closed the door. "I'll make this fast. I didn't appreciate your taking Ally off of suspension. What were you thinking?"

"Innocent until proven guilty." Will took a deep breath to slow his heartbeat. "I can't honestly believe she put laxatives in the brownies."

Packey crossed his arms. "Look, we can't put this camp in jeopardy. You know our numbers are down. We can't afford a scandal. Right now, most people still think we had a flu bug go through the camp."

"We also can't afford to toss out a good employee, either. She's a single mother doing an excellent job in the kitchen. We can't just make her give up her livelihood because of some unanswered questions."

Packey sighed, and for the first time today, he smiled at Will. "You're not thinking right, Will. We need to get to the bottom of this. If you let her back into the kitchen, you'd better be willing to be the fall guy if she's guilty. Is that worth your job?"

Will gripped the back of his neck, digging his fingers into tight muscles. "I believe in erring on the side of mercy. I'll put my reputation on this woman. She's extremely capable, and the kids love her. She's jumped into camp life."

"But do you really know her?" said Packey.

"Do you really know any employee's motives and mindset?"

"Okay." Packey uncrossed his arms and hitched up his belt again. "I'm giving you just enough rope. The only thing I ask is for you to supervise each meal, taste the food, and check the petty cash box at random."

*   *   *

Ally stopped into the office to drop off the menu for next week. "Oh, hi, Sarah, nice to see you."

"Hey, did he tell you the news?" Sarah perched on the corner of Will's desk, playing with his hair while he worked on some paperwork. He jerked up his head and playfully pushed away her hand.

"No." Ally turned to Will. "Are you holding out on me?"

"We set the date. June twenty-third of next year." He made the okay sign to Sarah.

"Congratulations, that's great." Ally stuck out her hand to shake.

Sarah reached out her arms. "Awww, just give me a hug."

Ally gave her a squeeze.

"We're having an intimate wedding at my parents' home,

and then he's taking a position at Casa Familia. He's always wanted to be a missionary, so this works out great. He'll be the personnel director for the orphanage, in charge of all the hiring and the paperwork. He's perfect, considering all the camp experience he's had."

Did he just get engaged, or get hired for a new job?

"Slow down, we're still talking, Sarah."

What happened to your dreams, Will?

* * *

"Can I have a minute of your time?" Justin, the lifeguard, leaned his head through the kitchen doorway.

"What's up?" Ally asked as she wiped her hands on a towel and stepped into the dining room. She looked forward to taking a quick break before the dinner crowd converged on her.

"Mrs. Cervantes—err, Ally—it's about your daughter. She didn't show up for swim lessons two days in a row, and that's not cool. I talked to one of her cabin mates, and they said she'd been hanging out with Danielle Klasinski."

Red alert alarms went off in Ally's mind as she rubbed her forehead. This was not good news. She knew Danielle. *Everyone* knew Danielle, and sweet and innocent weren't the top adjectives used to describe the precocious teen. Her parents gave her a lot of leeway and she took it, pushing the limits at home and camp. Simply put, she wasn't the kind of friend Kylie needed. For one, Danielle was thirteen going on eighteen. For another, she lived and breathed BOYS.

"Yeah, I noticed Kylie's been tight with her. She's a little too mature for her age."

Justin lowered his voice, "That's not the only thing. One of my assistants said she saw the two of them behind boys cabin C, getting friendly with a couple of guys. Danielle had her arm around an older camper, and they looked pretty cozy. Junior campers like Kylie know they can't hang out without adult supervision, and I just hate to see your daughter get caught up in something."

That night, Ally picked up Kylie from the camp. "Guess they found some campers missing-in-action during swimming today."

She looked at Kylie, who was busy fumbling around in her backpack. *I'll just wait this one out.*

Ally turned off the car radio, leaving only the sound of tires crunching over the gravel road. The trees marched by as the silence stretched out.

Kylie crossed her arms, and finally broke the silence. "Okay, I cut swimming today. I had a stomach ache, and just went back to the cabin to rest."

"Do you want to redo that statement?" Pressing her lips together, Ally kept her attention on the road.

"What do you mean? You don't believe me? Geez, Mom, you've gotta trust me! I'm not a little baby anymore. I'm not like Benjie. You don't have to know exactly where I am every minute of the time."

Ally swallowed a lump of fear the size of a golf ball and

gripped the steering wheel for support. She glanced over at her daughter, whose mouth was set in a defiant line. "Look, you're not a baby anymore, and that's why I'm worried about you. I'll give you one more chance to tell me the truth."

"Okay, okay, Danielle and I took off 'cause we're sick of swimming. We just needed to talk."

"So, just the two of you took off to talk?"

"Well, we ran into a couple of guys from Cabin C. She had to talk to her boyfriend. It was kind of an emergency. No big deal."

"Yes, *big deal*. You had no right to cut swim lessons. And what's worse, you're twelve, hanging out with a thirteen-year-old who has a sixteen-year-old boyfriend. That's not a good combination."

"I *knew* you hated Danielle. She's been the nicest person at the camp, and now you have to diss her. Why can't you leave me alone?"

"As long as I'm your mother you're going to have to stick by my rules. I gave you one pass when you took off from swimming, but I'm not putting up with this again."

Ally pulled into her aunt's driveway, and before she could turn off the car, Kylie jerked open the door and fled into the house, probably to go lock herself in her room.

When Ally passed by her door, she heard Kylie talking on the phone.

"Yeah, Dad, she's trying to control me. She doesn't want me to grow up and have any fun."

Ally put her ear to the door and heard silence, and then, "Yeah, I guess you can talk to her, she's home now. Yeah, I love you too, and miss you lots."

Rage exploded like a bomb throughout Ally's body. "Open this door immediately," she hollered.

After a few seconds, the door creaked open a couple of inches. Ally pushed it so hard it bounced against the wall. Everything in her wanted to slap her daughter. Ally stood with hands on hips, glaring at her firstborn. "Don't you ever phone your father like that and give him a one-sided story."

"At least he listens to me, and doesn't think I'm just the slave around here."

"Slave?"

"Yeah, I'm just good for babysitting Benjie. You don't want me to have any fun."

Ally's mouth opened to respond, but nothing came out. She knew anything she would have said she would have regretted.

Kylie continued her spiel. "I'm always handcuffed to Benjie. I can't be a regular kid. Dad understands. You don't."

Ally stifled the urge to scream, *You don't have any idea,* but instead she dug her fingernails into her palms.

Kylie flopped onto the bed and buried her head in the covers.

Ally sat beside her. "Listen, I thought we got this all ironed out. I didn't realize I'd put such a burden on you."

"I'm Benjie's second mom."

Ally paused. "Yes, I guess you could say that. I have counted on you to always help me." She put her arm around her daughter. "Please look at me."

Kylie grabbed a Kleenex, blew her nose, and lifted her head.

"I didn't realize I'd done this. You've always been such a help to me, and I don't know what I'd have done without you. I'm sorry, Kylie." Ally grabbed another Kleenex, and wiped a tear from the corner of her daughter's eye.

"It's okay," Kylie bleated in a hoarse voice. "I love Benjie, and I do want to take care of him, but—"

"But I dumped too much onto a little girl's shoulders."

"Mom!"

"You know what I mean. Now, I want you to do something for me."

"What?"

"Come to me when you are mad. Don't just call up your dad."

Kylie nodded.

Ally continued, "And another thing. After this camp session ends, you're grounded."

*   *   *

"So, when's the big move?" Ally asked Don.

They both lingered after lunch, enjoying the relative quiet of the camp while half of the teen boys finished up their three-day hiking trip.

"I don't know, but here goes the end of our quiet coffee break." Don pointed to a train of backpackers shuffling back to the lodge. A sunburned Will headed up a group of twenty boys equipped with backpacks and looking bedraggled and hungry. "Ask him."

"Okay, guys, drop your packs here and head inside for a late lunch," Will ordered.

Ally heard a dozen thuds as the lodge porch shook with the weight of the campers' dust-covered packs. *They must be exhausted. I've never seen teenage boys so quiet.*

She waved to Will. "Hey, you okay?"

He lowered his body one painful inch at a time until his rear hit one of the porch steps. "You try it sometime. These guys eat like horses. I thought we'd brought enough food, but we ran out this morning. Only stuff edible left was a couple bags of trail mix." He made a gagging sign. "If I never see a bag of raisins, sunflower seeds, and peanuts again, I will be a happy man."

"Losing your touch, boss? What happened to the eternal Boy Scout?" Don asked.

"He grew up and decided he liked regular meals. You know, like real eggs, and mashed potatoes not made with water." Will leaned back onto his pack and closed his eyes as he basked in the early afternoon sun.

"Too tired to move into the new house this weekend?"

Will sat up, a curious look crossing his face. "Sorry, Don, I forgot to tell you I wouldn't be moving yet. Too much stuff going on. Maybe in a week or so."

Something wrong in Sarahville?

"Well, just let me know. Right now, I need to fix the office air-conditioning unit or Betty will withhold my paycheck." Don took off his baseball cap, wiped his forehead, and put the cap back before yanking open the lodge screen door.

"Stories, I need to hear stories," Ally demanded as she poured sunscreen into the palms of her hands and smeared it over her arms. It wouldn't calm down her freckles, but she didn't need sunburn *and* freckles. She put on her shades so Will wouldn't notice her staring at his eyes twinkling amidst his three-day beard growth. For an hour, he regaled her with tales of rescuing boys from white rapids and almost stepping on a snake. She laughed as he shared how they filled his sleeping bag with shaving cream the last night of the trip.

The backpackers' chatter coming through the screen door, and a lone woodpecker hammering on a nearby tree, made her want to hold the moment in her head. Was it the lazy heat and the afternoon of freedom that made it magical? Or had it something to do with being around Will?

She tilted back her head to catch a light breeze rocking one of the hammocks back and forth on the lodge porch. "Back to moving. Aren't you going to move in? You can still live in the house by yourself even if Sarah isn't sure about the date."

"Who told you?" Will crossed his arms around his chest.

"And anyway, she's trying to figure out God's will for her life."

"God's will, my eye. That girl's sweet, but as flaky as Stew's famous pie crust."

Will bit his lower lip. "Do you think you just might want to butt out of this one?"

"No."

"I figured so. It isn't any of your business."

"I'm your friend, and I care what happens to you."

Will tilted his head. "Touching."

"I'm serious, Will. Maybe you don't want to be with a woman who has had a difficult time committing."

Will looked down and played with a hangnail on his thumb.

"You keep telling me God put you guys together. Maybe, maybe not. Wouldn't God give her that same feeling? Isn't that how it's supposed to work? I don't know—don't have much experience with this. I just found a guy I liked and married him. Never thought about any 'God's will' stuff."

"Early staff meeting tomorrow." He picked up his backpack and hitched it onto his shoulders as Betty came through the front screen door, clothed in the loudest fuchsia and purple Hawaiian shirt this side of the islands.

"Welcome back, Daniel Boone." She handed Will a telephone note. "Make sure you call her back by the end of the day." She headed back inside.

Will nodded absently as he readjusted his backpack. "You may be the most direct woman I've ever known."

"Hey," said Ally with a shrug, "I'm just trying to point out the obvious. Isn't getting married supposed to be something pretty exciting?"

Will groaned as he put down the backpack and sat down next to her. "I'm going to get your opinion whether I want it or not."

Windburn reddened his cheeks, and deep circles darkened his eyes. Did the weariness come from more than just staying up with the senior guys, telling ghost stories?

Okay, now she was about to become a bona fide buttinski. She scooted closer to look him straight in the eye and, to her amazement, he started blinking and looked away for a moment.

"As someone who's just come out of a bad marriage, I only know what doesn't work. I'm sure you have dreams."

Will let out a long sigh. "Um, a—a woman who'd give me companionship, someone who'd make me laugh and keep me grounded. And I guess, from a spiritual standpoint, a woman who'd pray for me and have the same vision I do. Someone who could work with me to be the hands and feet of Jesus." He paused and swallowed. "Sarah's a wonderful Christian woman, and she does pray for me—"

"Yes, I like her."

Will put on his baseball hat and stared out towards the lake, avoiding her look.

"Sorry, I guess I just say too much. It's just that I don't ever want you to have to go through what I went through."

"Okay, okay, I'm not up for this, but shoot—"

"Well, I was crazy about Bryan, and we had a happy marriage for several years. It's when Benjie came along— Bryan started pulling away from us. He acted bored and spent a lot of time at the office, just when I needed him most. I started to nag him about spending more time with Benjie. I wanted him to be there for me, but he kept leaving the marriage, emotionally. It hurt a lot."

Will looked up from his perch on the steps. "I'm sorry. Must have felt like ten backpacks on your back."

"You could say that. I tried to balance a successful career and two kids while Bryan seemed to slip away a little at a time. One day, I realized he didn't care about much of anything anymore. I just dug in my heels and kept trying, all the time realizing I was only irritating him." Ally paused. "Can you imagine me irritating someone?" She curled her lips into her most innocent smile.

"Ally, if you irritate, it's only because you speak the truth. That's what makes you the person you are. Don't ever change that about yourself." Will leaned over and patted her arm. "Honesty is a trait desperately lacking in our world."

He studied her face as if looking for answers to his troubling questions. She saw a fleeting look—tenderness?— but it evaporated away as his expression morphed back into camp director mode.

"Hey, don't forget to pick up our order at P and W," he reminded Ally as he turned to go inside the lodge. "We're almost out of bread and hamburger buns."

* * *

The law offices of T. S. & C. covered the fifth floor on Riverview Center in Grand Rapids, the top commercial real estate in the city. The view overlooked the Grand River, and on summer days one might see workers sitting out on picnic tables, eating their lunch.

Ted sat in his leather desk chair on the top floor of the building, reading the letter Will Grainger sent. It seemed that Camp Surrender had decided to turn down their offer.

"They don't know who they are dealing with." He crumpled the letter, and stabbed his letter opener into his desk blotter. "But they'll find out."

* * *

Will telephoned Sarah and cancelled lunch; he was needed in the kitchen to help. He grabbed a large chef knife and chopped celery for tuna salad sandwiches.

"This look chopped up enough?" Will asked Ally.

"Looks pretty professional to me. Why don't you start working on peeling the hardboiled eggs?" Ally pointed to a pan of eggs cooling in the sink. "You're picking this up pretty quickly for a man who doesn't even know how to operate a microwave."

"Hey, watch it. I make a mean peanut butter and jelly sandwich." Will winked at Ally, and whistled a camp song.

"Where did you learn to do that? It's beautiful. I've never heard such great whistling."

"My dad taught me when we'd go for walks. It took a lot of practice. I even taught Don to whistle. It's gotten me through some tough times."

"Whistling?"

"When my mother died, I'd go out to the woods behind our house, sit and look up at the sky, and think about her. Sometimes I'd imagine she'd ask me for a tune, so I'd make up one for her. Sounds kind of strange, I guess."

"No, it's sweet."

Will lowered his gaze and gave an exaggerated sigh. "Sweet isn't very manly."

"Well, you're kind of a mixture of manly and sweet." Ally grinned at Will, and he returned the grin, holding her gaze so intensely that she had to look away. Looking down, she returned to frosting a chocolate cake. *He has the kindest eyes I've ever seen. I could tell him anything.*

Betty entered, and placed a few invoices on the counter. "Good to see you back in the kitchen, Ally. We've all missed you the last couple of days." She walked to the table where Benjie was busy coloring, and sat next to him. "Looks like a red car, Benjie. Nice job."

Benjie looked up at Betty. "LLX 132." He reached out and patted her on the arm.

"You're amazing, kid." Betty chuckled. "I'd better stay straight with the law." Grabbing bottled water out of the cooler, she flapped out of the kitchen in her flip-flops.

Ally grabbed a clean spoon and scraped the side of the icing bowl to take a sample. Wiping her hands on her apron, she stood back to admire her creation. "You know, this cake reminds me of the time I ate one three-layer chocolate cake in two days."

"What were you thinking?"

"I was about to get married to Bryan, and we had a big fight, something stupid he said about my mother. Anyway, I broke up with him and self-medicated with Demon Dark Chocolate Sour Cream Cake."

She took the spatula and empty frosting bowl, put them in the soapy water, and then looked up.

Will stared at her in disbelief. "What did you say?"

"I ate an entire cake."

"I know, but what was the name of the cake?"

"Demon Dark Chocolate Sour Cream Cake. Why?"

"You wouldn't have, by chance, purchased that cake at Jolly's Groceries in Menlo Park?"

Ally put her head in her hands and groaned. "Yep, I shopped there a lot."

She knew what was coming next, and covered her face, peeking through her fingers. Will had a strange look. She grabbed the frosting bowl and tossed it in the sink. Turning on the hot water, she squeezed the dish soap into the water.

Will tossed the empty pop can into the recycling bin and sauntered towards the sink. "Funny, I used to work there while I was an intern."

Ally concentrated on the dishes as she dumped the clean bowl into the rinse side of the sink. She pulled a frying pan up from the soapy water and scrubbed it furiously.

"I knew you looked familiar when you applied for the job. You're that girl! The one who kept buying our bestselling cake." He slapped the side of his pants. "You were something else."

Ally looked out the window above the sink, wondering why she hadn't called in sick this morning. Her stomach started to knot up in the usual configuration. His learning her identity was not in her plans.

"Yes, that was me. I was pretty full of myself in those days."

"But, wait, there's something else that's been bugging me. Did you ever summer here with your parents?"

Ally kept her eyes down, concentrating on scouring the now shiny pan.

After a few seconds of painful silence, she decided she'd better look up. She had dreaded this moment.

"I was afraid you'd figure it out. Yep, and you're that Will who tormented me and my sister all summer. And, now that I'm in full disclosure mode, that was me that tripped in the restaurant a few months ago."

Will let out a low whistle. "You're *that* Ally from California? You're kidding. Well, that explains a lot of things. But why did you keep it a secret?"

Ally wiped soapy hands on her apron and tucked a straggle of hair behind her ear. "I told my aunt I just wanted a fresh start. Seems kinda silly now."

His finger pointed at her. "You're little Ally? Wow." Will shook his head.

He leaned his elbow on the counter and propped up his head with his right fist, studying her as if looking at a different woman. He was probably trying to reconcile his past mental picture of her with the present reality.

Finally, Will snapped his fingers as if he'd just had a revelation. "I think God has an appointment with you this summer. He had a reason for you being here."

Ally gulped. Her face burned with humiliation, and yet she felt the relief one encounters when being found out.

She fished around for the right words, but as she searched Will's face, she knew she didn't need to answer him. What had begun as embarrassment made way for a new emotion. The tight knot in her stomach, her constant companion for the last few months, started to unravel. Something inside kept telling her to just let go.

Benjie, still coloring at the kitchen table, put down his crayon, crawled off of his chair, and toddled over to stand by Ally. Grabbing the hem of her blouse, he jerked it up and down to get her attention. Ally squatted down to his level to see what he wanted. He said nothing, but tilted his head sideways.

"What is it, honey?"

He was quiet for a moment. Then he opened his mouth, and in a slow, deliberate manner said, "Mama, 'God cares for you.' I Peter 5:8."

Will knelt beside him. "Does Benjie love Jesus?"

He looked at his mother, and then back at Will. He beamed. "Yes."

"The sirloin I had craved all week is just sitting on the bottom of my stomach like a Lake Michigan shipwreck," said Will as he walked into the office. Betty and Ally looked up from the mailing they were sending out.

"Not a great night?" Ally slid a brochure through the stamp meter.

"She said, 'You just don't understand, I have been away too long, and I have to get back. I can't make any big plans yet.' She's going back in a week. Says she's got a lot of staff problems at La Casa Familia. I guess I pictured a romantic evening with her, not butting heads over a wedding date. She claims she's made a commitment to the kids and can't let them down."

"Can't some other staff member handle some of the issues?" asked Betty.

"She says she needs time for a transition. I told her, 'This isn't a transition, it's a marriage.'" He pounded his hands down on the desk, and papers went flying.

244

Betty walked up to him, and put her arm around Will. "Well, coming from a forty-year perspective, I'd say she has pre-wedding jitters. You'll work things out."

*   *   *

It was early September, the beginning of the conference season. Will, Justin, Betty, and Don spent the day reorganizing the craft cottage.

"One more camp season over," said Betty as she loaded paints and plastic lanyard strings into a cardboard box.

Will walked in with plastic bins of glue and markers. He set them down on an ancient craft table covered thick with layers of poster paint and glitter, and stared out the window. "Seems like I've spent most of my life on this lake."

"Didn't your grandfather own the cottage directly across from the camp?"

"Yep. I remember watching the sunset from his porch. He had two neighbors who kayaked in the evening, and they'd always wave."

"Any more news on wedding plans?" asked Betty.

Will shrugged and picked up a broom to sweep the floor. Don and Betty scrubbed a summer's worth of craftiness off of the tables. They worked quietly 'til Betty broke the silence.

"Don was telling me you used to be homeless."

He leaned on his broom.

"Hey, not trying to be nosey," said Betty as she sat down to sort out beads.

"No, it's part of my story." Will put down the broom and plopped down astride a chair. "Guess it's proof of God's tenacity. You know I went to school in California. Wanted to shake off my small-town identity. Kinda test out the world."

"You were raised in a Christian home?" Betty asked.

"Oh yeah. But the West Coast kept calling my name. Ended up going to UC Santa Cruz by the beach."

"Beautiful area," Don added.

"Yeah. Got into the whole lifestyle. Profs encouraged us to do whatever it took to 'expand' our creativity." He shook his head. "Translated meant 'experimenting with all kinds of drugs.' Lots of fun for a while. Became a total hedonist."

"A what?" asked Betty.

"You know, pursuing pleasures."

Ally appeared in the doorway with a platter of tuna fish sandwiches and a bowl of potato salad. "Can I get in on the conversation?"

"Might as well know my darker side," Will answered. *How do I get myself into these conversations?*

"I can't believe you have a dark side," said Ally.

"Not proud of it. Still, God brought me through." He ran the palms of his hands on the sides of his jeans, and continued. "At first I thought I'd found nirvana—great weather, redwoods, and the Pacific Ocean."

"Lots of people end up in California looking for something," added Betty.

"Don't know I thought that far ahead. Just enjoying life."

He looked at the four of them. "Do you want to hear all of this?"

"We'll love you no matter what." Betty patted his shoulder as she picked up another plastic bin of beads to put back on the shelf in the craft closet.

"Had a lot of friends, or at least that's what I thought while I was buying the good stuff. Funny how they all disappeared when I flunked out of school after three semesters. I moved out of the dorm with three other flunkies who were looking for work. I at least had a part-time job at a bike shop. Things were okay until they shut off our electricity, followed by our water." Will felt his throat go dry as he remembered the incident. "Well, Murphy's Law kicked in. Whatever could go wrong, did."

"Why didn't you call your dad?" Don asked.

"Pride. I knew he was proud of my grades, and I didn't want to disappoint him. So I lived on the beach, under an overpass, wherever it looked safe. Learned where to find the best half-eaten steaks, dumpster diving behind the nicer restaurants."

"Gross." Don made a gagging noise.

"You do what you can to survive. I started to notice how the veteran street people knew the good places to flop at night. The pastors at some of the local churches would open the doors and let us bed down when the weather got cold. I panhandled at the boardwalk. And I learned something."

Will looked past his friends and out the window of the craft room as the memories of those days came flooding back.

"What?" asked Betty.

"The kindest people were those who would buy me a burger and shake, and add a 'God bless you.' Even through my drug-fogged brain, I saw the face of Jesus."

"So what finally got you back on your feet?" Ally looked at Will quizzically as if she couldn't believe his story.

"Showed up at Twin Lakes Baptist Church. Heard they had food. Christmas." Will paused and looked down at the floor. "Started thinking about my family back home, my brothers and dad, and how when my mother was alive she always played *Oh Little Town of Bethlehem* on the piano before we had Christmas Eve supper, and how she had this great meal for all of us. And there I am, smelly, hungry, and rain-soaked, with a black eye from some panhandler who thought I'd invaded his territory."

"So, did they feed you?" asked Justin the camp lifeguard. Will noticed Justin never missed a meal.

"Yeah, but that's not the amazing thing. This weird dude with a ragged beard down to here"—Will pointed to his sternum—"and wearing this dirty black raincoat motions for me to come stand under his umbrella. He looks me dead in the eye and says I need to call my family. Freaked me out. I followed him into the church, and he unlocked the office for me to make a call."

Will raked his hands though his hair. *I'll bet I bawled for ten minutes on the phone.*

"Is that when you headed back to Michigan?" asked Betty, stacking a pile of newspapers.

"Nope. Somehow got my degree from San Jose State University, and then worked as an intern for a church a half-hour south of San Jose."

"Were you tempted to stay?' asked Don.

"No, heart's always been in Michigan. Got a call about the camp position, and moved back a few years ago."

Will turned and looked at Ally. She had a dumbfounded look on her face. *Now you see, I'm an imperfect man.*

CHAPTER
TWENTY-TWO

Conference season started with an AA retreat on the second Friday of September. Friday night, the group leader announced campfire time, and the group of fifty ambled down the short trail to the fire pit.

Benjie emerged from the kitchen, a candle lighter in his hands.

"What do you have?" Kylie asked her brother as he flapped his hands in excitement. "Oh, I get it—that's for the campfire. Benjie, you're not supposed to have the candle lighter. Let me have it."

She tried to pry it from his grasp, but he dropped to the ground and curled into a ball, like a tightly-rolled porcupine hiding his treasure.

"Give it to me right now." Kylie pulled his arm away from his body and uncurled his fingers. She grabbed the lighter.

Benjie let out a blood-curdling scream and flew into a rage, coming after his sister with fists and feet.

"Mom! Benjie's playing with the candle lighter," she

hollered to her mother ahead of her, who was laden down with boxes of graham crackers, Hershey candy bars, and bags of marshmallows. Several of the attendees turned and looked at Benjie as he grabbed Kylie around her knees.

"Hey, mom, you might want to referee this," Kylie heard an older woman inform her mother, and wanted to die.

Ally threw down her pile of stuff, flew into the brawl, extracted Benjie, and gave him a swat on his behind.

"Kylie, go on ahead."

Still breathing hard and shaken, Kylie took a few steps away, and then looked back. Her mother took her brother by the shoulders and knelt down to his level.

"You know I've told you not to even touch that lighter, and you're not to hit your sister. She was only looking out for you. Are you listening to me?"

Kylie watched her brother kick a large pinecone in the middle of the path and then slowly raise his head to meet his mother's look.

"Do you want to spend the night in the cabin?"

His gaze darted back and forth.

"If I see you with the lighter again, we'll just go home. Is that what you want?" Mom waited until Benjie finally met her eyes. Kylie thought she saw a tiny shake of his head.

"One more outburst, buster, and we're heading home." Mom pulled Benjie up to walk beside her. "I don't care if you can't tell me anything, I don't care if you don't learn to read or learn algebra, but you are going to learn to mind me. Do you hear me?"

Benjie looked at her, but didn't respond.

When they reached the campfire, Mom and Kylie passed out some more fixings. Benjie followed right behind, and sat on Mom's lap when she finished.

"Fire, fire," he cried, bouncing up and down, pointing to the growing flames.

"The boy definitely likes a good bonfire," said one of the group members with a chuckle.

For the rest of the night, she held Benjie on her lap while the AA group sang old folk songs, like *Blowing in the Wind* and *Hang Down Your Head, Tom Dooley*. Not a particularly musical group, the attendees still had belted out the words with gusto. Kylie thought the songs were dumb, but she loved sitting around the fire. She just wished her brother wouldn't keep embarrassing her in front of others. *I'm sick of having to always explain my brother to people*. One thing she liked about her new camp friend, Carson, was he didn't care what kind of brother she had. He never asked stupid questions.

About twenty minutes later, Mom stood up with Benjie. "It's probably time to get this guy to bed."

"Hey, I'll walk you guys back to the cabin." Will put down his roasting fork and dusted off his jeans. "It's pretty dark along the path since one of the outdoor lights burnt out. I'll have to get Don to get that fixed in the morning."

"I can lead," said Kylie. "I'm not afraid."

"I guess you didn't see that raccoon fighting with that skunk back there." Will winked.

Kylie grabbed his arm. "Well, maybe we can walk it together."

The four of them walked silently for a few minutes with only a dim flashlight to cut the darkness.

"I didn't realize how dark it got," said Mom. "Ouch!" Her foot tripped over a tree root. She grabbed onto Kylie to catch her fall.

"Whoooooo!"

Kylie jumped and shone the flashlight up to a tree branch on her right. About twenty feet up, a pair of shining amber eyes peered at them. "Wow," she exclaimed, "it's good luck to see an owl."

They stood mesmerized by the great bird.

"Mr. Don told me it's hard to see an owl. They hide."

"Let's get going, it's late," said Mom, yawning.

It had been Kylie's first week at her school, and it had been stressful for both of them. Kylie pointed the flashlight back on the path. They were almost to the junior girls' restroom. Will halted, and put his fingers to his lips to shush the group.

"Did you hear something?" he asked.

They stopped talking and listened. A twig snapped somewhere behind their cabin.

"Stay here." Will had already grabbed the flashlight out of Kylie's hand. She was glad Will was around to check things out.

The three of them huddled in a tight knot watching him sprint toward the cabin where the family would be staying. He circled around the dwelling's perimeter. The only sound they could hear was his tromping up and down in the underbrush. After about three minutes, he came back.

"Coast clear. Didn't see much, but I know I heard something. If you run into Big Foot, give me a call. If you don't get a cell signal, come knock on my door. I'm sleeping here tonight."

After unlocking the cabin door and flipping on the lights to make sure no nasty night creatures had crawled inside, he waved goodnight. Kylie shivered as she watched him go back down the path. His room behind the office was kinda far away.

*   *   *

Once Ally helped Benjie into his pajamas and settled Kylie next to him in the double bed meant for the summer camp counselor, she slid down under the sheets in the twin bed next to them.

Within five minutes, both Kylie and Benjie were out cold, but Ally tossed and turned. She remembered she'd had a can of Coke a couple of hours ago. She knew better than to drink caffeine after seven at night. She got up, and put on her cowboy boots and the old brown plaid bathrobe with the ripped pockets, wondering why she'd sold so many of her good clothes before leaving California.

Opening the screen door, Ally walked out on the tiny porch. Two twig chairs flanked either side of the door. She settled into one, watched the quarter-moon in the sky, and searched overhead for the Little Dipper. Then her gaze went to the handle to find the North Star. She used to love astronomy.

The world went mute until she heard the loon's melancholy lilting tune. In an eerie voice, it cried for its mate to come home. The sound put goose bumps on the back of Ally's arms. Maybe she was the only one on the lake to hear it. Was the loon lonely too? The cry stopped, and she wondered if the two loons had finally met.

The calm lasted a few minutes before Ally's thoughts, like a favorite poison, seeped back to arguments with Bryan. What a night for reruns. She'd memorized each cold and uncaring word he'd fired back at her during their last arguments.

But halfway through rehashing the final conversation that ended their marriage, Ally paused. *What am I trying to prove, reliving that inane moment? I must be sick.* She tried to push her mental stop button, but the old conversations kept tumbling out.

Another voice interrupted her muddled thoughts. Was she going mad, hearing voices in her head? 'Forgive him, for he knows not what he does.'

What? Forgive Bryan, the coward of all time? Forgive Bryan, the man who barely communicates with his own flesh and blood? Forgive?

'Yes, forgive.'

Ally stood up and paced the porch. *Scuffity-scuff, scuffity-scuff.* Her boots created a rhythm as she tried to wrap her mind around the words she just heard.

"I can't forgive! This man doesn't deserve forgiveness."

She looked to the right of the porch to a wood pile with an ax stuck in the top of a log destined for firewood that Don had accidentally left. Something rose up in her, and she grabbed the axe handle and jiggled it out of the log. She eyed her target. Six feet from her stood a large pine tree to the right of the porch. With uncontrollable fury, she ran to the tree and whacked the axe against the trunk. *Bam, bam, bam.* Over and over, she pummeled the blade into the tree trunk with every ounce of anger she had stored up. She didn't stop until she had gouged a large indentation in the trunk.

"That's what I think of you, Bryan!" she shouted at the tree.

Out of breath, she collapsed at the base of the tree, sitting in a pile of pine needles, weeping. Even the strong scent of pine needles didn't comfort her. She didn't know she had such a backlog of tears. "Bring 'em on, I don't care," she screamed to the empty woods, her fist shaking in the night air. "I'm beyond broken."

For what seemed an eternity, she lay crumpled at the foot of the tree, her hands reverberating in pain from her chopping. She put down the axe and flexed her hands back and forth to disseminate the dull agony of her pounded muscles. Then she stood, her body trembling as she grasped her bathrobe sleeves and wiped her flooded face. A strange sensation deluged her body. Starting from her toes, the feeling ripped through her legs, her stomach, and her arms until it met her brain. Something or someone had turned off her thoughts, replacing—yes, replacing—turmoil with a tranquility that infused her whole being. Something had somehow exchanged her anger and bitterness for a clean calmness.

The tiny whispery voice returned. 'Forgive him, for he knows not what he does.'

Ally groped around the base of the tree in the dark to find the axe she'd flung on the ground. She held the tool close to her breast and felt the cool metal against her chest. "I'm sorry." She took a deep breath. "It's okay, Bryan."

She remembered a talk about forgiveness that Will gave around the campfire at teen camp. He told a story about how a guy, the head counselor at camp, had fallen in love with another counselor. Even though the camp strictly forbade any romantic involvement, all the staff could see they were smitten with each other, and many of the kids would tease and try to get them together. The two counselors would seat their kids together at campfires, and they'd pass little notes to each other when they thought the campers weren't looking. The guy even carved both of their initials underneath the steps of the lodge. Everyone knew they were meant to be. When they left in the fall to go to different colleges, they promised to write—and they did, once a week. But soon the girl's notes became fewer and fewer. She wouldn't return his phone calls, and when he did reach her, she made excuses why she hadn't written. She had a lot of term papers to write, she worked too many hours at her waitress job, etc.

When he found out she'd been dating another guy in her hometown, they had a terrible fight and she broke up with him. For two years, he harbored a secret little box in his mind that he'd pull out, rehashing the ugly memories. Will told the campers to picture the box, dirty, with a broken hinge and a deep gouge on the top. Even with its ugliness, the young man still had a morose pleasure when he opened that box. It made him feel noble, comparing himself to his unfaithful girlfriend who had turned against him. She was the evil person. One day while reading his Bible, he read a verse about forgiving someone seventy times seven. He'd always tried to ignore that verse, but this time it haunted him day and night. He couldn't study, and he lost his appetite. When he finally let go of the bitterness and forgave her, it felt like he'd been let out of jail.

"Unforgiveness is a mighty strong prison, and the only combination to unlock the door is letting go and forgiving," Will had said. "Forgiveness is perfume in the nostrils of God."

Ally looked at the gouge she'd carved in the tree trunk. "I can't forgive him, but You can, Jesus. I give You my bitterness. Please unlock my prison door."

She lay there, enjoying the peace and knowing she'd done the right thing. She finally rose, went back to the cabin, slid under the covers. *I know things will be different.* She settled on the pillow. For the first time in months, she looked forward to the future.

*   *   *

Benjie woke. Still night. He sat up in bed and flapped his hands. Mom and Kylie, deep in sleep, didn't notice him jump out of bed and put on his flip flops.

"Staaa!" Benjie growled in desperation, trying to shake his mother, but she just rolled over in her bed.

His sister didn't even move. Benjie's hands flapped fast and faster. He turned the wooden latch on the door and sprinted out of the cabin. As he glanced back, he saw tiny flames flickering around a woodpile right next to the cabin.

"Campfire," he yelled, and ran around in circles in front of the cabin, confused and frightened. Then he stopped, remembering. Will would help his mother and sister.

Benjie darted toward the lodge and saw a car drive off toward the road. He jogged up the porch stairs. The front door didn't budge. He needed a key.

Maybe he could bang on the door? Benjie curled his fist into a ball and knocked first on the door, and then on the large glass dining room window that looked out onto the lake. *Bam, bam, bam.*

Nothing.

Benjie looked back at the fire. *Hurry.*

The flames had spread onto the ground and were headed to the side of their cabin. His hands flapped even faster.

He raced around to the kitchen porch where he played during the day, and tried to pry open the screen door. It, too, was locked.

A tiny hole in the screen had ripped above the door handle, so he put his finger in the opening and tugged. The hole grew larger, but the edges of the screen pierced his finger and made it bleed. He had to be brave. Grabbing one side of the hole, he pulled with all his might, and ripped an opening large enough for his arm. He thrust his arm through the hole and reached for the latch. It was too high for him.

He looked around. Don had left his toolbox by the door. Benjie dragged the box over to the door and stood on top of the lid. The extra inches allowed him to unlatch the door handle. He flew through the kitchen, down the back hallway to Will's room. Benjie banged on the door, using his hands, head, elbows, knees—any part of his body that would make a noise.

After a few seconds, Will stuck his head out. "Benjie! What on Earth?"

"Stopp, drwop, and woll!" Benjie repeated, "stop wdrop and woll!"

"What are you trying to tell me?"

Benjie just shook his head and paced back and forth in front of the door. He had to tell Will about the emergency.

"Are you saying you saw a fire?"

Benjie nodded.

"Take me, little buddy." Will seized a sweatshirt and shot out of the door, following Benjie down the hall and out the building. He grabbed Benjie's hand, and they flew down the gravel pathway.

Fire had consumed three large trees to the right of the cabin, and then moved to the cabin. The roof wore a reddish-orange halo of flames. More cabins were about to catch fire.

Will pulled out his cell phone from his jean pocket and twice tried to phone someone, but that person must have been asleep because Will just closed the phone again. He grabbed Benjie by the shoulders. "Go knock on Don's door, the maintenance building. Say 'fire.' Do you understand! Say it."

Benjie paused a minute. He didn't think he could do this.

Will grabbed him by his shoulders and looked him straight in the eye. "I know you can do it, Benjie."

"Fire!" Benjie blurted, and he felt his mouth turn up in a victorious smile.

"Go!" shouted Will as he gave Benjie's lower back a shove.

Benjie felt his heart pounding almost as fast as his feet pounded the ground. He would find Mr. Don.

*   *   *

Will sprinted back to the lodge, snatched the fire hose, and threw it into his suburban. He floored it all the way back to the fire. Will tried the door of the cabin, but could hardly touch the knob. It felt like a smoldering iron.

"Ally! Kylie! Can you hear me?" Will screamed over the roar of the flames.

He heard a faint voice whimper—"In here."

Will couldn't tell if it was Ally or Kylie, but was relieved to hear someone's voice. He grabbed the water hose and screwed the connecting valve to the outside spigot near the junior girls bathroom. With a flip of his wrist, he turned on the spigot, but only a weak stream of water came out. The water pressure had always been low at camp.

His heart banged against his ribs as he realized the horror of the moment. The flames had started to cover the shingles. In a few minutes, the roof might collapse. He ran to the back of the burning cabin and banged on the window. Smoke clouded the view.

He ran around to the front again and caught sight of the camp truck. Don sat in the driver's seat with Benjie in the passenger side. Behind him, a local Lake Surrender volunteer fire department truck followed.

Two firemen began pumping water from the lake. Two others jumped out of the cab of the truck, one with a hatchet in his hand.

"Where are they?" he asked.

"I can't see through the windows," Will shouted.

"Look at that yellow smoke leaking out of the windows. Looks like a backdraft," one of the firemen hollered. "We'll have to cut into the roof."

Will understood. Opening the door or window would

cause too much oxygen in the bedroom and lower the chances for anyone to come out alive.

Two firemen headed toward the left side of the cabin and threw a ladder against the building. They scaled up the ladder to the roof. Chopping between two of the roof's joists, they created an eighteen inch wide opening to let the heat and smoke escape. They scrambled down the ladder and smashed the bathroom window on the left. Glass crashed to the ground.

A fireman scrambled up the ladder and through the window. Two other firemen and Don held a hose and fought flames on the roof and other side of the cabin.

Will saw Don's arms shaking and jogged up to take over his duties.

"Let me relieve you."

Don took Will's place holding Benjie's hand.

As they pointed the hose skyward, Will prayed, "Lord, let it not be too late."

Benjie ran up and tried to grab the hose, too, trying to help. Two strong arms hoisted Benjie onto his shoulders as one of the firemen returned him to Will. The boy hugged Will's head. "It's okay, Benjie. We're getting Mommy and Kylie help."

Betty and her husband pulled up in a Ford Bronco. "We heard the police radio. Is anyone in there?"

"Ally and Kylie," Will answered.

Betty's mouth dropped open. "Oh, dear God," she said. "Oh merciful God."

Will surrendered his hold on the hose, and steadied Benjie's legs as the boy kicked Will's chest. The small group watched the bathroom window in expectant horror. Every second that passed put another knot in Will's stomach.

"Even if they haven't been burned, the smoke inhalation could kill them," said Don.

"Hush." Betty glared at him. No one wanted to go there.

Finally, a head of long brown hair and a body with a long red nightshirt appeared.

"Kylie!" shouted Benjie.

"Stay right here, Benjie," Will ordered as he set the boy on the ground.

Betty grabbed Benjie's hand. Will ran to the window, hands clenched, and waited at the bottom of the ladder until the fireman stepped on solid ground. Who knew what the firemen would carry in his arms. Would they both be alive? Will stretched out his arms, and the fireman lowered Kylie into his waiting arms. Her face was covered with soot, and she was breathing shallow, but she was still alive.

Don put a blanket down on the ground for Kylie. By now, the paramedics had arrived. They pushed everyone else out of the way, and one of them had oxygen ready to cover her mouth. Slowly, Kylie's breathing became stronger as she came to, choking and gasping for air.

"Praise God!" shouted Betty.

Ally's auburn hair appeared through the opening as a big

burly fireman cradled her in his arms.

"Watch that glass," one hollered as they maneuvered Ally though the jagged opening. Too late. An edge of the broken window caught her arm and sliced a deep cut in it. They lowered Ally to the ground and a couple of paramedics hovered over her, giving her oxygen, taking vitals and bandaging her arm. Will watched them work, but saw no visible reaction from her.

No. No, not Ally.

"She's pretty bad. We'll have to rush her to Community. We'll take the girl, too, but she's better off."

"Come on, Benjie, you're coming with me." Will buckled Benjie into the passenger side of the truck. He put the truck into gear and followed the flashing lights of the paramedic van.

CHAPTER
TWENTY-THREE

Ally squinted and blinked against the bright light. She saw a figure walk over to the blinds and dim the room.

"You gave us quite a scare last night."

Ally drew her eyelids completely up, viewing a smiling Will. His eyes had an achy tenderness.

"I've told you for years to quit smoking those Swisher cigars," a higher-pitched male voice chimed in.

Ally turned her head. Bryan. Her heart sped up, and she wiped her sweaty palms against the sheets. Things must be bad if Bryan was here.

"What are you doing here?" she asked. *And what's wrong with my voice?* It sounded thin and reedy. "What am *I* doing here?"

Bryan and Will looked at each other.

Will put his hand over his mouth, and Ally thought he paused a bit too long before he explained. "Your cabin caught fire. Both you and Kylie got out, but you have second- and third-degree burns. Kylie's okay. She had some minor injuries and is at home with your aunt, but you need to stay in the hospital a few more days."

"Where's Benjie? Where's my baby?" Ally had a faint recollection of him talking about something in the middle of the night. She thought he'd just been talking in his sleep.

Will leaned forward in his chair. "Benjie is the reason you and Kylie are alive. From what we can piece together, Benjie smelled smoke and ran to get me. My guess is he tried to wake you, but you were too deep in sleep. He figured out a way to rip open the back screen porch off the kitchen at the lodge and open the door. From there, he ran to my room and woke me up. I couldn't understand what he was saying. He just kept repeating 'stop, drop, and roll.' You know, the fire drill the kids learned at camp."

"He's been fascinated by that drill all summer. I got tired of hearing it. How would I ever have thought that would have saved my life?"

"Well, I guess you won't ever get tired of it now." Will smiled. "Benjie's probably going to be awarded the Junior Fireman of the Year for Lake Surrender."

"Kylie's holed up in Aunt Nettie's bedroom," Bryan said. "Your aunt insisted Kylie have her king-size bed and the view of the lake while she recuperates. Kylie's milking it for all it's worth. Benjie's lying on a sleeping bag right next to her, and won't leave her side."

Ally offered a tiny grin, glad the kids had each other. "But Kylie is going to be okay?"

"Yes, her burns weren't severe. Benjie's rattled, but if he has his collections with him, he'll keep busy," said Bryan. "I just spent the day with them."

Ally paused. She wanted to know more, but the pain medication in her IV made her drowsy. "I just need to ask one more question." She closed her eyes. "How did the fire start?"

The room grew quiet. All she heard were the soft footsteps padding up and down the hallway outside, and the noises from a game show program on the TV in her room.

They're not telling me something. Oh dear God, what could go wrong now?

Will cleared his throat. "Well—"

"Let me take it from here," said Bryan.

"It's kind of complicated," said Will. "Why don't we talk about it later when you're rested?"

"How about we talk outside a minute?" Bryan motioned toward the door.

The two men exited the room. Their voices carried from the hallway.

"Let me handle this," Bryan argued. "I know what's best."

Ally ignored her sore throat and rallied her feeble voice. "Bryan, Will!"

Both men rushed back into the room.

"Don't fight."

"We're not, just had to get some things straight." Bryan shot an angry look at Will before turning back to Ally.

"Why don't you wait until she feels better?" Will asked.

Ally's heart started pounding. "What aren't you telling me?"

Bryan pulled up a chair beside the hospital bed. "You know I'm not one to sugar-coat problems. I'll just give it to you directly. The fire department is looking into arson as the cause of the fire. Some anonymous person sent in a tip saying they'd seen Benjie playing with matches several times this summer, and maybe the autistic boy set the fire. It sounds ridiculous, except for the fact the investigators found a box of matches on Cabin B's front porch."

"That's a lie, a dirty lie." Ally tried to scream, but she couldn't raise her voice above a loud whisper.

She sat up in bed and hit the nurse call button. A petite young nurse raced into the room.

"You're awake, Ms. Cervantes."

"You bet I'm awake, and I want my cell phone. I'm going to phone that fire department and give them a piece of my mind." Her mind was screaming, but her voice only whispered.

"Ms. Cervantes, you've been through a great shock, and you're in no frame of mind to talk to anyone." The nurse uncapped a syringe, tapped it, and injected a light-colored liquid into the IV. "How about I just give you a small sedative?"

"How about I just leave this hospital. Looks like while I've been camped out here, my son has been accused of arson."

"Look, Ally"—Will held up his hand—"it was an

anonymous tip, and the fire department has to check our leads. They won't even finish the investigation for several weeks."

Ally settled back down into the bed.

Will continued, "Benjie wouldn't do that. He's our fire safety kid!"

Bryan shot Will a warning glare. "Didn't take you long to move in on my family."

The nurse looked back and forth between the two men. She leaned down and murmured, "Do I need to call security, Ms. Cervantes?"

Ally shook her head. She didn't want this to escalate by putting Bryan even more on edge. With an uncertain glance back at the men, the nurse capped the syringe and left the room.

Ally watched Will's jaw tighten. He rubbed the sides of his jeans before he answered.

"Yes, Bryan, I do know a lot about your son. He's a terrific boy, and he made this year's summer camp a joy. The staff loves him, and some of the campers write letters to him after they leave. I give a lot of credit to his mother for his being so well-adjusted."

"Yeah, as if an autistic child can ever be considered well-adjusted."

"He broke into the back door of the kitchen, got me out of bed, and in his own way, he told me about the fire. You wouldn't have a daughter if your son hadn't raced to get help. So don't give me any crap about your definition of well-adjusted."

Ally blinked at the heated exchange. She hadn't seen this side of Will before.

Bryan's face turned pink, red, and then purple. He shot several unflattering comments at Will, along with an obscene hand gesture, before storming out. He almost knocked over a woman who had just arrived.

Will looked up, and surprise crossed his face. "Sarah."

She placed a brilliant bouquet of lilies and carnations on the nightstand, then leaned over and squeezed Ally's hand. "How are your children?"

Will spared Ally's voice by relating what Bryan had said about the kids. They talked some more about Kylie and her recovery, and this year's camp stories.

"I've had a great summer at camp and learned a lot," said Ally in a raspy whisper, blinking to keep awake. "It's rotten that this had to happen. I'm worried about Kylie."

"Kylie's just fine," Will said. "She's her old self, and from what I hear, she loves the extra attention from Aunt Nettie and her dad."

"And what about Benjie?" asked Sarah.

Ally could lose custody. Officials could easily accuse her of being an unfit mother who let her disabled child play with matches. She'd seen it before in California. Losing him would be her worst nightmare. Especially this summer, when she had him nearby most of each day, she'd felt a fierce protectiveness she'd never known before.

"Just get well." Sarah gave Ally's hand another squeeze.

"Things have a way of sorting themselves out, and I'm confident Officer Kirkwood will check every inch of that cabin for clues." She handed Ally a water cup with a straw. "Get well as soon as you can so the upcoming conference attendees won't have to eat baked beans and hot dogs for dinner."

She and Sarah laughed at the idea of Will trying to handle institutional cooking, and then Ally faded as she lost the fight against the medication and fell asleep.

She had the strangest dream. She was still at her old house in California, sitting at the head of a table surrounded by firemen. She kept passing around pans of chicken enchiladas and refried beans, and the men kept making her run to the kitchen to get more hot sauce. Flying around and eating hot Mexican salsa made her, at one point, put her head in the freezer to cool off. Benjie and Kylie, oblivious to the guests, played croquet in the front yard. Her mother drove by and waved. "Have a Green Peace steering committee meeting," she yelled through the open window as she sped past.

Ally woke, her throat and head burning up. She pushed the help button, and a nurse scurried into her room. As she struggled to swallow a couple painkillers, her mother and father walked through the door.

"Oh my," she croaked.

"Oh my, yourself," said Dad.

After bending to kiss their daughter, her parents sat down in the two empty chairs. "We were so worried when Nettie called. We caught an early morning plane. We're sorry we couldn't get here until this afternoon." Her mother unbuttoned her suede jacket.

"It's afternoon already?"

"Tuesday afternoon." Dad shook his head. "Those pain meds must be kicking in pretty well." He leaned over Ally, and brushed back her auburn bangs tenderly. "You gave us an awful scare. How are the kids?"

"I think they came to visit, but now I think I dreamed it."

"Actually, they were here yesterday evening. We'll try to get them tonight after dinner. Nettie insisted on our staying at the house, but we thought it would be more convenient to stay right by the hospital," her mother informed her. "The kids are doing great. Benjie is flying around the house. I think he's overly excited about everything going on."

Any change, good or bad, would stir up Benjie. Ally wished she could just go home and be with her children. They needed her. But she'd be here a while. Each time she brushed her legs against the top sheet, she winced. Her legs throbbed and had started to blister. Most of the time, the nurse wanted her not to cover her limbs and let the air get to them.

Ironically, though, the fire prompted family togetherness. It brought her parents to Michigan.

She closed her eyes as her parents talked about the plans they had made with Bryan to take the kids to the beach and the miniature zoo in town. Mom also had a shopping trip planned with Kylie as soon as the doctor agreed. Ally listened as they recounted their anniversary cruise, and she pried her eyes open when Mom whipped out pictures for Ally to "ooh" and "ahh" over.

Then her parents stopped talking and exchanged an odd look. *What's going on that they aren't telling me?* Ally barely remembered any of the conversations she'd had in the last few days. What else had gone wrong? Oh, that's it, something about Benjie. But what? Hadn't he gotten help and saved them? She had a sick feeling in her gut.

Dad leaned over the bed and grabbed her hand with both of his. "You know they are still investigating the cause of the fire. They ruled out a faulty wiring system for the heater. They are now thinking the fire was either set by an arsonist, or—" Her father winced to keep back any emotions. "Or maybe the fire was an accident." He swallowed. "Honey, I might as well tell you. They think Benjie might have been playing with matches inside the cabin."

"No, no, no. That's impossible. There weren't any matches in that cabin."

"That's not what Sally, one of the board members, said. She told them how some staff members noticed Benjie had an abnormal interest in matches," Mom said. Ally hated how her mother's mouth set in a grim little line when she thought she was right. "Honestly, you know that kid loves fires."

"How could you even think that, Mom? I checked that cabin through and through before we settled in for the night. The cabin was clear of anything other than our duffel bags and pillows. I can't believe you'd think that."

"You have your hands full with that kid," her mother shot back.

Ally pulled herself up in bed, fighting the pain medication that had doped her up. Everything in her wanted to lash out. "Just what exactly are you inferring here about 'that kid'?"

"Dear, calm down. We know you are overwhelmed by life because of one child. You have so much talent and ability, and we hate to see you shortchange yourself."

Ally took a big breath. "I've had one of the most peaceful and interesting summers of my life. In spite of a divorce, losing a home and a job, I'm starting to clear my head, get some direction in my life, and here's the shocker: It might even include God. Yes, Mother, I'm turning into a right-wing holy-rolling Jesus Freak." She paused to catch her breath, and then pushed herself off of her pillows and leaned into her words. "And about Benjie—I want you to hear me loud and clear—Benjie didn't set the fire. I know you'd love to accuse him, Mom, but he didn't do it." Her entire body shook with fury and pain, and she collapsed on the mattress.

"Ally, you know we just want the best for you," said Dad. "We'll talk about this later. For right now, just rest. Look, we love Benjie and don't want to see him in trouble. Maybe he just needs a more structured environment than you can offer." He paused. "What if you and Kylie just came home and stayed with us—"

"You forget I have *two* children." Ally glared.

"We've been talking to the director of a wonderful new institution in the Bay Area. They are doing fabulous things with autistic children. It's a residential facility only about twenty minutes from our house," said her mother.

"Mom, you're more worried about saving the whales than your own grandson."

"Hush up, Linda, this isn't the time," Ally's father said.

"You've already tried Benjie and found him guilty in your Court of Perfect Children. Couldn't even wait until the Fire Inspector's report is finished," Ally said.

She reached over to rip out the IV tube attached to the top of her right hand, but a nurse had just walked in to check Ally's blood pressure, and grabbed her wrist.

"You'll both have to leave," she announced. "You're upsetting the patient." The nurse narrowed her eyes in a warning look.

Ally's mother got the message and gathered up her purse.

"We'll talk later," Dad said as they left.

Ally turned to face the wall.

CHAPTER
TWENTY-FOUR

Two days later, Fire Marshall Inspector Josh Kirkwood pulled his van up to the charred remains of Cabin 2. The bathroom still had a couple walls intact, and the shower and wash basin remained, but the rest had burned down to the foundation. The small pump that the camp owned didn't produce enough water pressure to put the fire out fast enough.

Josh and his men walked around the perimeter, overturning any stone or pile of debris they found. Then they sifted through ashes and the two duffel bags that had been rescued. Other than a burnt t-shirt that said *Lake Surrender Sizzles*, a couple of pillows, some bedding, and a melted plastic bag of Benjie's button collection, nothing else surfaced to alert the team to arson.

"Well, men, let's call it a day. Can't seem to find any evidence, but my gut still tells me it's arson," said Josh.

The men took the few items found in the cabin for further testing and carefully slid them into plastic bags. The three men were headed toward the truck when Conner, a rookie, glimpsed something. He turned on his heel and walked back to the demolished cabin. About five feet from the southeast corner, where the porch steps used to be, he bent down, and let a handful of scorched dirt sift through his fingers.

"Hand me a pair of tweezers, quick," he hollered to the two other guys.

He grabbed the instrument from his coworker. Gingerly, he dissected a pile of rubbish. In the middle of the pile lay two cigarette butts. He delicately moved partially-burned cardboard, holding his breath that it did not fall apart.

"Oldest trick in the book. Put a lighted cigarette into a matchbox. This brand of matches is pretty old-school, the kind my grandmother used to light her gas stove when the pilot light went out." Conner grinned. "Ohio Blue Tip."

"Jackpot! The rookie scores." The fire chief exchanged a fist bump with the young man. "Now we've got the beginnings of a case. Good job, Conner."

*   *   *

Four o'clock on the last Friday of September, Aunt Nettie poured coffee for the fire chief as Ally, just home from the hospital, sat on the porch sofa, wrapped in one of her aunt's crocheted afghans. The late afternoon sun streamed in through the screen on the porch but gave little warmth. Sweater weather had arrived. Benjie settled into his mother's lap.

"Now, you need to use your best behavior for Inspector Josh. He wants to ask you some questions. You be a big boy and help the nice fireman, just like you helped us the night of the fire."

Did she see a flicker of understanding in Benjie's eyes?

She nodded to Josh. "Go ahead with the questioning."

Josh pulled out a kid's plastic fire helmet, and put it on the table. Benjie's eyes grew big and round. He loved hats.

"Benjie, we are so proud of you at the fire department. You helped rescue your mother and sister. We want to give you an official ride on our truck. Sound good?"

Benjie beamed as he focused his gaze on the prize.

"You could help your buddies at the fire department. You'd like that, wouldn't you?"

Benjie sat very still, listening.

"If you help us, we'll make you an honorary fireman."

Will, Nettie, Kylie, and Ally's parents stared at Benjie. Bryan, absent as usual, had returned to the West Coast for business after seeing Kylie and Ally would be okay. What Benjie did or didn't say might change their family forever. Ally glanced over at Kylie, who looked like she was holding her breath.

"Okay, Benjie, buddy, did you see anyone around your cabin on the night it burned down? You remember, the night you found Will and told him, stop, drop, and roll?"

"Sto, dwap—and wowol," Benjie repeated.

"Yes, you did that well. Who did you see around your cabin when you woke up that night?"

All waited for some clue from Benjie.

"Mama wants you to help the fireman," Ally said. "We need to catch the bad guy. I know you can help Inspector Josh." Ally took Benjie's hand and rubbed it softly in hers.

After a few moments of silence, Will whispered something to Josh. Josh nodded.

"Benjie, what's my license plate number?" He leaned toward the boy, smiling.

Benjie's lips turned up at this game. " JRR182."

Will gave Benjie a thumbs-up. "That's right! Can you remember the license plate of the man who started the fire with the box of matches?"

"JRK666," Benjie blurted, "brrrrrrrrrrrrirp."

"That's one of his car motor sounds," said Kylie. "He has five."

"Why five?" asked Josh.

"Well, one for a sports car, one for a truck, one for an SUV, one for a motorcycle, and he loves to make one for cars that lose that thing—what do you call that, Mom?"

"A muffler. Cars that have lost their mufflers."

Josh wrote it down. "Thanks, buddy." He put the firefighter's helmet on Benjie's head. "I've got to run this license plate number. I'll let you know when I have something."

"Let's keep our fingers crossed," said Ally's mother.

"It's a done deal," Ally answered her, a little too quickly.

* * *

"I think we've got a lead in the camp arson case," Josh announced as he walked into the police chief's office.

Chief Reynolds turned around in his chair, a Dr Pepper in one hand and a bag of tortilla chips in the other—his usual mid-afternoon snack. "Hey, you just caught me on my coffee break, but shoot."

"I'm just like the Canadian Mounties—I won't sleep until I get my man."

Two minutes later, they pulled up a name to match the license plate, a local man. Josh dialed his boss at the firehouse to report the news.

Next stop on his search was the local Midas muffler shop. After waiting about six minutes, Josh hollered out, "Hey, anyone here?"

A short little man about forty emerged from the garage. "Waddaya want?"

"Information. I'm from the arson unit in Lake Surrender, and we're doing an investigation. I need your records for the last week to see if any of your customers had a muffler job done." He handed the service manager his card and told him to email him any information.

Granny's Olde Tyme Shoppe was next on his list. The store boasted selling things of a bygone era. Josh pushed open the front door with the tingly bell and walked past old potbellied stoves, canning equipment, and hand-crank ice-cream makers.

Josh walked up to the counter. "Blue Tip Ohio Matches?"

he asked an elderly woman who looked like Granny and was quite hard of hearing.

"You tip? No, you don't need to tip here." She looked confused.

Josh smiled politely, and then walked the aisles until he found what he was looking for.

"Anyone been in here recently to buy some of these?" He waved the box of matches in front of her.

"Bison? No, we only have elk and deer meat here. We keep it in the freezer."

Josh sighed. Very slowly, he tried again, raising his voice. "Have you sold these recently?"

"Oh, my dear, yes. A gentleman came in here about a week ago, and said he needed eight boxes. He said he was going camping."

She gave him a description.

Thank you, Granny. We might make you an honorary fireman, too.

*   *   *

"Thought you might want something unhealthy for a change." Will thrust the bag of donuts at Aunt Nettie as she opened her screen door.

"Nothing like sugar and grease to heal a body." She laughed, and waved her hand toward the sofa where Ally lay, watching an old Tom Hanks movie.

"Hey."

"Hay is for horses," Ally answered. "I was just craving one of those chocolate-glazed numbers. Where's Sarah? I wanted to see her."

Will took a seat on the sofa. "She and her mother went away to Saugatuck for the weekend," he answered, looking out the window at Kylie and Benjie playing Candy Land on the picnic table.

After catching up on what was going on with this week's conference with the Michigan School Board Association, Ally asked Will more about the wedding. "You'll be leaving the camp?"

Will poured a cup of coffee. "Staying here."

"I thought you were going to be working at that orphanage in Mexico?"

"Plans change." Will looked at Ally, but she knew he wasn't seeing her. In an instant she got it.

"I'm sorry, Will. When did it happen?"

He examined the dirt under his thumbnail, and then rubbed his hands on the side of his jeans. "Week ago."

"I'm sorry. Really."

Will put down his coffee mug and winced. In spite of herself, she charged ahead. "What happened?"

"I finally realized her heart was back in Mexico, and it always would be. We're still friends but she felt called to be in Mexico." He pinched his eyes together. "I feel foolish." He stood. "Look, I'm waiting to hear the results of Josh's investigation, so I'd better get back to camp. Let me know when you hear anything."

He left. Her burns couldn't hurt as much as his heart did at that moment. She said a little prayer for him. *Some women are just clueless.*

*   *   *

Hal Schwindleman seemed edgy on Thursday morning. He'd just shown a beautiful five-bedroom house out in Elk Rapids to a couple from Ann Arbor who were looking for a summer home for their extended family. They seemed like good prospects, and had cash to plunk down, a pipe dream in this economy.

But at the office, three cups of coffee and two Danish rolls later, his jitters increased. He phoned his golfing buddy, Charlie, to set up a golf date that afternoon. He sorted the mail and checked his email for a message from Johnson in Detroit. Nothing yet. Johnson had better come through. Hal had put his neck on the line, big-time.

He clicked out of his email as the front door opened. Hal looked up to see the county sheriff and two deputies in front of him.

"We're looking for a Hal Schwindleman. Would you know where we could find him?

"Who's looking, and why?"

"He's wanted for questioning in an investigation."

"Hold on a minute, and I'll see if I can get him." Hal's hand trembled as he pushed away from his desk "Hey, Nancy, have you seen Hal?" he yelled as he headed through the doors that lead to the back office.

He kept going 'til he hit the back door of the building, and then sprinted to his Ford Taurus. He looked out of the rearview mirror. All clear. Within thirty seconds, he had peeled out of the parking lot, headed for the highway.

A flashing red light appeared behind him, and the squad car followed him into Traverse City. After a backroads chase and near-collision with a combine, the police finally pulled him over. Hal's face dripped with sweat.

"We're taking you downtown for some questioning. Yeah, just like in the movies," said the sheriff. Hal slid into the back seat. He could kiss Boca Raton goodbye.

*   *   *

Josh grinned. "It just came in on the police frequency. They've got Hal down at the station for questioning. He denies even being in the area the night of the fire, but guess which license plate number he has?"

"Yes! Can't wait to call Ally." Will dialed the phone and relayed the message, getting a shriek of joy from the other end of the phone line. Ally put Benjie on the line. "You're a hero, buddy!" Will smiled. "You're a hero, someone who is brave and has helped someone else."

Ally spoke on the line again. "Whatever you said, it put the silliest grin on his face."

Same here.

"So"—she hesitated as if gathering her thoughts or her courage—"what's the story?"

"Evidently, Hal had been working behind the scenes for a Detroit land developer," Will explained. "The company, T. S. & C., had their eye on the plot of land adjacent to the camp. They planned to build a large five-story hotel on the land, even though they had publicly announced plans for only a few modest cabins on the lake. Everything moved along smoothly as long as I and the board okayed the purchase. They knew the camp had financial struggles this year, and they increased their offer on the land until it was irresistible. Only one problem—the camp decided not to sell to them, but to Don's club. Suddenly the project had to be shelved, and T. S. & C. Development wasn't too happy. They tried scare tactics. Remember the near-explosion of the water heater? The board almost caved, but in the end said no to the offer."

Will sucked in a short breath before continuing on. "This Grand Rapids-Detroit group wasn't used to not getting their own way. One of the big shots started coming over to this side of the state, and made Hal's life miserable. They put pressure on him to get the deal done. Finally, he agreed to start a fire after the summer session had ended. He left the cigarettes in the matchbox. He thought the camp would only sustain a small structural damage, and the investment group thought that by the time the camp had to do the repairs, we'd be bankrupt and have to accept their offer. But then you and the kids decided to have one last sleep-over."

Ally let out a slow, shaky breath.

"The county prosecutor has Hal up on attempted manslaughter charges."

Nettie's voice came over the line; she must have picked up an extension. "I never liked that Hal. He always seemed to be about himself. What a slime bag."

Will chuckled, hearing Benjie yelling, "Slime bag, slime bag, slime bag."

"You tell 'em," hollered Aunt Nettie. "Good judge of character."

*   *   *

The late October sun with its diluted strength filtered through the camp's kitchen window. Outside, a sprightly breeze danced more leaves to their death.

Ally, scooping cookie dough onto a baking sheet for a Chamber of Commerce luncheon, felt a shadow over her. She looked up. Stew stood in front of her. She examined the scrawny cook who had decided to come back to work after missing in action for two weeks. "What planet did you drop from?"

"Hey, that's no way to greet an old co-worker. I just had some business to attend to in Texas. Will has a short memory. I notified him at the beginning of the summer that I'd be gone for several weeks." He ran his hands through the few strands of hair he had left, and then flashed a fiendish grin. "Can't believe you lasted the entire summer."

Ally remembered how much she couldn't stand that mocking, patronizing smirk. She narrowed her eyes and planted her forefinger in the middle of his chest. "Did you tell him you would take the camp recipes with you when you went?" she hissed. *I sound braver than I feel.*

He pushed her away. "Sounds like you did alright for yourself, missy. I heard you made some legendary brownies they're still talking about." Throwing back his head, he guffawed, slapping himself on the knee.

"Well, *I'm* still talking about them." Will lounged in the doorway, hands in his back pockets. His eyes flashed anger. "I want your recipe before you leave town again."

Stew's eyes narrowed, but he kept on with his banter. "Hey, I'm not the pastry chef. Talk to the little gal here."

Will strode across the kitchen in two seconds flat. He grabbed Stew's shirt collar. "You're a sorry excuse for a cook, let alone a human being. I know you put the Milk of Magnesia in those brownies." His grip tightened on Stew's shirt, and Ally saw a dark look slither across the other man's face. Will loosened his grip, and Stew staggered.

"Not saying I did, not saying I didn't. But you're just standing up for that girlfriend of yours. Guess by now you got two women on the string."

As in slow motion, Ally watched Stew slide his hand into his jeans pocket. He retrieved a pocket knife that he flipped open with his right hand.

"Watch out!" she screamed, but not before the knife

nicked Will on the left side of his face, leaving a three-inch gash. The cut grew wider as the blood oozed out and dripped down Will's neck.

The cookie dough spoons in her hand clattered to the floor as she darted toward the two men. She came alongside Stew and kicked his shinbone. He winced and held his leg, dropping the knife.

Will took a step and punched Stew. The man fell with a dull thud, his pack of Camel cigarettes skidding across the linoleum. Will knelt down on Stew's back and pinned his arms down while Ally fumbled in her apron pocket for her cell phone. She dialed the police.

"I've got your back!" Don raced into the kitchen with a shout. He joined Will in keeping Stew flat on the floor, immobile. He cursed and bleated like a baby goat, but he stayed put.

"Don't you dare move," Don growled in his ear with the authority of a seasoned law professional. Stew started to raise his head, but Don slapped it back down.

Ally looked out through the dining room window. Two Lake Surrender cops pulled up, sirens ablaze. She stepped aside as the armed officers barged into the kitchen.

"Nice job," one said, nodding to Don and Will. They pulled out a notebook and asked Will, Ally and Don some questions about the incident.

As the police led Stew away, he shouted at Ally, "You took away my job, you stuck-up Californian. I'm not finished with you yet."

"Well we're finished with you," Don shot back, following Stew outside as the cops took him away.

Will slumped into a chair. Ally grabbed a kitchen towel and dabbed at the wound. Will had turned two shades of pale under his summer tan.

She walked over to the shelf above the stove and grabbed the dark blue metal first aid kit. Kneeling down by the chair, she wiped the cut clean with antiseptic. She tried to steady her hands, but they shook as she held the gauze against his chin and put tape over it.

"There, you're going to live." She grabbed his arm, and didn't let go. "Thank You, Lord," she said under her breath.

Will opened one eye. "Did I hear you say what I think you said?" he whispered before grimacing from the pain.

"You mean the part about 'you're going to live'?"

"That's not the part I'm talking about."

Ally felt her eyes crinkle as she smiled. "I guess camp has been rubbing off on me. Don't tell my parents."

She lowered her head, and then looked into Will's dark eyes. An electrical charge shot through her body, and she felt a tender longing she'd not felt for months. *Where did that come from?* "I guess I need your friendship more than I realized. It's been a humbling year." Ally realized she still had her hand on his arm, and pulled away. "Oh, sorry. I'm used to calming Benjie when he's upset."

"Don't stop, that's just what I need. Mmmm." He closed his eyes.

"Did you have any inclination Stew could be violent?"

Will shook his head, and let out his breath slowly. "Never saw that coming."

"Don't think you'll need stitches. Did I say you gave me an awful scare? The kids need you around a little longer."

A gentle questioning look passed over his face. Will opened his mouth and then shut it.

"What?" asked Ally.

Will paused. "And do you?"

"Do I what?"

"Need me around?"

"More than I realized." Ally squeezed his shoulder. "Say, you flirting with me?"

"Fishing for possibilities."

"Possibilities?"

Suddenly she felt like the air had just been sucked out of the room. What was he asking her? It wasn't just a casual silly question.

Ever so gently, and careful to avoid the injury, she planted a tentative kiss on his bleeding cheek. "That's to make it better."

*　　*　　*

Another rejection letter. Well, at least I won't be holding my breath for another possible opening. She picked up the letter and put it in the trash can when something occurred to her. *Do I want to go back into the publishing industry?* The pressure and stress to produce. A nice easy job so she could spend more time with Benjie doing his therapy and help Kylie make a smooth transition into her teens sounded more appealing. *Man, have I changed.*

She could see a difference this summer, taking short breaks from cooking to work with her son. Aunt Nettie had worked wonders with him, too. He'd stopped his spinning in circles except for rare occasions, and Aunt Nettie had gotten him to look people in the eye more. He was using new vocabulary words. Between Nettie's patience and Kylie's enthusiasm, he had added twenty-six new words to his speech this summer. Even the professionals back in the Bay Area couldn't have done that.

In her life before camp, Ally could barely get home from work and fix dinner by 6:30. Maybe—no, she had to be honest. She hadn't left a lot of extra time for Bryan. It pained her to be that truthful, but she knew she had let her job absorb most of her waking day. She had blamed a lot of their marriage failure on Bryan's not accepting Benjie's disabilities. But, with the perspective of the last eighteen months, she saw things she'd previously avoided. Could they have ever made the marriage work?

She wanted to just move forward and get Benjie the most help she could, even if she had to stay with Aunt Nettie the rest of her life. Being back in Michigan had given her a single focus: to be the best parent she could to both her children.

"Jesus, if You're the God of second chances, please let

me have another to be the mother I need to be. I'm sorry my priorities got so out of whack." Ally wiped a tear from the corner of her eye. "I ignored You, and now I see what an emptiness I had in my life. Please take my fumbling, awkward prayer and make it into a heart steady for you. Take my life and make it count."

CHAPTER
TWENTY-FIVE

Gene Nilsen, mayor of Lake Surrender, proclaimed the Festival, November 1st, Benjie Cervantes Day. Ally dressed him, Kylie, and herself as scarecrows for Lake Surrender's float in the annual parade. Aunt Nettie came as a farmer, Will as a wood chopper, and Don joined a few other Native Americans in their traditional costumes.

Ally and Kylie sat at the front of the float, with Benjie sitting in his sister's lap. Will, Don, and Betty and her husband sat behind them on the hay-filled bottom of the float. Ally watched her son mesmerized by the crowd. She looked for any signs of fear, but he seemed to be eating up the applause and shouts of "There's Benjie, he's our boy!" He wore a big firefighter hat on top of his scarecrow costume. Around his neck he sported a long chain with a large key, *Town of Lake Surrender* imprinted on it.

Behind them, the Lake Surrender High School Honor Band played *Shine On, Harvest Moon*, and behind them the Garden Club followed with a float made entirely from orange and yellow chrysanthemums. The local bakery's float looked like a large frosted pumpkin cake, and the owner passed out free pumpkin cookies.

Don and his Dads Club's float had replicated a pond growing rice. Next to it, a Native American woman stirred a pot of cooked rice. On the side was a banner reading "Celebrate the Lake Surrender Youth Planting Project. Donations accepted!" Don beamed as he waved, and pretended to harvest rice from the pond. The club planned to start their project next spring.

All civic organizations and local businesses had a float in the parade. The one obvious omission this year was Lakeshore Realty. Because of the arson investigation, the management decided to be low-key and avoid any publicity. Hal Schwindleman's name had been dragged through the front pages of the *Traverse City Eagle Record* enough times for him to become a poster boy for criminal real estate dealings. Hal, cooling his heels in the county clink, was enjoying jailhouse food while he awaited his trial. The Wayne County sheriff in Detroit chased leads on the shaky investment company. Hal kept mum about his involvement.

Aunt Nettie leaned over to Ally, and whispered, "I'm so glad you're here. Lake Surrender got a whole lot better when you moved here." She squeezed Ally's hand.

A couple of neighbor kids held a banner—"Benjie's Our Hero"—and they cheered when the float went by. Ally's heart swelled with pride. *I'm so proud of my boy.*

Ally turned around and tapped Will on the shoulder. He'd been pretty quiet during the parade. "You okay?" she asked.

He nodded grimly, but looked straight ahead. "Tell you later."

Aunt Nettie changed seats with Kylie so she could be on the side of the road where she could see her friends from school. A whoop and a holler made Kylie jump up and down as she saw her class, twenty-five kids, waving little flags.

The parade ended at the high school parking lot. The driver, Packey, parked right next to the Rotary Chili Cook-Off booth, where half the town stood lined up for the prize-winning Vic's Venison Chili.

"Come on!" Kylie grabbed Benjie's hand, and the siblings hopped off of the float and headed for the corn dog booth, but not before begging for a few dollars from Ally.

"I'll meet you there in five minutes. You hang onto your brother."

She sat still on the truck bed float, keeping her hands under the hay for warmth as she watched the kids run off.

"Well, it's the end of the line." Will was the only other one left on the float but, instead of climbing down, he slid his hand underneath the hay and touched hers. "Sorry, looking for my cell phone."

He pocketed it and stood, extending his hand to help her up. In spite of herself, Ally felt a spark of pleasure. "Think you can take an hour or two off?" he asked in a quiet voice. "Can Nettie take the kids home?"

"Um, yeah," she answered, not sure of what he wanted.

After making arrangements for the kids to get home, Ally and Will found his Suburban. He opened her door and helped her up the step, and then got in on the driver side to start the engine. Ally saw they were headed out east of town.

"Looks like you're heading toward your house. Did you finally move in?" Why was she chattering like a magpie? *Calm down.*

"You'll see."

The tires crunched over the gravel road. Finally, he pulled into the driveway of the grey stone cottage.

"I want to show you something." He grabbed her hand and pulled her running through the front gate and around the side of the house 'til they arrived in the backyard.

What on earth?

They stopped in front of a thirty-foot oak tree, its branches spread low and wide. The trunk had a ladder with ten steps that led up to a platform with a three-foot wall around it and a gradual-sloping tin roof over the top.

"A tree house!" Ally exclaimed. She stepped on the first step to test her weight, then scrambled up to the top landing.

Will followed her. They sat for several minutes on the large pine wood platform, swinging their feet and enjoying the last moments of sunshine before the sun turned in for the day.

"Looks like you missed a pile." Ally pointed down at the wind-whipped pile of maple leaves that had been raked and left to scatter again.

"Kind of a lonely time of year," he finally remarked. "Good time to reflect."

Ally still didn't know where he was going with this.

"I'll say," she said.

He seemed to be in another world. Finally, Ally ventured, "You didn't ask me up here for tea—"

He turned to look at her. "Ally, thanks for being my friend. I need that right now." He looked at her with shining eyes, the kindest eyes she'd ever seen. "I've learned a lot from you this summer, how to be gracious under pressure."

"No, you were the one who helped me through the hardest time of my life, and didn't ask anything in return except cooking a zillion camp dinners."

Will chuckled. "We had quite a summer—maybe my best."

"Even with the turmoil at camp?"

He lowered his gaze. "There's always turmoil—that's just life. No, what made it one of the best summers of my life was getting to know you. It hit me a few days ago. I've never known anyone gutsier or braver than you. You jumped into a job, and in a few weeks acted like you'd done it for years. But more than that, I am grateful to God for our friendship. I only wish one thing."

Ally looked up at him, and couldn't look away.

"I wish that I had become your friend years ago, when we met and played together. I remember looking at you and thinking, I like that girl, she has something to her."

Ally shivered as the wind kicked up. "The feeling's mutual. I really needed a friend this year."

Will locked his hands together and stretched them above his head. "I guess I feel kinda foolish about Sarah."

"You're talking to the queen of foolishness."

"She'd been in my life for so long, I guess I just thought—"

Ally kicked the side of his boot. "Can't fault you for trying. Sometimes you're just not feeling it."

"Huh?" He kicked her back.

"The spark." Ally snapped her fingers, and he laughed. She pointed over to the house. "But you got a house out of it."

They both sat breathing in the quiet beauty of the backyard trimmed out in brilliant colors. A dozen geese flew overhead, heading for warmer parts.

He nodded, and ran his hands through his hair. "Could live here forever."

Ally poked him in the ribs. "I can see you as a wobbly old man with a gray beard and a cane, chopping wood out back and keeling over from a heart attack."

"Not a bad way to go." He tweaked her ponytail like he had in third grade. "Think you'll stay a while in Lake Surrender?"

"Can't get rid of me yet. Feel like I'm starting to figure out this God thing. For the first time in my life, I'm focusing on something besides Ally Cervantes."

"How's that going?"

"Hard. I hate to admit it, but I didn't try as hard as I could have in my marriage. But there's something even harder that bothers me. I've never told anyone this."

Will raised his eyebrows.

Ally looked up at him and then down at the chipped nail polish on her thumbnail. "I always felt guilty about Benjie. I wondered if he came out the way he did because of something I did." She paused as she watched a squirrel zip up a tree to hide more wintertime nuts in his storehouse.

"I'm listening."

Ally swallowed hard. "I think about something. He had a lot of shots given to him, bunched together when he was an infant. Lots more than Kylie had."

"Ally, quit beating yourself up. You don't know what caused his autism. But no matter what happened in the past, it's gone."

"Just gone?"

"Gone."

Ally blinked away a tear as she reached over to give his arm a squeeze. "Thanks."

Will turned to her. "Sometimes it's hard to receive forgiveness. But it's there for the taking."

"Guess I need to start taking."

* * *

CHAPTER
TWENTY-SIX

She slipped the sixth turtle cheesecake into the oven in preparation for the weekend Christmas open house, set the timer for fifty minutes, and then sat on a stool, the camp tabby cat swishing by her feet. She reached out to pet the animal, but he fled down the hall in heavy pursuit of some mouse pie. It was now so quiet, she could barely remember the constant activity almost four months ago. Did she actually cook meals for two hundred campers the whole summer? She could almost hear the roar of the campers waiting for meals, and the singular voice with which they sang grace. It seemed eons ago.

Now she could look out on the back porch and see nothing but a light snowfall, like a milky glaze over the floor, the light from the roof shining on it as millions of tiny snowflakes twinkled in an attempt to show off their beauty. It was like they wanted to be on stage. Funny how different a place looks in winter.

She buttoned up her cardigan sweater; her inner

thermometer still hadn't adjusted to the cold. Nevertheless, the snow enchanted her.

Abruptly her cell phone interrupted the serenity.

"Hey, Bryan, long time no hear," she replied in a monotone, fiddling with the spatula on the counter. "Suppose you have a great weather report from California."

Though Kylie kept her informed, Ally hardly heard from Bryan. He'd been trying harder with the kids since the fire.

"Sunny and warm."

Ally looked absently around the kitchen for any dishes she'd missed washing. She grabbed a couple of measuring cups and tossed them into the soapy dishwater.

"Well, there's been a reason I've been sort of bad about communicating. I've had some stuff to deal with." He paused. The phone sounded dead in Ally's ear.

"You still there?" she asked.

He mumbled something, and Ally caught a crack in his voice.

She put down the dishrag and jerked to attention. "What's wrong?"

"Give me a minute." Another long pause, and then he whispered something into the receiver.

"You been drinking?"

"Just hold on," he replied. "I forgot how impatient you are."

Ally held her hand over her mouth to hold back a snotty comment.

"Anyway I've just been to the doctor, and he told me why I've been having some intestinal pain."

"What did he say?"

"Actually it wasn't Dr. Kerner. I went to a specialist. An oncologist."

"What are you saying?" Ally's hand started to shake.

"I've been diagnosed with pancreatic cancer."

She gripped the stainless steel counter to keep her balance. "Are you positive?" she said softly as her throat went dry. A forgotten sense of tenderness arose from buried memories. "Can you get a second opinion?"

"I got the best care in the Bay Area. My uncle in Kansas knows the head of the oncology department at Stanford University. Looks like this is the bad kind of cancer—if any kind is good."

"How about chemotherapy?"

"Yes, could have it but I'm in Stage IV. It's the doctor's opinion it might not matter." He sighed.

"You're kidding."

"No, prognosis is a year or a few months."

Ally sucked in her breath. "What? No! How can that happen? You've been such a health-nut all your life."

"Looks like that didn't count for much." His voice lowered. "Wonder what does count anymore. Hold on—my doctor's beeping in."

Ally whispered a prayer.

"Sorry, have to go for another consultation. Ally, can you do me a favor?"

There was a strained vulnerability in his voice she hadn't heard for years. Where was that cockiness and self-assured manner? *Trials have a way of bringing one back to the basics.*

"Okay."

"Tell Kylie for me. It'll be better coming from you."

"Of course."

"One more thing—" He took a long breath. "I'm sorry about the way I handled myself this summer. I was wrong. I should have stood up for Benjie when they thought he started the fire."

"You made me mad, assuming our son—" Ally stopped short. Why was she starting the argument all over again? She knew better. "Just forget it. We were both stressed out."

"I do love Benjie, in my own way."

Ally looked at the snowdrift piling up against the back porch door. *Kind of like Bryan's life.* His life had always been a gentle powder snow that he could ski over without a hitch, always coming out ahead. But now those snowflakes settled into an icy snowdrift that wouldn't budge. She had the choice of pouring warm water over his heart, and at least melting some of the ice.

"Bryan, I forgive you." Ally paused to get rid of the tremor in her lips. She wanted to stop there, but something kept compelling her to continue. "And I forgive you for our breakup."

There, she said it. It was one of the hardest things ever to get past her vocal chords and out of her mouth.

"You do?"

Once she said it, she felt every muscle in her body relax. "I don't go around saying things I don't mean—you know that, Bryan." She swallowed. "To be honest—"

The radio pumped out *Angels We Have Heard on High*.

I could use an angel just about now.

"To be honest, I had a big part in the breakup too." Her heart pumped briskly as she waited to hear Bryan's reaction, but it was quiet on the other end of the call. "Bryan?"

"Yes, I'm here. Just taking in what you said."

"I've been thinking—I was sort of a workaholic, too. To be honest, I got home pretty late a lot of nights. And maybe I just expected you to jump in and be the perfect father to Benjie."

"Thanks, Ally." His voice faded away for a second. "You don't know how that's helped me."

"Or me." She grabbed a red-checked tea cloth from off the counter and wiped the corner of her eyes. A sense of compassion she hadn't experienced for Bryan for a long time deluged her heart, watering all the dry spots in her soul.

* * *

Kylie held Benjie on her lap, her face white with shock.

"Maybe they made a mistake." She hugged Benjie tighter, rocking her brother back and forth as Ally sat down next to them on the sofa in Aunt Nettie's living room. "Can't he go to another hospital? Maybe they mixed up the tests where he went."

Ally hit the remote control and turned off the television. Somehow *Celebrity Dancing* didn't seem important right now. "Kylie, sweetie, I know it's hard to believe. Your dad has always been so healthy."

"We need to pray for him. He probably doesn't know anyone who will pray for him."

That's probably true but—" Ally stopped when she caught a look at her daughter. Something was brewing in Kylie's mind.

"Who's going to take care of him? He lives by himself, and his relatives live in L.A."

"I know, but he'll probably hire a private nurse. He has great insurance that covers round-the-clock care." Ally reached out to grab her daughter's hand, but Kylie jerked it away.

"Mama!"

"What?

That's not what I'm talking about. Who's going to make him dinner, and read to him when he can't sleep? Who will see he takes his medicine?" Kylie's voice grew louder and higher. "He needs me, Mom."

"It's true he doesn't have relatives nearby, but he is planning on hiring a nurse. What are you getting at?"

"I want to go live with him, and take care of him. I could go back to my old school, and live with him. Come on, Mom—"

"That's crazy. You're too young."

Kylie put Benjie on the floor and stood. "I'm twelve. That's not a baby. I could ride the bus to school and then take it back to Dad's condo. Mom, he's the only dad I have." She folded her hands together as if praying.

My child, trying to be a mother.

"Kylie, that's sweet, but taking care of a cancer patient is a full-time job for an adult, let alone a twelve-year-old girl."

"Mom! He might only live a few months. You've got to let me spend time with my dad."

Ally sighed and drummed her fingers on the coffee table. "Well, maybe you could spend a week with him during Christmas break."

"A week. What good would a week do? In camp I learned to always ask what Jesus would do. Well"—Kylie canted one hip and crossed her arms—"what would He do?"

"You're being unreasonable."

"Am I, Mom? Or am I just trying to follow Jesus? Think about that."

"Think about what?" Ally tucked her hair behind her ears, wanting to control more than a few stray strands.

"If you've decided to follow Jesus like you told me, you need to forgive Dad. Otherwise you're just a phony."

Ally opened her mouth but snapped it shut as she eyed her daughter's crossed arms.

The room grew quiet, only interrupted by Aunt Nettie's cuckoo clock reminding them of the late hour. Midnight wasn't a good time to make big decisions.

*   *   *

The next day, the wind blew with razor-like cruelty as Ally and Benjie walked through the snowy nature path behind the camp lodge. With two days working on the food for the big weekend party, she needed to take a break and collect her thoughts. Her eyes stung from the ten degree wind that hunted her down, and every joint of her body ached with the insistent arctic blast that came down from Canada. How she longed for mild California winters where she barely needed a sweater to ward off the cooler temperatures.

As she tromped through a foot of new snow, images of Bryan flashed through her mind: pole vaulting in college, dumping her into the fountain near the college cafeteria, and taking her to a football game on their first date.

They'd been set up by another couple, and the four of them double-dated. What she remembered was Bryan's smile as he shared his dreams of making it big in the business world. When he dropped her off at her apartment that night, she felt a spark and knew she'd be seeing a lot of him. A year later, they were married.

They brought Kylie home from the hospital to their first little house near California Avenue in Palo Alto, and Ally remembered many late nights as they took turns soothing Kylie in an old yellow wicker rocking chair in the kitchen for the two o'clock feeding.

Other memories she tried to block, but they pushed to

the front of her mind: their trip to Europe; grilling parties on the patio with business associates and school friends; the late nights when Bryan came home after spending too much time at Mulligan's Pub after Benjie was diagnosed with autism. The angry words they flung at each other as he pulled away from the marriage.

Don't go there. Delete, delete, delete.

I saw him in a rosy haze, never seeing the real Bryan. I wonder who the real Bryan is. Will I ever know? All I know is he is scared right now.

Her boots crunched in the dry snow as she grabbed Benjie's mittened hand. He pointed to a tiny chickadee shivering on a branch, and waved to the bird.

Ally remembered hearing about how Judas had a place of honor at the Last Supper, even though he planned to betray Jesus. Well, hadn't Bryan betrayed her? Maybe, but didn't she betray him, too? Did they both betray their marriage by putting everything else first? Were they both a sort of Judas toward their marriage, going after the pieces of silver instead of real family life as they betrayed their own relationship?

Benjie reached out to break off an icicle from a tree and put it in his pocket.

Maybe Kylie is right—real forgiveness has feet and hands. But what does that mean with Bryan, Lord? How much do You require of me? Haven't I already forgiven?

But she knew the answer. The answer didn't live in logic or what was fair. It lay in a tender area where one moved beyond the lowland graveyard of bitterness to the icy mountaintop of praying for one's enemies. She saw how she had painted Bryan as the enemy. But, to be honest, she had not paid attention to her marriage.

"Forgive seventy times seven," Jesus said. Ally had made a commitment in the summer: she'd either completely disregard this Christian thing, or jump in and never look back.

She dialed Will's number. His voice resonated throughout the phone, and at once her hand stopped shaking.

"Got a minute?" she asked.

"Got all day for my favorite cook. What's up?"

Ally sighed contentedly. "You know you're good medicine for me?"

"Yep, just what the doctor ordered. But you sound funny. What's going on?"

"I want to run something by you, but I need to talk to you in person."

"Sounds kinda serious."

"Can you meet me at The Bookworm at eight tonight? I need to see you."

"Likewise. But what's going on?"

"We'll talk tonight," Ally whispered.

*　　*　　*

Ally watched Will step out of his Suburban parked on Main Street. *What would I do without you, Will Grainger?*

You're my rock. She waved.

"Missed seeing that red hair," he yelled as he jogged toward the curb.

"Thanks," she laughed. At least someone liked her hair color. Will opened the door, and Ally slipped inside. He followed, placing his hand on the small of her back. The gentle pressure guiding her toward the café gave her a warm glow. They found a corner table, and ordered two tall mugs of coffee.

Dressed as elves, bookstore associates wrapped packages and rang up sales. The main counter displayed a colorful collection of Christmas books, and the store smelled like some employee had sprayed a whole can of pine needle potpourri throughout the building.

Will grabbed a green-frosted Christmas tree cookie from a plate that the waitress had placed in the middle of the table. "Okay, shoot. What's up?" His deep brown eyes shone, as if he expected good news.

She looked down at a missed crumb on the table cloth. *Lord, give me the right words.*

She placed her mug on the table and nibbled on a lemon bar. "I have a theological question for you."

"Umm, maybe I'd better phone my old seminary professor."

"No, seriously, I need to know what it means to forgive someone."

"Forgive?"

"Yes, to truly forgive someone."

Will propped his chin in his right hand. "Hmmm. Allowing God to work in your heart and move beyond the problem—"

"I know that, but do you think God sometimes calls us to do something for that person, something we don't want to do?" Ally twirled the corner of her scarf until her finger turned red, the circulation cut. She untangled her finger from the scarf.

"Out with it. Is it something I said?"

"Of course not."

"Is this about Bryan?"

Ally picked up her spoon and stirred another packet of sugar into her coffee.

Will reached for the plastic container that held the sugar packets. "Now I know there's something wrong. You never put sugar in your coffee."

She continued to stir, the spoon clinking against the sides of the cup. "I've been thinking and praying a lot lately, especially for Bryan and this cancer thing." She looked down the aisle to the front of the store. Seeing Will's face right now might keep her from continuing. "I think I should ask Bryan to live with us. He needs someone to take care of him."

Will pulled his hand away from hers. "Why would you do that?"

"I'm trying to do the right thing."

"And you think that includes taking care of him?"

Ally held up her hands in defense. "I didn't pursue this idea, it pursued me. It's haunted met since Kylie begged me to let her go take care of him in California. Of course, I couldn't let her go, but I've been thinking—it could be the last Christmas the kids spend with their father. I've talked with Nettie, and she's fine with it. We'd rent a hospital bed, and clear out the small bedroom off of the living room. Bryan could be around the kids for the last few weeks of his life. Do you think I'm crazy for thinking about this?"

Will studied his empty coffee mug.

"Do you think it's a good idea?"

"Ally, I'm not the one to ask." He dug his thumb nail into the palm of his right hand and looked away.

"More coffee?" The waitress had sidled up to the table.

"No thanks," they both answered.

God, stop shooting arrows at my heart. She took a big gulp of air and continued. "I think I should do this."

"It's very unorthodox," said Will, looking straight into her eyes. "But so are you, Miss Ally."

"It will feel weird at first."

"You're telling me."

"Not to mention awkward."

` "Surely there's someone else to help him."

"I want him to know what I've learned this year."

"I understand." His eyebrows drew together in a frown, contrasted with the jolly Christmas carols playing on the overhead speaker. Did she detect a hint of jealousy pass across his face?

He stood up, check in hand to pay the cashier. "Do what you must."

*   *   *

The plane slid down the runway, landing safely only because of the veteran pilot's experience. Because of the ice storm, the flight came close to being cancelled. Fortunately, the weather warmed up just long enough to squeeze in another couple of flights to Traverse City before Christmas. Just like the landing, the drive to the airport had been a white-knuckle one.

Kylie and her friend, Krista, stood by the baggage claim, holding a sign: "Dad—Welcome to Michigan." Ally and Nettie watched the ramp as the passengers arrived.

Behind two college-aged boys hauling a couple of backpacks and snowboards, a dark-haired fifty-something woman pushed a wheelchair carrying what looked like a shriveled-up middle-aged man.

Ally sucked in her breath. Bryan!

He was only a remainder of the man she'd been married to, his body boney, his once-broad shoulders slumped forward. His face, bloated from the meds, hid his normally chiseled good looks.

Ally clenched her jaw for fear of blurting out something. *How could this be Bryan?*

"So good to see you, Bryan," said Nettie, and kissed him on the cheek. She handed his travel companion an envelope.

"Thank you. We'll take it from here."

"Where are those wonderful children of mine?" Bryan held out thin arms.

Kylie dropped the sign, and she and Benjie ran to him. Tears poured down his cheeks, but Ally saw no embarrassment. *You're not the same man.* "No sad, no sad," said Benjie, hopping up and down next to the wheelchair. Ally leaned over and gave a side hug to her ex-husband before grabbing the handles to push the chair.

"You look tired. We'll get you home."

He raised his eyebrows. "That sounds so funny. Home has always been California."

"Well, from now on, home is where your children are," she said, hoping she sounded cheerful as she steered the chair toward the exit.

Nettie and Kylie grabbed a couple of bags from the luggage conveyer and fell in line next to her.

*   *   *

Ally walked past Bryan's room and saw the door open. Will had volunteered to help in the evenings. He had just wheeled Bryan into his room to put him to bed for the night. Even with Bryan's weight loss, Ally still couldn't lift him, so Will came over each night to settle him in. In the bathroom he found a wash cloth, and brought it to Bryan to wipe his hands and face. After brushing his teeth, he handed Bryan a glass of water and his pain pill. Now she watched Will slide his arms under Bryan's boney frame and lift him into bed.

Humbled, grateful, she turned away and went to clean up the after-dinner mess.

* * *

"Why are you doing this?" asked Bryan, frowning.

"I do this for extra money in the winter to supplement my income," Will cracked. "The pay is great for nurses' aides."

"No, seriously."

"Seriously?" Will peered out the open bedroom door and saw Ally piling the plates from dinner to carry into the kitchen. He gestured toward her and then turned back to Bryan. "I've learned from her how to become the hands and feet of my Savior. She's quite a woman."

"I know. Realized it too late." Bryan winced. "Figuring out a lot of things I missed."

"Hey, we all screw up in life. It's being human."

Bryan pulled up the sheet around his neck and riveted his gaze on Will. "It's worse when it's your family. I wasn't there for them, especially Ally, when they needed me." He lowered his voice to a hoarse whisper. "It haunts me—choosing career over my family."

Will sat down on the bed next to Bryan and handed him a glass of water and a pain killer. "Your children love you a lot."

Bryan nodded.

*　　*　　*

"Another helping of trifle, Bryan?" Betty leaned over with a spoonful, ready to replenish his plate.

Bryan patted his stomach. "Thanks. Great food, but I don't have much of an appetite anymore. Better give that recipe to Ally and Nettie. This might be the best Christmas dinner I've had yet."

"Sweet-talking will get you everything, Bryan."

Nettie looked up from making coffee in the kitchen. The soft rumble of the dishwasher assured everyone had their fill of holiday goodies complete with ham, scalloped potatoes, orange sweet potato casserole, and green beans. The dessert menu included English trifle along with blueberry and pecan pies.

"Presents, everyone, forget the dishes." Kylie stood on one foot and then the other.

"Presents, yes," said Benjie in his mother's lap.

Will joined Ally on the loveseat, Bryan next to her in a wheelchair.

The next hour they spent undoing wrapping paper and oohing and ahhing over each gift. Ally received a new winter coat from Will and a scrapbook of family photos from Bryan. Kylie piled up her new collection of CDs along with jeans, a couple of tops and a tiny pearl necklace from her father. Benjie's gift was a photo of a trampoline Bryan had ordered in time to be installed next spring. With Ally's bank account meager, she had taken up knitting, and everyone in the room received a hand-knitted scarf.

"Ally, this scarf is gorgeous," commented Betty, admiring the variegated green and blue yarn. Ally chuckled to herself. Little did anyone know how many times she had to rip out rows and start all over. Knitting had become a practice in patience.

After watching A Christmas Story together, Betty and her husband gathered up their presents and left. Ally took Kylie to her best friend's house for a while, and drove to the store for coffee and milk while Nettie settled Benjie for the night.

As Ally came through the back door from the garage to the kitchen, she heard the two men talking. Something told her not to interrupt them, but the old curiosity bug got the best of her, so she sat silently on a stool in the darkened kitchen.

"Nice fire, Boy Scout," she heard Bryan say to Will.

"You betcha. I'm the best in this area."

"Kind of wish I'd been more outdoorsy in my life. Too late now."

She heard Will get up and put another log on the fire. Thud. "From what I've heard you've had a pretty cool life. Self-made businessman in the Silicon Valley, and a scratch golfer to boot."

"Not too important any more. Funny how things come into focus when you're counting out your days. Wonder who will care about what I achieved when I'm gone. Seems to me it's more about people than success."

"If you've figured that out, you're way ahead of the game."

The fire crackled and then let off a big pop.

Bryan cleared his throat. "And, while we're alone, I want to say thanks for the friendship. I don't know what motivates you to help me—I mean coming over here every night—but whatever it is, you're a better man than me."

Ally strained to hear Will's answer, but only heard the tick-tock of the cat clock in the kitchen.

"Not at all. I've enjoyed getting to know you, Bryan. You're a pretty cool guy."

"You're easy to talk to. I don't usually tell people much about what I'm thinking but I sort of need to unload."

"Shoot."

"It's a guilt thing. I'm really feeling crummy about this divorce and not being able to provide much for the kids and Ally this last year. It's kinda eating me up. Do you understand?"

Ally imagined Will nodded, but she didn't hear an answer.

"I feel so guilty."

She drew her breath in. *I never knew he felt that.* She leaned her body sideways on the stool so her head would be in the opening from the family room to the kitchen and she'd get a better listen.

The kitchen door to the garage flew open, and her daughter flipped on the light. "Hi, Mom, got a ride home from Mackenzie's mom. Hey, why are you sitting here in the dark?"

*   *   *

Will called Ally. "Wear something nice, it's New Year's Eve."

She was just going out to eat with him, but something in his tone made her insides dance.

After she settled Bryan and the kids down for the night, Ally ran to her closet and found a deep forest green silk strapless dress she had worn to a friend's elegant wedding in San Francisco a few years ago. It still fit, even after all the cooking and tasting she'd done in the last few months working as the camp caterer. She dug through her closet for the matching heels. In a top drawer she found a crystal necklace with matching drop earrings. Would this be too overdressed for Traverse City? She decided she didn't care; she wanted to do glamorous for a change.

Will showed up in dress slacks, tie, and a sweater. "Holy moley, is this the woman who cranks out dozens of flapjacks for two hundred campers at six-thirty in the morning?" He held open the car door. "You clean up nice."

"Thanks."

At Marco's Restaurant, they were seated in a corner booth, and the hostess lit the small candle in the center of the table.

"Guess I'm a little overdressed for Traverse," she said.

"I'm not complaining. Seriously, you really look great tonight."

Ally took the compliment in and savored it. She couldn't remember the last time a man had given her one.

She tilted her head to the side. "Aren't you going to order?"

Will had been eyeing her and didn't even hear the waitress ask a question.

He glanced down at the menu—"Antipasto and guacamole. *Err*, I mean toasted raviolis"—and resumed staring at her.

"Are you okay, William?"

He didn't answer. Instead he fumbled around and found her hand under the table. "There, now I can concentrate. Guess I've never seen you in a dress. You do have legs."

"And arms and fingers. Yes, I'm normal."

"Wouldn't call you normal in that dress."

He tore off a piece of bread from the loaf and gently fed her a piece. It might have been the best piece of bread she'd ever eaten.

They ate in silence, enjoying the Chicken Marsala. When Will had finished the last piece, he put down his knife and fork.

"You're looking so beautiful tonight. It's going to make what I have to say that much harder." He took both her hands in his. "I need to ask you something."

Ally shivered in anticipation of his words. "I'm all ears, my friend."

"I want your opinion on something. I just got a call from Sarah."

"Didn't think you and she still talked."

"Not much. She called over the holidays to wish me a Merry Christmas. Anyway, while she was on the phone, she mentioned the orphanage, Casa Familia, has been wanting to start a camp. She had volunteered me because of my experience." His grip on her fingers tightened. "I care a lot for you and for your opinion, so I wanted to run the idea by you."

Ally looked down at her empty plate. "When would this be?"

"As soon as possible. They want to get a small camp up and running for summer." He continued to outline some of the things he'd be doing, and then he stopped.

"And you want to know what I think."

"Hey, Al, you know I care about what you think. I love the idea of a camp, but I hate to leave Bryan and mainly you. I've come to depend a lot on your opinion."

Ally mulled his words around in her head. *But why now, when I need your friendship? How am I going to take care of Bryan by myself?*

But, even as she thought that, she knew the right answer. "It matters more what God would have you do. We answer to Him first. If I've learned anything from you this year, I've learned that lesson." She gently removed one hand from his grasp and placed it over his. "When would you leave?"

"In about ten days. Ally, I'm torn. I've become very attached to that red hair."

*   *   *

Will put his arm around Ally and walked her to the front door. Under the roof of the front porch, safe from some of the flurry of the New Year's snowflakes, he took her muffler and wrapped it gingerly around her neck to keep out the cold.

"I've never met anyone like you, Ally." His fingertips, ever so gently, traced her eyebrows and down the curve of her nose, and lingered when they reached her lips. "You know I'm going to kiss you, don't you?"

Ally saw his eyes crinkle, and her heart sped up. "You know I'm going to kiss you back."

He leaned closer to her, and she caught a whiff of his lime shaving lotion. His head tilted toward her, and his lips pressed gently against hers. Her shoulders relaxed.

"I come with a lot of baggage," she whispered in his ear.

"Don't we all."

CHAPTER
TWENTY-SEVEN

The heavy snows of mid-January blew in right on time, blanketing Lake Surrender with two feet of the white stuff. Any romantic novelty of the winter wonderland had ended when Ally drove the icy streets and stayed home during snow days for Kylie and Benjie.

Irritated and feeling cooped up in the house, Ally drove to the grocery store to grab some ingredients for a mocha cake she'd been eyeing in a women's magazine. She returned, mixed the ingredients, and slid the cake into the oven. Nothing could cheer her up. Tonight was the last night she'd see Will for a long time.

He knocked on the front door, and Ally raced to open it.

"Got your passport?"

Will patted his shirt pocket. "Where are the kids?'

"Kylie, Benjie, Will is here."

They came flying down the stairs and almost knocked Will over.

"Adios mi amigo, Vaya con Dios," Kylie blurted out.

"That's all I know in Spanish. It means 'goodbye my friend, go with God'."

Ally turned toward her daughter. "You learned that just for Will?"

Kylie beamed.

Bryan, sitting on the sofa, turned his head. "Can't believe you're going away."

"Not to worry, I've lined up a couple of guys to help you. They're great."

"But they're not you," Kylie lamented, trying to be a grownup by holding in her tears.

"You know I'll be back before summer, silly." Will patted her shoulder, but his gaze didn't stray from Ally's face.

Everyone talked small-talk, not wanting to deal with goodbyes. Finally Bryan asked if Will could lift him and put him to bed, and asked Ally to get him an extra pillow upstairs.

Ally headed downstairs with the pillow, and started to walk in the family room but stopped.

"Man to man, I'm facing something scary and not prepared. I'm just going to cut to the chase. I'm afraid I've missed something in life and now I'm facing death."

"Well, don't miss this." Will slid his thumb and finger into his shirt pocket and extracted something metallic. "I've been saving it for you." He placed it into Bryan's limp hand, then pressed Bryan's fingers shut around it.

The man brought the cross up to his face and scrutinized the necklace. "I've always thought that's a crutch for weak people." He fingered every inch of the cross. "Anyway, I can't, it's too late."

"It's never too late," said Will.

Bryan turned his head toward the wall, and then looked back at him. "I want whatever Ally and you have. I know it's for real."

*　　*　　*

On high doses of morphine to lessen the pain, Bryan drifted in and out of coherency the next few weeks. On his good days, he'd crack jokes and tell Kylie stories about his childhood. He spent hours at the kitchen table with Benjie, lining dominoes into long intricate roads only to be bowled down in a matter of seconds. He would give the thumbs-up cue, and Benjie would tap the first domino. Father and son giggled at the reaction. Often Benjie sat on his father's lap as Bryan read him the same Bible story over and over again. One night, Ally found the two of them fast asleep on the loveseat next to the wheelchair in his bedroom, Benjie's head resting on his father's thin shoulder.

I'm a spectator to a miracle. You do love your son.

*　　*　　*

On February fourteenth, Bryan put on his heavy parka, sat in his wheelchair, and hollered from his bedroom, "Push me out to the porch, babe."

The kids were asleep, and the day's accumulation of

snowfall had ended. Five inches of snow had covered holly bushes, maple tree branches, and the front steps. Ally could see the ethereal beauty as the streetlight's beam lit up the scenery, backlighting the glistening snow like a movie. Ally pushed him to the edge of the porch railing so he could take in the scene. Gingerly she tucked an afghan around his frail body. Bryan pushed himself up on the handles.

"Careful," she said, trying to support his arms.

He turned to her, his eyes shining. "Ally, I want you to help me out of the chair. There's a dry patch here in front of me."

Bryan wrapped his arms around her shoulders; but, instead of standing up, he lowered his body down in front of the wheelchair.

"Here, let me help you stand up," Ally suggested.

Bryan shook his head, and continued kneeling on both knees. His hand shook as he grabbed one arm of the wheelchair for support.

"What on earth?"

"Humor me." He shifted his weight until he felt stable. Ally locked the wheelchair wheels in place.

Bryan grimaced as he turned his body until he could face her. Ally looked into the disease-worn face of a once-handsome man. Now his skin hung down from his cheekbones, and his eyes seemed not much more than deep hollows. He cleared his throat.

"You know I don't have much time," he started. "No,

hear me out. I *know* I don't have much of my life left. I want
to use whatever time I have left to restore our relationship."
He paused a moment and coughed. "Ally, I know I've been a
jerk for the last few years, and I want to apologize."

Ally opened her mouth to say something, but he raised
his hand to silence her.

"No, I know who I've been. Nothing like having death
know your name and address to realize what a life you have
been given." He closed his eyes to squeeze shut the tears. "I
never appreciated my family as much as I have in the last few
weeks, and I want to thank you for your kindness in letting
me stay here."

"I did it for the kids."

"I know." He grabbed Ally's hand. "I'm on my knees for
one reason."

Ally gasped.

"No, it's not what you think. But I want you to remember
this moment. If circumstances were different, I would be
here asking you to remarry me."

Ally shook her head. "But circumstances are different." A
tear dripped down the tip of his chin. She grabbed a Kleenex
and gently patted away the tear, and pushed back the hair on
his forehead. "It still means a lot to me, Bryan."

Then she lifted up the hair on her neck. "I want to show
you something." She turned so he could see her neck clearly.

Bryan chuckled. "Well, I never thought *you'd* get a tat."

"Wanted to prove to the world I was a free woman. I could

do whatever I wanted. No one would control me." Bryan started to say something, but she continued on. "It took coming to a camp—becoming a cook and serving others—that taught me freedom. You might say I found my freedom at the bottom of a twenty-gallon cook pot."

*   *   *

She opened her laptop and clicked onto her email. Just as she hoped, she had a message from Will. His emails were rare because he had a weak Internet connection in Mexico.

Dear Ally,

It's been a hard week laying all the foundations for the new camp. It will house only forty to fifty kids and five staff members. We're starting small and building from there.

You should see the excitement the kids have when we explain they will be able to go to a real rancho in the campo (a camp in the country). So few of them have been anywhere. I'm happy to be a part of these kids' lives.

It's not to say things are easy. Time moves slowly down here. For example, we say a clock "runs", but in Spanish a clock "walks". Timetables are arbitrary, and if some workers come a half a day late, "no problema". We're just glad they showed up that day. I'm learning to chill and be on God's timetable.

You probably think I forgot, but I did remember it was Valentine's Day. I'm not very good at the mushy stuff, but

*you know I miss you and think of you often. So many times
a day I want to share something, but then I remember you
are thousands of miles away.*

*How's my Benjie boy? Does he ever talk about me? I
miss Kylie and hope she is doing well in school. She's one
smart kid.*

I'll sign off now.

*Con mucho Cariño, (that's Spanish for "with much
affection)*

-Will

She picked up the framed photo she'd taken of him last summer. He was sitting on the porch steps of the camp's main building. He had a backpack and sleeping bag by his feet, and a three-day beard on his face. His deep-set eyes smiled back at her as she had snapped the picture. "Dang you, Will. I didn't plan on loving you."

*   *   *

The next day, Ally waited until the house was quiet. She was hoping to still find Bryan up as she needed to give him his pill. She tapped on the bedroom door and waited until she heard a hoarse "Come in."

She settled beside him on the bed. "Here's your pain pill. Hope you can sleep well tonight."

Ally held the glass in one hand and supported the back of Bryan's head with the other. His brow crinkled up in pain. Today hadn't been a good day for him. He took a sip of water, and it ran down his chin and onto his pajama top. She wiped his chin with a dry washcloth, and dabbed at the wet shirt.

"Now, just scoot down into that bed and let the pill do its magic."

He obediently slid down, and almost as soon as his head touched the pillow, his eyes closed. He muttered something, but Ally couldn't understand what he was saying. She knelt down by his left side and pushed the hair off of his sweaty forehead, noticing how the hair had begun to thin around the hairline. Cancer had aged him beyond his years. Ally bit her lip to give herself courage as she blinked back tears.

"Did you ask me something?" She leaned close to his ear. "I'm here to help you be comfortable."

Bryan shook his head as if he had something else on his mind. He held out his hand, and she felt the long boney fingers surround hers.

"Please pray—" He paused to catch his breath.

Ally threw her body down on top of the blanket as the tears flowed down her cheeks onto his hand. They poured as a reminder of the death of her marriage, death of her career, Bryan's illness, and now saying goodbye to him. She raised her head as an errant tear raced down the tip of her chin. Usually she hated to cry in front of anyone, but she had no shame anymore. Let the flooding begin.

Bryan pulled his arm out from underneath the blanket and reached for a Kleenex from the box on the bedside table. "Here, sweetheart."

Just hearing the broken tenderness in his voice turned up the velocity of tears, and now she sobbed into the tissue. After a minute she wiped her face with the back of her hands and turned to look at Bryan. "I'm so sorry about everything. I didn't—" but Bryan put his fingers against her lips to shush her. No longer did his eyes have the achy uncertainty of a man unsure of his future. Instead she saw shining eyes of peace.

*　　*　　*

The twenty-ninth of March broke clear, full of sun and promise in spite of the heavy snow shower the evening before. The snow had melted on some side streets and refrozen, into ice making the roads treacherous.

Ally, Kylie, Benjie, and Aunt Nettie stood across from Bryan's relatives, a handful of distant cousins, aunts, and a stepfather he had barely remembered.

The strain of taking care of her ex-husband through the long winter had added some gray hairs. Many nights Ally had sat and held his hand as he tossed and turned in bed. But the results produced a stronger faith because of it, an unshakeable peace in God's plan for her life. Somehow, caring for Bryan yielded the best kind of inner peace, something no one could ever take away from her. She had seen her ex-husband, a proud man, soften as he faced death with courage and hope.

They buried Bryan in the little church cemetery next to Lake Surrender Community Church. Several members of the church stood watching the last few shovelfuls of dirt thrown on the walnut casket. Kylie and Benjie placed a red rose on top of the casket as Pastor Jeremiah read from the book of Isaiah.

"But those who hope in the LORD will renew their strength. They will soar on wings like eagles; they will run and not grow weary, they will walk and not be faint.' Let us pray. Father, we commend our brother to Your loving arms. Bryan, who for the last few months of his life suffered greatly, is now in Your presence. He now soars like an eagle. Amen."

Pastor Jeremiah closed his Bible. "We did not know Bryan long, but in the short time with us he became part of our church family. The last months of his life, while he lay in great pain, he spent listening to the Bible. Many of you in the congregation came to read to him, talk to him, and be the hands and feet of Jesus in his last days. We came to see the joy of the Lord on his face. He will be missed by his family and all the members of our church."

"I want to stay here a minute and talk to Dad," Kylie waved her mother on.

Aunt Nettie, holding Benjie's hand, slipped her arm around Ally's waist as they walked back to the car. "You're a woman of great courage, and you've handled yourself with grace throughout Bryan's stay with us. I'm proud of you."

Ally wrapped her arm around her aunt and leaned on

Nettie's shoulder for comfort. They stood together watching the mourners get back in their cars.

After a moment, Nettie said, "I had a call from Will this morning. I told him the burial was today. He said he'd call you a week from tonight at seven o'clock."

True to his word, he phoned.

"Thanks for the call—it's been a tough day," Ally said as she sank down into an easy chair in the family room. "Yes, they're handling it okay, but Benjie's confused. I know you meant a lot to Bryan in his last days."

"My prayers are with you," Will said.

"I feel them. Listen, Will, I just don't feel like talking right now. Maybe in a few days." She powered down her phone and, after getting Benjie to bed, went to her room for the night.

*   *   *

"No quiere un poquito de desayuno?" asked a smiling, rotund woman. One of the kitchen workers, she stood waiting to take Will's order of huevos and tortillas. He loved the fried eggs, the black beans, and the fresh tortillas used to scoop up the beans, and ate them every day since his arrival at the camp.

Will took another slug of coffee and put the mug down on the bare wooden table. "No gracias, no breakfast for me today."

He had no appetite. His mind was on his friend Bryan and

how he would miss him. The few weeks he'd spent helping Bryan, they'd developed a friendship. Since Will had been in Mexico, Bryan had sent a few emails, asking questions about the Bible, and Will had seen a real change in him. Now he was gone. Such a short life.

Will ached for Kylie and Benjie.

But, when he tried to talk to Ally last night, she seemed distant. He knew she was sad about Bryan. After all, they had been married a while and shared two kids. Did she still have strong feelings for her ex?

Haven't heard much from her. Does she miss me?

If she only knew how much he longed for her. He'd drop everything and be back on the next plane if he didn't feel convinced God wanted him to finish this project. But he was two to three months away from getting the simple cement and tin building up and hiring someone to run the camp. He owed it to the kids in the orphanage to give them an experience in the campo and a true vacation.

Sarah passed by the table and dropped off some mail before heading to her makeshift office. She had come from Guadalajara to Pajaro Valle to check on the progress of the kitchen and main hall. Tents would be used until funding came in for cabins.

What he thought would be an awkward relationship ended up being good. The two of them worked well together. Will noticed one thing missing: he'd lost any spark of interest in her. He'd finished a chapter and had moved on.

No bitterness on either of their parts. That, he attributed to God's grace.

He pulled a yellow legal pad from his laptop case, but couldn't concentrate on his plans for the day. He flipped over to a fresh page and started writing.

Dear Ally,

I'm sitting here in the middle of a beautiful jungle, longing for the snows of Michigan. Can't believe I'm missing the entire winter. It's actually hot here among the plátano trees. I've seen some ugly snakes that the workers kill with a machete, so I make sure my tent is secured at night. The food is simple but delicious. I've had my fill of mangos, papayas, fresh tortillas, and even barbacoa— barbecued goat. I do miss ice cream and brownies, but I am eating healthy. You'd be proud of me.

I'm sorry to hear about Bryan's death. He was a good man, and your children will see him on the other side. He and I became friends over the few weeks I took care of him. I will miss him.

If I didn't feel like I needed to finish this project, I'd hop on the first plane north. I miss you terribly. Didn't realize how much you and the kids have become a part of my life. I still see you in that green dress you wore on New Year's Eve. Wow. Don't get rid of that one. Or, if I close my eyes, I can picture you standing on the porch at the lodge in your jeans and apron, waiting for us to get back from the backpack trip. Were you worried? I hope so.

I pray for you every day. I'm excited to see what will become of our relationship.

So thankful for your friendship,

Con Mucho Cariño,

Will

P.S. I laugh now when I think of how you came to the camp interview and were very indignant about my opening the door for you. You are Miss Independent, and I love you for that. But as our friendship has grown, so has my desire to take care of you.

P.P.S. I miss your red hair.

*　　*　　*

"Well if you aren't a grinning fool," said Nettie as she walked into the kitchen with a bag of groceries for Easter dinner.

"Just another letter from Will."

"Another one? Lately you two have been mailing each other letters several times a week. Can you have that much to say?"

"Plenty. I've got four months of snail mail piled up on my dresser."

"When is he supposed to come back?"

"Building has been delayed, and he might not be back until midsummer. I miss him terribly."

"Have you told him that?"

"Well sort of."

"Sort of?"

Ally pulled frozen vegetables, whip cream, and rolls out of a paper bag. "I'm not wanting to rush it. It's funny, but since we only communicate with letters—the phone service is terrible—I feel like I'm getting to know him better with each letter. He's got his funny side I saw with the campers this summer, but he can also be pretty deep and philosophical."

She handed a can of soup to her aunt to put away in the cupboard.

"Will's one of a kind. They don't come any finer than him," said Nettie.

*   *   *

"Mama."

Ally looked up from the movie she'd been watching on television. "Something bothering you?"

"No, I just miss Dad. I'm so glad I will see him again."

Ally held out her hand to her daughter and pulled her next to her on the sofa. "I know, honey."

"Can you get me that Kleenex?"

Ally reached over to the box on the side table and handed one to her daughter. "It's okay, it's important that you cry."

"Every day, I wear the necklace he gave me." Kylie looked down, and fingered the lone pearl hanging on a gold chain. "It makes me feel closer to him."

"I understand."

Kylie looked up. "Is it bad that I miss Will, too?"

*　　*　　*

Early June was her favorite time of year, and Lake Surrender didn't disappoint. Ally took a coffee break from inventorying the camp food for this year's program, and pushed open the creaky screen door that led out to the lodge's front porch. Her hands wrapped around a cup of java, and the mug gave just enough warmth to fend off the cool spring air. She put down her mug on top of the porch railing and stood leaning against it, watching Don lean the canoe paddles up against the craft barn. He was preparing to give them a fresh coat of paint. A quiet tat-a-tat of a red-headed woodpecker echoed among the oak and maple trees just starting to sprout greenery.

I am a blessed woman. She waved to Don. *I've found peace in this simple life.*

Don dipped his brush into the paint bucket.

It's been a hard year but a good year. She felt stronger in her faith, and knew she could make a life for her and her children. Yes, she battled the melancholy from Bryan's sickness and death, and she missed Will, but she'd learned a surrendered life was a good life, and when she put her head down on the pillow at night, she thanked God for His goodness.

*　　*　　*

"Ah Mom, I've *got* to have a new pair of jeans."

Ally cringed at her daughter's whining, and looked up from the desk in her bedroom where she sat paying bills. She was thankful she'd been able to continue working during the off-season at camp, but with her modest salary she still had a tight budget. But when she glanced at Kylie's jeans hem an inch above the ankle, she reluctantly looped her purse strap over her shoulder.

It had been two months since Bryan's death and she felt blue today, at loose ends. Even spring, with its offering of cheerful daffodils, sweet smelling lilacs, and baby ducklings on the lake didn't lift her spirits. Ally especially didn't relish shopping for a picky teenage daughter. She couldn't believe Kylie had turned thirteen last month.She got the kids into the car and mechanically jabbed the key into the ignition. *Please don't let this be a shopping trip that takes up the complete Saturday afternoon.*

Turning onto Main Street, Ally tapped her brakes to check if they were grabbing the road. They'd been giving her some trouble lately.

"Mom, quit doing that," Kylie growled in her mother's ear and then turned to look out the windshield. She let out a shout. "Hey, there's some cool big letters in the store windows."

"Probably just something left over from the Memorial Day sales."

Kylie wiped the morning's fog condensation off the window with her hand and pressed her nose against the glass. "No, every store has only one letter in the window, and the letters are red."

Ally sighed. She could care less about some big marketing campaign in downtown Lake Surrender. What she wanted was to go back home, put on her slippers, and hold a hot cup of Red Rooibos tea. That was her big plan for the evening.

Kylie pounded her hands on the leather neck rest to get her mother's attention. "Mom! You have to go around the block again before we stop at Panama City Jeans. I mean it, you have to do it!"

"Kylie, you're wearing me out."

"Do it," repeated Benjie.

"You're both ganging up on me again," but she flipped on the right blinker at the next street. Driving around the block, she circled back to the beginning of Main Street and started the route again.

"Now drive real slow."

"For heaven's sake, I'm not in the mood for little games."

"Mom, you'll be glad you did this."

Ally turned her head sideways to the passenger seat and saw a big grin rip across her daughter's face.

"Now, as you drive real slow, look at every window on the left side, and say the letter you see in the window."

"Okay—looks like the first one is a *w*."

"Keep going."

"I, an *l* and another *l*, and then nothing in the next window."

"Okay it starts up again. Y, an *o* and a *u*."

Ally frowned and wondered if Kylie was in on some secret. "Looks like there's another empty space and then *m*, *a*, *r*, *r*.

Kylie, you're smarter than me if you have this one figured out. Okay, a y and then another empty space, then—oh, wait. I think this is the last part, an m and an e."

They drove past the final store on the left. With a start, she read her name in the window, just above the name of the store, the Bookworm. "What on earth?"

"JUST PARK IT, MOM!" Kylie yelled.

"I'll park you in your—" Ally started to reply, but Kylie looked so stirred up she just complied and maneuvered the Audi into the nearest parking stall.

"Mom, you're an editor and you can't even spell. Look, I wrote it down. Ready?"

Ally leaned over her daughter's shoulder, noting how Kylie seemed to be sharing an inside joke with herself. She had gone from exasperated to exuberant in three seconds.

"Okay I'm paying attention."

"It says, 'Will you marry me?' Go see him, Mom."

Numbly, Ally pulled on the door handle and stepped out to a view of Will Grainger sauntering out of the door of the shop, his arms full of her favorite yellow roses. Wearing a deep tan and full beard, he had a smile the width of Lake Surrender.

Will enveloped her in a huge bear hug, the bunch of yellow roses smashed between them.

Ally's legs shook like a California earthquake as his grip tightened around her. "But I thought you were in Mexico."

Will drew back a little and caressed her cheek, then whispered, "I came back early. I missed you. You're who I want. I want your red hair surrounding me when I embrace you each morning, and I want those wild dancing eyes to send me off to work. I want to hear your laughter when I call you at lunchtime, and to hold you last thing before I go to sleep. There's no one else for me."

Ally felt his hands wrap around the sides of her face as he tipped her head up. "You are a wanted woman, and I'll never be able to get you out of my system. I love you, Ally Cervantes, all the wonderful, awful, vulnerable, joyful, irritating qualities that make you, you."

Ally started to open her mouth to reply but Will covered it with his hand. "Shhh, for once let me be the one with the words. I've rehearsed this for a month."

He gazed at her like someone who had just been given a drink after being found alive on a desert island. She delved into those dark, kind eyes. "I loved you when I was eight, and I love you at thirty-eight. And to quote one of your favorite lines from a famous bear named Winnie, 'If you live to be a hundred, I want to live to be a hundred minus one day so I never have to live without you.'"

He grabbed her by the waist and swung her around and around. "Say yes you love me and you'll marry me, or I won't put you down."

Liquid laughter bubbled out of Ally's throat as she formed the words "Yes" on her lips and then shouted out the word.

"She said yes," Benjie hollered from a tiny opening in the car window. "She said yes."